Family Heir:
A Bigfoot Novel

By Sara M. Drake

Sara M. Drake

Family Heir: A Bigfoot Novel

Edited by Jennifer Jensen (www.literallyjen.com)

Cover art by Paramita Bhattacharjee (www.creativeparamita.com)

ISBN 978-0-9903724-0-0

To Jen, for believing!

Chapter One

Brent rubbed his temples and leaned back in his chair. The pictures of women, torn apart in the most brutal fashion, had begun to blur together. He had no better idea of what had killed them now than he'd had eight hours ago. He did not know if he could look at those pictures much longer. Nothing he had seen during his time in the military had prepared him for this level of gore. He couldn't imagine anything that would have prepared him—not even a childhood full of watching horror movies. This was his first case as an agent for the Bureau of Hominid Affairs— otherwise known as BHA—and he found himself longing for the simplicity of an assignment in Afghanistan.

Around him, the familiar sounds of the office diminished. He knew it was getting late. The thin walls of the cubicles did little to absorb the noises created by over forty people in a large room. Only in the evening did silence descend. The clickety-click of keyboards quieted as people shut down their computers. The normal office chatter drifted toward the elevator as people began to trickle home. Brent tried to enjoy the peace, but the pictures still stared back at him with dead eyes.

"Hey," Jan said as she popped her head around the cubicle wall. "We're heading down to Pop's Bar. You coming?"

"No, I still need to work on this," Brent said, turning his head toward her voice.

Jan came all the way into the small cubbie, her helmet-like, curled gray hair framing a round, wrinkled face. Brent watched her face as her grin slid away, washed-out blue eyes widened, and her whole face tightened. Brent reached out and keyed back to previous pictures, giving Jan time to take each one in, time to register the full problem.

The first victim, a young woman caught backpacking, had been dismembered and sliced into such small pieces that identification had relied on the fingerprints from her ring finger. The FBI had some luck on this case; she had worked as a secretary on an army base, so her prints were on file. The second and third victims had been a mother and daughter; the DNA had confirmed that much. They had been torn into unidentifiable parts and the FBI could not match the DNA with anyone in their database. Four more victims had been found in a deserted recreational area; they had been an average, middle-class family out picnicking. The son's face had been the least damaged, allowing investigators to identify the family. The last three had been found on a hiking trail; a mother and her two daughters. The husband had reported them missing and identified the bodies. In total, ten victims. Each reduced to nothing more than piles of meat.

"My husband and I worked a case like this back when we were young enough to work the field. Of course, that was back at the FBI," Jan said, twirling a curl of hair around her finger.

"I'm sure you solved it easily, but this one has me stumped," Brent said, hoping to cut off one of Jan's infamous and constant stories about her days of glory.

"Don't let it bother you; we all start someplace. My husband and I struggled for a year before we really got the hang of it," Jan said, adjusting her glasses. She laid a hand on his shoulder as she bent over him to peer at the screen. "Maybe I can help."

"I'd appreciate it," Brent said. Jan might be annoying, but she knew her job better than anyone he had met. She and her husband had been field agents for over three decades before health problems had landed them in desk jobs. Jan had come to work for the BHA, but her husband still worked at the FBI.

"Possible werewolf," Jan said after several long moments, "but that doesn't match the norm."

"I'd concluded that much," Brent said. In fact, that was all he had concluded. The werewolves were ruled out, but that told him nothing about whom or what had killed these people.

"The police and FBI have no leads?" Jan asked. "I could call my husband and ask."

"No. I checked with the FBI already," Brent said. They had sent him their files, which had amounted to little more than the identities of most of the victims. "What do I do next?"

"Pass it over to one of the Hunters," Jan said, smiling down at him.

"Shouldn't we do our own investigation first?" Brent asked.

"For standard vampire or werewolf crimes,we hit the field. But if there are complicated circumstances, we need the help of the Hunter Families," Jan answered. "Even my husband and I had to call them in if we had a hominid case."

"Why? Aren't we supposed to handle all hominid crimes?" Brent asked, turning to look at Jan.

"Look, I know that's what's on the recruitment posters, but the truth is that the world is a stranger place than we can ever guess at," Jan said. "Every year the government finds a new species of hominid, and every time that happens the Families already know about them."

"I thought they taught us everything," Brent said. "I had a Hunter as an instructor at the academy."

"The Hunters keep telling us that they will not reveal species who have not already agreed to come forward, and that the remaining species have gotten better at avoiding scientific detection," Jan said.

"We just do vampires and werewolves and leave the rest to unorganized civilians?" Brent asked.

"Yep, that's the bottom line. They've been doing this for ages and we're still the new kids in town," Jan said with a laugh. "They've been at it for longer than even old folks like me."

"So I call in the Hunters without doing anything more than having stared at pictures for hours," Brent said, shaking his head. It felt like admitting defeat.

"That would be my recommendation," Jan said. "Part of this job is knowing when you're in over your head."

"How do I call them in?" Brent asked.

"Forms, lots of forms," Jan answered with a chuckle. Brent shook his head. Typical government procedure. The answer to almost everything seemed to be to fill out a form which would lead to yet another form. He had often wondered if he should be filling out paperwork just to take a bathroom break.

"Which forms?" he asked with a sigh.

"BHA 1067, 701, and 442, to start with," Jan answered. Brent scribbled the numbers down as she talked. "The 1067 goes straight to the chief, the 701 to finance, and the 442 to legal."

"If you want to go out with the Hunters, you also want a BHA 882 and a 339. Both of those go to the chief," Jan said as he finished scribbling.

"Of course I want to go out," Brent said.

"Then do the paperwork," Jan said. "The chief will want you to get the field experience."

"How long will it take?" Brent asked. "How many more women will die while I push paperwork?"

"That depends on you. Get a hold of everyone and charm them into approving this right away—you could be out of here tomorrow. Let those forms go through the system on their own, and it could take a month."

Brent moaned. He hated trying to be persuasive just to get people to do the right thing. This late in the evening, he would have to call them at home. Never a good time to get cooperation. The Bureau chief, Dr. Ellison, seemed reasonable, but Carl in legal could be a nightmare. He glanced at the picture on the screen. These people deserved justice. This killer needed to be stopped. He did not have much choice. He nodded, looking up at her.

"Good boy," Jan said, ruffling his hair. "Hey, Mike! Let's help Brent get this ball rolling before we leave."

Mike's blond head popped over the cubicle wall to Brent's right. He smirked down at them, his blue eyes glinting in the overhead lights.

"What, the baby agent can't do his job?" Mike sneered.

"He just needs a little help," Jan chided.

"Do I need to burp him and change his diaper, too?" Mike muttered.

"You don't have to help. I got this," Brent said, glaring up at Mike.

"Sure you do. You've been sitting there doing nothing all day," Mike said. "Must be nice to have only one case at a time. Looks like you can't even do one without Grandma Jan helping."

"Mike, just see if you can't get ahold of Peggy. Then bat those gorgeous eyelashes at her or flirt or whatever you do to get her to roll over," Jan snapped.

"Only because you asked so nicely," Mike said, winking at Jan before his head disappeared.

"Just ignore him," Jan whispered as she patted Brent's shoulder. "Now, you start filling out those forms. I'll call the chief's office and see if he's still in."

She backed out of his cubicle, which was too small to turn around in for a woman of her girth. A moment later, Brent heard her voice on the phone with the chief's secretary. Brent listened for a moment before turning back to his computer. He called up the forms and began filling them out. He had gotten halfway through the first before Jan reappeared.

"What do I put in block 5?" Brent asked, trying to decipher the form.

"The explanation's on the back page," Jan said. "Let me do a few of those for you."

Brent nodded, happy to share the load. The two of them divided the forms and got to work. The office had become silent, and the only lights still on were their own. Jan sent her last form to him and headed out, leaving him alone in the cubicle farm.

Chapter Two

Forty-five minutes, fifteen phone calls, eight e-mails, and five forms later, Brent had everything completed. All I'm missing is a partridge in a pear tree, he thought. Brent had learned more about shortcutting the bureaucracy during the past hour than he had during the past six months on the job.

He stood and stretched, looking for anyone who could advise him on what to do next. Jan's last instructions before she'd left had been to make sure all of the forms went through, but he had no idea how to track them. The phone on his desk rang, interrupting his thoughts.

"Agent MacKrae," he answered.

"This is Chief Ellison's office; he'd like you to report here immediately."

Brent walked down the empty rows of cubicles, eerie in their silence. Outside of his cubicle area the lights had been turned out by departing employees, leaving him to navigate by the red lights of the emergency sign. The chief's office sat at the end of the building one floor up from Brent's desk, the lights from within pouring into the darkened hallway. Brent moved a little faster, eager to get away from the shadows.

Brent entered the chief's office, blinking a little at the brightness. The small room looked like every government office Brent had been in: standard issue furniture with standard issue decorations. A faux wood desk and expensive office chair took up most of the space. The walls and shelves held knickknacks and plaques that had been collected over several years of federal service.

"So, Agent MacKrae, this will be your first field assignment?" Chief Ellison asked.

"Yes, Chief," Brent said.

"Do you know Patriarch Bullend?" the chief asked.

"By the title, I assume one of the werewolf leaders," Brent said. What was this? Had he been called in for an oral exam?

"Yes, the Wyoming spokesperson," Chief Ellison said. "I have already had two requests from him to call in the Venators on this; in fact, he already processed the legal paperwork to call them in at the local level."

"The Venators are the largest Hunter Family in the West, aren't they?" Brent asked.

"Yes, and they will be the ones you will be working with on this case," the chief said. "The hominids still trust the Hunters more than they do the BHA. We've had fifty years to prove ourselves, and quite honestly, the Hunters still get better results."

"Yes, sir," Brent said.

"I want to change that, but we have a long way to go," the chief continued. "So here's how this works. From the government's perspective, you are in charge of this case. In reality, the lead Hunter will be in charge. Follow his directions, learn everything you can."

"Yes, sir," Brent said.

"Unofficially, you have a secondary assignment," Chief Ellison said.

"What's that, sir?" Brent asked.

"The FBI National Security Branch has seen an uptick in chatter from the radical hominid rights groups," the chief said. "They suspect that there might be violence directed at the Hunter Families."

"What are they expecting?" Brent asked.

"There hasn't been enough information to predict an attack, but the FBI asked for our help. Keep your eyes open and report anything suspicious to the FBI." The chief handed him a card. A quick glance showed him the FBI symbol. Brent tucked it into a pocket.

"Also, you are authorized to take any actions you feel reasonable to protect the Venators," the chief added.

"Sir, if the hominids trust the Families so much, why would they want to take them out?" Brent asked.

"The Hominids Equality Movement and People for Hominids are groups run by humans—no hominids involved," Chief Ellison explained. "They have been quite vocal in their opposition to the Hunters, viewing them as a separate and unequal justice system."

"I thought the Hunters worked under the same laws that bounty hunters do," Brent said.

"Yes and no," the chief said. "Simple werewolf or vampire cases almost always go through traditional channels. However, for everything else, justice depends on the Hunters. The case in Maine last year with the mermen set off the rights groups."

"Those two mermen who were raping and killing tourists?" Brent asked.

"Yes. We didn't have a cell designed to hold merpeople, and the Hunters had no choice but to kill the suspects," Chief Ellison said. "The local mer king supported the Hunter's actions, but the hominid rights group held it up as a case of brutality and oppression."

"So now the FBI fears some form of retaliation?" Brent asked.

"Essentially," the chief said, nodding.

"Sir, I'm not sure I am the best agent for this case."

"You'll be fine," Chief Ellison said. "Just follow the Hunters on the primary case and keep the FBI informed on anything else."

"Yes, sir," Brent said, restraining the impulse to salute. Old reflexes died hard.

"Now, you have a plane to catch," the chief said as he turned back to his computer.

Brent nodded, accepting the dismissal, and made his way back out of the office. He had just enough time to get packed and to the airport, so he would have to use the flight to do some research on the rights groups. The case horrified him enough before the addition of possible terrorist plots.

Chapter Three

I looked around the bar as I waited for my date to get back from the bathroom. Tiny tables standing chest high dotted the floor; men and women in their jeans and cowboy boots stood around talking. Booths lined the walls; they were the only places you could sit down unless you were up at the bar itself. Most of the booths held couples making out, though a few had larger parties. I swept the room with a glance again. Still no sign of my date.

Who would have thought that a man would have a smaller bladder than I did? This must be at least the third bathroom break he'd taken. Maybe he was doing drugs? That would be just my luck! My first foray into the world of dating had been a complete disaster so far. There was something to be said for marrying your childhood sweetheart. Wait—I'd tried that and it hadn't worked. I growled low in my throat, eyeing the other customers in the bar.

The thick cigarette smoke made it difficult to see the rest of the room, which always troubled my inner paranoia. After all, who knew what could be hiding in a place like this? Okay, I did know. Vampires wouldn't be caught dead in a low-class bar like this, and werewolves couldn't stand the crowds. Yet I'd seen other creatures in the world—enough of them to keep me vigilant—especially since my job was to deal with the ones that had gone bad. I knew that the worst trouble likely to happen here would be yet another fight, human versus human.

My cell phone vibrated and I glanced down to see a text from Lisa. She had been my rock since the divorce. Twenty-one was way too young to get divorced. Lisa had been the only one to stand by me as I cried for weeks on end. She'd come and packed all my things up in the dead of night, offered me a place to live after things feel apart.

@ BBQ PIT, 2 BACK 2 APT, C U LATER

I rolled my eyes at Lisa's text. I should have known. All of her dates seemed to end back at our apartment, and most of the time I couldn't avoid listening to the grand finale. I'd been hoping she would bring her Date of the Week to meet up with me tonight; it looked as if I was on my own. I texted Lisa back, letting her know I would not be bringing my date home with me, and then tucked the cell phone into my purse.

I hated first dates. And really, what type of man chose a bar for a first date? One who wanted to get laid more than find true love, would be my guess. A little backup would have been nice. If I had to listen to one more boring sports story, I was going to deck the guy and walk out.

I glanced around the bar again, hoping to see my date returning. I'd just tell him thanks for the beer, and then head home. Maybe I could be sound asleep by the time Lisa and her date got noisy. I should have listened to Lisa's advice: Don't date jocks. Maybe I'd try one of the science majors next. I'd been a pariah in high school; the small school had no love for the Families. However, the community college had been a complete change; the students seemed to think wrestling vampires made me someone they all wanted to know. Dr. Lyman had said it was because I was exotic here, whereas at home I was just considered weird. I still didn't understand what the difference between the two was, but I'd take it.

A sudden tension filled the bar. Like a wave of silence, the noise level dropped as heads turned. The women admired, and the men tensed for possible problems. Following the movement—or lack of movement—I had no trouble finding the cause.

Tall, toned, and terrifying, Troy made his way straight toward me without even a glance at the women who eyed him with obvious hunger. His leather trench coat billowed out as he walked, showing off skintight jeans that accentuated one of his finest features. Of course, he thought the amazing upper body muscles earned the attention but, well, any lady with eyes couldn't help but look a little lower. Yep, my ex-husband never failed to raise the pulses of women, and I wished at least one would catch his attention before he reached me.

The restraining order didn't seem to faze Troy much. He didn't hesitate to follow me everywhere. Someday he would get a new woman or a job, something that would keep him from trailing behind me like a lost pup. The sooner, the better. How long was he going to keep this up?

I spotted my date, a blond basketball player a year older than I was, trailing in Troy's wake. I could almost see the thoughts going through his head as he decided my company wasn't worth facing down Troy. I sighed. Man number four that Troy had scared off. Thank goodness the local college offered a steady stream of men interested in dating a woman who could kill werewolves; there were plenty more men out there—some of them even lining up. Maybe one day I would get past the second date. If I got lucky, I might even find one capable of a little bit of romance. Or had I just watched too many chick flicks?

Troy slid into the seat across from me, keeping his head bowed with his coffee-colored bangs hiding his eyes. I resisted the urge to offer to cut his hair. A few months ago I wouldn't have hesitated. But that was before. Before the fight to end all fights, before the hospitalization, before the arrest, before I knew I shouldn't be around him. Still, I knew he hated letting strangers near him with sharp objects. No matter how he hated bangs, he hated haircuts more. I guess a few months weren't enough to kill the instinct to take care of him.

"What do you want?" I snarled at Troy to cut off my train of thought.

He glanced at me through his bangs, his puppy-brown eyes begging me not to be mad.

"Really? Not even going to say hello," I muttered, fighting to stay mad.

"Hello," his deep voice was so quiet that I struggled to hear him over the country music. His shoulders slumped, as if the effort to speak took all that he had.

"You did realize I was here on a date?" I asked, glaring at him.

Troy glanced around the bar, checking out the men as if looking to find my lost date.

"Oh, don't bother; you scared him off already," I muttered. I remembered the last time he'd scared off a man by hanging outside my apartment until my date had dropped me off. I growled, showing him a little teeth in the process.

Troy hung his head even further, refusing to meet my eyes.

"What do you want?" I asked again, trying to keep the anger from my voice.

Troy glanced at the door, then back to me.

I felt the anger break free, a desire to shake him until words poured out, making me long to jump across the table. Remembering the advice of my anger management therapist, I counted to ten and looked at him again. A rumble of rage rattled in my throat. Nope, not enough. I closed my eyes and counted to twenty. When I opened them, the

17

anger still pounded through me, seeking an escape. I closed my eyes again and pictured hitting Troy with a bat. No, can't go down that road. A Styrofoam bat! That will do the trick! I mentally pummeled Troy with a Styrofoam bat until the anger calmed. In control once more, I looked up at Troy.

"All right, let's go," I said, standing up. I managed a quick tug to make sure the miniskirt covered me before stepping out from around the table. The heels I had borrowed from Lisa were at least an inch taller than my normal date shoes. I stepped forward, eyeing the floor and trying to keep my balance. I grabbed my clutch purse off the table, the small thing just large enough to hold the essentials: wallet, phone, keys, lipstick, and a .22 pistol.

We made our way through the crowd, which parted before Troy like waters before Moses. I always wished I could have that effect; instead, I was the one that people walked into without noticing. We reached the door and Troy held it open for me. The heat of Wyoming summer hit me as soon as the door shut behind us. Even the little clothing I had on felt like too much. I took a deep breath of air, enjoying the dusty, smokeless air. Troy's black pickup truck sat next to my beat-up pink VW Beetle. Side by side, it looked like my tiny car could fit into the bed of his Chevy, making me feel even smaller than normal. Troy took a few long strides, leaving me behind with just a few steps, and opened the passenger door of his truck for me. Through the open door I could see two shotguns, a large army duffel bag, and a shopping bag sitting in the backseat.

"So this is work related?" I asked.

Troy nodded and headed toward the driver's side. I debated walking away, getting into my car, going home, and taking a long hot shower. However, college cost more than I had expected and I had almost run out of money from our last job. We might have gotten divorced, but he was still my partner.

I shook my head at my own stupidity and boosted myself into the truck. If there was a way of getting into a tall pickup in a miniskirt without flashing people, I hadn't discovered it yet. I peeked through the window to see if anyone had gotten a view of my purple thong. Nope, empty parking lot. Lucky me.

"Can we swing by my apartment to get my gear?" I asked as he started the truck.

He shook his head and began to pull out of the parking lot.

"Do I at least get to know what the job is?" I asked, trying to dampen my irritation.

Troy opened the center console and pulled out a stack of papers. Without taking his eyes off the road, he handed them to me.

I glanced at them; standard apprehend-and-arrest paperwork. I glanced over the form. My name jumped out at me. Kelley Mallard and Troy Mallard were listed as the authorized executioners, with me in command. That was odd; Troy always had command. Ten dead from unknown attacker, suspected werewolf, but DNA evidence not a match. The victims had been slashed with claws, bitten, and dismembered. The path of attacks indicated that the murderer kept to the mountains but seemed to be heading southwest, either toward Idaho or Utah. The warrant had been signed by the governor of Wyoming, the pack Patriarch of the Yellowstone tribe, and the vampiric liaison to the Wyoming congress. Everything seemed to be in order.

"What's the hurry? Why can't we take thirty minutes for me to get my gear?" I asked.

"Page six," Troy said.

I turned to page six and began reading. The victims had all been families; mostly mothers and their children. The last victim had been an infant less than a year old. The attacks had been escalating in brutality, and the police worried that the media would begin to put the cases

19

together soon. The Patriarch, Old Seth himself, expected Troy and me at the reservation tomorrow for a briefing.

"So if we stop at The Range tonight for supplies, we can just get there before Ma and Pa set all the alarms?" I asked as I put the papers aside. I didn't know who named our Family's ranch, but it came straight from the stupid song Home on the Range. Aren't we the clever ones. "No chance to leave in the morning if we want to get to the reservation on time."

Troy nodded.

"And you expect me to hike out to The Range in this outfit?"

I stared at the four-inch heels I had kicked onto the floor and tried to imagine the mile walk to my parents' house from the driveway. As I was contemplating the possibility of Troy carrying me, his arm snaked back to the rear seat and pulled out the shopping bag. He dropped the bag on my lap. I glanced inside and saw a stack of clothes.

"Eyes on the road," I said as I pulled out a pair of jeans and glanced at the label (size 8). Moving as fast as possible, I peeled the skirt off (size 4) and slipped on the much more comfortable jeans. I wondered if Troy had forgotten my size or remembered that I preferred my working pants a size or two too large. I glanced over at him and caught him staring. He shifted his eyes back to the road, but the appreciative grin remained. I rolled my eyes and turned back to the bag.

I pulled out the T-shirt and a sports bra fell out. A glance showed me that the bra was 34C. I smiled to myself as I took off my blouse and push-up bra. He had remembered my sizes and preferences. It might not be romantic, but after the date I had been on it sure felt like it. I pulled the sports bra and T-shirt on, feeling ready to get to work. At the bottom, I found a pair of tennis shoes and a belt. They were cheap, but they'd do the trick. I pulled the shoes on over my bare feet (since he had not thought to buy socks).

"So you had time to buy clothes for me, but not enough time for me to go to my apartment?" I asked. I began threading the belt through the pants loop, feeling a little undressed without my gun holster.

"Tracking you," he said as his arm crossed over my lap to open the glove box. He pulled out his Colt .45 and handed it to me. I pulled the gun out of the holster, checked that the safety was on, and popped the clip out. A quick glance at the bullets showed me that they were Hunter's Special, the only trusted brand of ammunition for hunting both werewolves and vampires. Other ammunition makers marketed special bullets, but none of them were effective. They either didn't have the right mix of silver and pinewood, or they wouldn't fire reliably. I slid the holster onto my belt and finished putting it on.

"Tracking me down took too much time?" I asked, feeling better around Troy now that I had on working clothes and not date clothes. I picked the discarded outfit off the floor of the cab and tossed them into the shopping bag. I took more care with my shoes, placing them between the folds of the miniskirt where I could be sure they wouldn't get scratched. Lisa would kill me if I damaged these; they were her favorite club pumps.

He nodded.

"So you weren't just stalking me?"

He shook his head.

I rolled my eyes at him and pulled out my cell phone. I had better make the necessary phone calls before we were out of range of a cell tower. A quick call to work let them know I was off on a Hunter assignment and didn't know when I would be back. Chances were I wouldn't have a job when I got back. I tried to comfort myself by thinking it was only part-time minimum wage.

It was a shame, because I liked working as a receptionist at the psychologist's office. Dr. Lyman was the best boss I had ever had, and the rest of the staff had adopted me. They brought me home-cooked food for lunch and offered unwanted advice. The best part of the job was that I could listen to all their stories of work as mental health counselors. I shook my head clear and hit speed dial again.

"Do you know what time it is?" Lisa's voice screamed at me over blaring music.

"Obviously not your bedtime!" I laughed at her answering shriek of mock outrage.

"Bad date?" she asked as the background noise lowered. I guessed she had stepped outside.

"Yes. Troy," I answered.

"Again?" Lisa screeched.

"This time with work," I answered quickly, to cut off her normal rant about my ex.

"So you're going out of town, armed to the teeth, with your ex-husband? And you think this is a good idea?" Lisa asked seriously.

"I know, but it's still my job," I said.

"Your job is to get through school so you can stop doing this crazy stuff."

"But I'm not there yet," I said, wondering what life would be like with a nice job that came with an office and a steady paycheck.

"Only shoot at the bad guys, okay?"

"Of course," I said, smiling. "I'm not that crazy."

"Is that what your therapist says?" Lisa giggled.

"Very funny." I muttered. "Are we good on bills until I get back?"

"Yeah, I can cover rent and nothing else is due. Just come home safe," Lisa said.

"You'll remember to feed Kitty?" I asked, thinking of my last weekend at my parents when Lisa had forgotten all about the poor feline we had adopted. Lisa did not like the critter much, but I loved having something warm and soft to curl up with at night.

"Of course," she said, and I knew she was rolling her eyes at me.

"I'll be back soon."

Chapter Four

I hung up and glanced over at Troy. He stared at the road, pretending not to hear my phone calls. I appreciated the thought, but the cab of the truck was too small for him not to hear every word.

He had hated Lisa since I started hanging out with her two years ago, and he hated her even more for taking me in after we split. Of course, the dislike was mutual. I never understood it, but it seemed to be a case of hate at first sight.

"Money problems?" Troy asked.

"No, I'm doing okay. The money from this job will certainly help, though. I don't want to take out student loans unless I have to," I said.

"Alimony?" he asked.

"No. I told you before, I'm not taking your money," I said, looking over at him. "We make the same on these jobs. You don't have much more than I do."

"Inheritance," he said, turning to look at me.

"That's blood money from all the abuse. I am not taking any of the money you got when your mom died. You know that." I turned away to stare out the window, wanting the conversation to end.

I didn't need him to take care of me. I could take care of myself just fine. Who did he think he was? I just wanted to hit him—hard. Of course, that was the problem; I spent a lot of time fighting the urge to beat him. I wanted him to hear me and to understand, even though I knew it would never happen. More than that, I wanted him to talk to me, tell me what he was thinking.

"Not mom," he said, interrupting my thoughts. I ran that through my head a couple of times, searching for a meaning, before my brain put it together. He meant he didn't think of his mother as his mom.

"I know; my family is your family," I said. "The divorce didn't change that. Ma and Pa practically raised you. They aren't going to disown you just because I did."

"Hate me?" he asked, his voice so soft that I wished he came with a volume control.

"No," I sighed, feeling my irritation drain away. "I can't hate you, even on the days I want to. We grew up together, and I can't imagine life without you."

"Werewolf?" Troy asked.

"Werewolf? What?" I asked, confused at the subject change.

"Case," Troy said.

"Oh, the job," I said. Thoughts of my complicated relationship with Troy fled in the normal adrenaline rush of facing a new job, a new challenge. "The report said that the DNA didn't show the werewolf marker. But what else kills like that?" I loved this part of my work—the mystery, the search for clues.

"Not vampires," Troy answered.

"No, they don't have claws," I said. "Though a berserker vampire might dismember a victim. Do you think a berserker would have the presence of mind to make it look like a werewolf attack?"

"Unlikely," Troy said, dragging out the word as he thought it through.

"But possible," I said, just to be stubborn. I glanced over the pictures of the victims. Gross. Still, looking closer at them, I could see the wounds had to have been made by claws. No vampires.

"Wendigo?" Troy asked, glancing at me out of the corner of his eye.

"Hmm, possible," I said, thinking about a case I'd heard about as a kid. The Wendigos kept to themselves, but when one had gone rogue it left a long trail of bodies before the Hunters caught up to him. "They prefer to prey on humans and have the claws for it. But, none have ever been spotted west of the Mississippi."

"Standens," Troy said.

"You're right; the Standen family would have let us know if a Wendigo had headed West." I said, thinking about the East Coast Families. Hunter Families had been maintaining the peace among the species once believed to be myths for longer than history could remember. The Standens had risen to prominence among the Families along the Atlantic Coast and acted as something of a senior Family among the Hunters in the United States. Of course, we never organized very well, but with the government's recognition of vampires and werewolves we needed a spokesman. The Standen Pa and Ma stood up and interacted with government agencies, representing all of us. In some ways, the changes had been good. The Hunter Families kept each other much better informed about the activity in their areas.

"What else could it be?" I asked, running out of possible hominids with claws.

"Dunno," Troy said.

Silence drifted between us and Troy reached over to flick on the radio. The horrible twangy country music that Troy loved came pouring out of the speakers. I wanted to snap at him to turn on something decent, but decided I'd try for a catnap instead. I pushed the seat all the way back and closed my eyes. I did my best to clear my mind and felt sleep begin to take me.

I heard a gunshot and felt the truck brake, heard tires squeal. I tried to bolt up, but the seat belt held me down. I struggled for a moment before remembering to relax. Dang seat belts! Sitting up with slow, deliberate movements, I found myself suddenly covered in glass as the truck came to a halt. I brushed it off my lap with my purse, listening to the tinkle as the pieces fell to the floor of the truck, glinting in the light from the dashboard.

A second gunshot and the sounds of more shattering glass echoed in the air. Troy grunted and the Chevy engine roared to life as it struggled to meet Troy's demands. I gripped the purse handle until I could feel my nails biting into my palms hard enough to break the skin. My heart pounded in my own ears as I tried to remember to breathe. Do not panic, I told myself.

I brushed the new collection of glass off of me and glanced over at Troy. He appeared to be favoring his right arm, but it was too dark for me to see if he had been hit.

"Are you okay?" I asked.

"Fine," he barked.

"Fine. Don't tell me. What do I need to know?" I shouted at him, the anger pushing the fear away. "I'm just your partner who's going to be depending on you as we hunt something that's clearly dangerous."

"Grazed shoulder," he answered, his composure cooling my anger.

"Okay. How long to The Range?" I asked. If he could stay calm, I refused to let myself act like a hysterical girl.

"Twenty minutes," he said.

"Do you think we were attacked by the same creature we are hunting?" I asked, my thoughts returning to the situation as the adrenaline fled.

"Or two," he said, voice tight and words clipped.

"Great. There might be two homicidal, sentient beings out there," I muttered.

"More. Humans." Troy said. I rolled my eyes at him. No matter what we had faced on these jobs, Troy insisted that humans were the most violent of the hominids. Some days, I even agreed with him.

"You know I don't mean the humans," I said, growling low in my throat. Troy just chuckled. His laugh relaxed me more than his calm had. Somehow, if Troy could find the humor in this, it couldn't be that bad.

"I mean almost all the hominid species we know, no matter what their evolutionary background, have been peaceful," I said, thinking out loud. "Even humans. It's rare to find one who turns into a true predator of hominids. So either we have an unlikely coincidence of murderers out here, or the one we thought we would start tracking tomorrow is moving faster than anticipated. Not only that, but changing methods."

"I know," Troy answered. The truck sped up and I glanced at the speedometer. For a man who hated going more than 5 mph over any posted speed limit, we were approaching 90 mph with no signs of slowing. Sometimes actions speak louder than words. Okay—with

Troy, actions always told more than words. This was bigger than anything we had dealt with before.

Chapter Five

Troy pulled the Chevy into the driveway of The Range, parking in the only free spot available. The gravel parking area looked like a truck convention: pickups, SUVs, and even a minivan were all parked in a semicircle. I eyed them, recognizing many of them, and began to get suspicious.

"What's up with this?" I asked Troy as I slid out of the truck. "Did someone call a meeting and not invite us? Did I forget something?"

"Don't know," he said as he grabbed for the duffel bag. He shifted the bag to his left hand and reached out for a rifle case. I grabbed the other gun while debating if I should try to get the duffel from him. Nah; if he wanted to do the manly-man routine, I'd leave him to it.

We walked around the stable. I swore it had been built by the original pioneers; the wood was warped and the nails were rusted. The familiar sound of the ponies was missing. I glanced in as we passed. Neither George nor Gracie, the family's two cart ponies, was in their stalls. I looked around for the cart, but it too was missing. I guessed someone had run supplies up to the house and hadn't come back yet. I looked for Troy and spotted him down the path, almost swallowed by the shadows. I did a short jog to catch up to him.

"Why won't Ma and Pa join the twenty-first century and just put a driveway up to the house?" I complained as I fell in step with him.

"No motors," he answered.

"No kidding. No motor vehicles past the old stables. I know the rule. But it's a stupid rule."

"Safety," he said.

"What, someone's gonna come raid The Range?" I muttered, looking up to wave at the security cameras. I could see three of them, but, of course, I knew where to look. Pa kept installing new cameras as the technology improved. From the main office at The Range, you could see every inch of land we owned. As if he wasn't paranoid enough, Pa had programmed the computers to alert him if any unknown hominid approached. I think Pa had perfected facial recognition software years before the government started using it. That's my Pa: paranoid computer programmer.

"Good exercise," Troy said.

"I don't need exercise," I said. "We need to get cleaned up, see how bad your arm is, and figure out why everyone's here."

Troy did not answer me, and I fell silent as we trudged along. The moon provided enough light to navigate the uneven path, making me grateful there was no cloud cover. I don't know why Pa would spend a fortune on security crap, but not waste a single dollar on some lights. Not that there was much to see, even in daylight. This part of the property held little else than rocks and some scrub brush. In the distance, we could see the glow of electric lights. Ma and Pa must have every light in the place on for us, or we wouldn't be able to see it at this distance.

Troy handed the duffel bag over to me, face paling as I took it. I pulled it on as if it were a backpack, not even pretending to be manly enough to throw it over just one shoulder. I looked at Troy, but he refused to meet my eyes. How deep was that wound? If it was bad enough we couldn't take care of it here, we would have to get back on the road to the hospital. Of course, the nearest hospital was about an hour away, so he had better not be bleeding to death on me.

"If you die on me, I'm going to kill you," I muttered to Troy's back. The freaking duffel bag felt as if it weighed around sixty pounds, and The Range was still about a quarter mile away. I tried to distract myself from the increasing pain in my shoulder by thinking of new creative curses to throw at Troy when I had breath to talk. Hairy-ape-man? No, not original enough, and insulting to apes. Neanderthalic moron? Boring! Not to mention I kind of liked Neanderthals—not that I knew any personally. After all, we were pretty sure they were extinct. Bug-brained bastard? Maybe.

I had been reduced to thinking about nothing more than taking the next step, sucking more oxygen into my burning lungs by the time we reached The Range, which looked as if it had been designed by Escher, if he had ever gone into architecture. The center stood three stories tall and looked like an old army fort, complete with battlements and cannons along the top. Four different wings branched out from the main fort at forty-five degree angles. One wing looked like the typical ranch house so common in Wyoming, the second looked like an old A-frame farmhouse, the third looked like a log cabin, and the fourth looked like a Victorian.

I managed the first step up toward the porch of the Victorian wing when I felt the duffel bag lifted from my shoulders. I shot Troy a glare, but was too exhausted to fight. Sure, whatever; he could have credit for dragging our gear up to the house while wounded. Who would believe me if I whined? I was pretty sure it was the first time since I was ten that he had let me carry anything.

"Kelley!" I heard the squeal a bare moment before my older sister flew through the door to hug me.

"Angie? I thought you were still in Salt Lake City taking summer classes," I said as I disentangled from her and we headed through the door arm in arm. Angie looked like a somewhat older and much more sophisticated version of me. In fact, she looked the way I had always wanted to be.

We shared the same blue eyes and rust-colored hair, only her hair had seen the loving care of a salon. Her porcelain skin, with just a touch of makeup, looked Barbie-doll perfect. I had spent too much time outside; the sun had darkened my skin, adding to my freckle collection. My hair, well...what can I say? At best, it saw the loving attention of one of the six-dollar haircut places that left me looking as if I had the style sense of a twelve-year-old boy. I longed for the day when I could put that much time—and money—into looking good.

"Oh, I'm just here for a brief visit. Ma made my attendance mandatory," Angie answered. I stopped my contemplation of our looks to consider again why everyone would be at The Range.

"Attendance for what? And why wasn't I invited?" I asked.

"You'll find out soon enough, sister-mine." Angie glanced at me with that glint in her eyes I remembered from childhood. Something was up, and I wasn't going to like it. Great. I thought chasing down a killer while getting shot at would be problematic enough. Now I had to add my own family to the list!

"Is Uncle Mack here?" I asked. It came in handy to have a doctor in the family when one hunted hominids, and Uncle Mack had been taking care of us for as long as I could remember.

"Sure, everyone's here! Including a few I haven't seen since our last attempt at a family reunion. Did you know Great-Auntie Bertha is still alive?"

"Bertha? Really? Did she bring Harold with her?" I asked, distracted by thoughts of the ancient couple.

"You know it! He's been telling World War II stories all night," Angie giggled. "Only I think his mind's starting to slip; some of them were X-rated!"

"No, really?" I asked, smiling at the image. Our great-aunt and uncle had crossed the centennial mark, making them the oldest Hunters in the U.S. Bertha wanted to win the record for oldest person alive and seemed healthy enough to do it.

"You'll have to go listen," Angie said. She glanced over her shoulder to look at Troy, who followed us like a large shadow. "Hey, what's wrong with Troy?"

"He was shot," I said, looking back to see Troy holding his right arm. "It's why I asked about Uncle Mack."

"Shot? Did you do it?" Angie asked, turning wide eyes my way.

"No," I said, glaring at her. "We had some trouble on the way here. Now go get Uncle Mack."

"Uncle Mack," Angie shouted. "Troy's been shot."

"Subtle," I muttered at her.

"You didn't think you'd get rid of me that easily, did you?" Angie said, grinning at me. "So, Troy, how's it going?"

"Fine," Troy mumbled from behind us.

"You dating anyone yet?" Angie said, head twisted to look behind her as we walked.

"No," he said.

"I could set you up with my roommate. She loves to talk, so you wouldn't have to say a word," Angie said, winking at me.

"No," Troy snarled.

"Angie, leave him alone," I snapped.

"I'm just trying to help," Angie said, trying to look innocent.

"No," I said as I elbowed her, "you're just being a pain."

Uncle Mack, bag in hand, appeared from a side hall and led Troy down the hallway toward the kitchen. I relaxed, knowing he was in good hands.

"How about you?" Angie asked. "Dating anyone?"

"A couple of first dates," I said.

"Well, find someone good enough to bring to the wedding," Angie said.

"Really?" I asked incredulously. "This is all about you?"

"Of course," Angie laughed. "I don't want you and Troy making scenes at my wedding."

"I don't make scenes!" I screeched.

"Whatever!" Angie said.

"I'll just bring Lisa with me," I said. Angie's wedding was in two months, to the man she had been dating for over a year. I had met him once on my last visit to see Angie. Why she had chosen September I didn't know, but it didn't leave much time for finding an appropriate plus one to show off.

"Perfect," Angie chuckled. "Lisa can find both of you a date."

"Really?" I rolled my eyes at her. I don't know why she was so obsessed with me getting a date. She was getting as bad as Ma.

"You're gonna love the bridesmaid dresses," Angie said. "You've gotta come to Salt Lake to try them on soon."

"I should be able to come over after this Hunt is done," I said, trying to think if I had anything important scheduled. I knew bridesmaid dresses had the reputation for being hideous, but I was excited to see mine. I hadn't owned a formal dress since elementary school.

We walked through the large doorway that separated the Victorian part of The Range from the original fort. The living room showed signs of recent inhabitation: glasses, cans, and cups on most of the flat surfaces. The spare chairs had been pulled out of the storage closet and a semicircle of folding chairs and bean bags had been arranged around the room's normal couch and recliner. The sounds of animated chatter drifted down the hall from the dining room.

"Cousin Letia says that the new vampire, Anabella, wants a couple of the youngsters for winter break," Angie said as we passed through.

"Is she nesting?" I asked, appreciating the subject change.

"I think so," Angie said. "Ma would know for sure."

"I don't remember the last vampire mating we had," I said.

"That's because you were in kindergarten, but it was quite the event," Angie said with a wink.

"What would you know? You weren't old enough to attend, either," I said, frowning at her.

"Hey," Angie said. "I was in second grade and much more mature than you."

"Ma still didn't let you go," I said.

"Well, we're both old enough to go this time," Angie said.

"If Ma will let us; they may not want a big audience," I pointed out.

I slowed my pace and Angie stopped to look at me as we neared the dining room. I shook my head, not wanting to explain why I didn't want to face them yet. My stomach knotted, warning me. Something big was up, and I wasn't going to like it.

Family Heir

Chapter Six

As I reached the door to the dining room my brother appeared, filling the doorway and part of the hallway with his presence. He had gotten all the height, somehow hitting the six foot mark by puberty. Not that I had been born when he hit puberty, but I'd heard the stories. He stopped growing somewhere around six foot three, while the rest of the family struggled for five foot six on a good day. His blue eyes glinted as he shot me a grin.

"Dave!" I threw myself into his arms. I hadn't seen him in years, not since he had moved East to join the BHA when I was twelve. Ma had him when she was still a teenager, and she and Pa must have decided to wait another decade before having Angie and me.

"Hey, kiddo," he said, setting me down and stepping back a little. "I have someone you need to meet."

A thin, athletic man stepped out of my brother's shadow. His brown hair glinted with bits of red in the hall lights and his bright green eyes sparkled as he gazed at me. His mouth slid into a slow smile which hit my hormones in their Achilles' heel. Oh my. I took a deep breath to try to find at least one coherent thought.

"Kelley, this is Brent," Dave said. "Agent MacKrae, I should say. He's the BHA agent on the case you're working."

"Hi," Brent said, extending his hand. I reached out in automatic response. His warm hand enveloped mine, shaking once with just enough pressure to let me feel his strength. I liked strong hands; it bode well for other strength.

"Hi," I said. I sought for something more to say but came up blank. I must have looked like a total idiot.

"And I'm Angie. Pleased to meet you," she said, shoving me far enough aside to grab Brent's hand. He shook it but just glanced at her, his eyes still fixed on me. She shot me a pouting glance before stepping back.

"I'm afraid I interrupted your family get-together," Brent said, still staring at me.

"Oh, we take in strays all the time," Dave said. He made a hand motion toward the door. I decided I had better take the hint and headed on in. The dining room held a long pine table lined with matching chairs. Giant platters of food, empty plates, and cups of all sizes lined the table. Pictures of generations of Venators lined the wall, dating back to the invention of photography. Not much had changed since I was born; they had merely added pictures of Angie and me growing up to the overall collection.

My eyes sought Troy from long-held habits. I found him tucked in a corner, wolfing down food one-handed. Uncle Mack stood nearby, talking to him, an intense expression on his face. The familiar faces of family, the majority of them bearing some shade of red hair with a sprinkle of brown, gray, and white mixed in, sat in small clusters around the huge wood table. Their plates sat abandoned as people filled with food began to fill up on gossip. A few groups had migrated to stand along the walls to talk, taking the chance to mix with relatives from the far ends of the state. It wasn't often that we all got together, and it seemed like everyone had made a festival of whatever this occasion was.

My two siblings shepherded me to the table, with the BHA agent trailing along behind us. Dave disappeared, and Angie shoved me into a chair. By the time she sat down, Dave returned with a plate full of Ma's chili mac. He set the plate down in front of me and slid into a vacant chair. I dug in, unwilling to let home-cooked food go to waste, even if it was past one in the morning. I had no idea if this counted as a second dinner or an odd early breakfast, but I stopped caring when the first bite hit my stomach.

Angie and Dave launched into a long discussion on the relative merits of their favorite bands and I let my mind drift. I could hear bits and pieces of the conversations around the table. The Cheyenne Aunts and Uncles debated with the Laramie branch about whether their local werewolves would be offended by disposable diapers as a baby shower gift. Werewolf tradition insisted on cloth diapers for fear the plastics might harm the infant. Further down the table, a group of cousins discussed the newest painting produced by the vampire artist who had settled north of Cheyenne about the time I had been born.

Aunt Bertha had cornered one of the cousins, launching into a long story about life during the Depression that somehow connected killing her own chickens for dinner and hunting a rogue werewolf. Uncle Harold fascinated an audience of adolescents with descriptions of the scenes from the concentration camps. He had been one of the Army soldiers that had liberated Buchenwald, where he had found vampires, staked in the open yard, who had died of burns from the sun. It had been a slow and painful death, but not as bad as the deaths of werewolves who had been the subjects of medical experimentation.

Pa discussed politics with his two brothers at the head of the table. They couldn't get together for longer than five minutes without launching into an argument about the latest from Washington. From what little I heard, they were upset about the bill before the Senate that would limit the Families' ability to Hunt.

"Why would it be a bad thing?" Angie said, thrusting herself into their argument.

"The hominids trust us to handle things," Uncle Mack said. "They don't trust the government."

"Our hunters could join the BHA like Dave did," Angie said. "Then they would be one and the same."

"That would cut into our income," Ma said, looking down at our end of the table.

"We could diversify," Angie said.

"Those MBA classes are going to her head," Dave whispered to me. I smiled back at him.

"How?" Ma asked.

"Since those of us who don't hunt all go into businesses to serve the hominids, why can't we expand on that?" Angie asked. "If we certified businesses to work with the hominids, charging the businesses for the honor, we would help everyone out."

"No. Families help hominids; that's the way it's always been," Uncle Mack said, glancing at Pa for support.

"But the hominids need more than we can supply by ourselves," Angie said. "Wyoming has more registered hominid voters than human, and the numbers grow every year."

"Wyoming has more cows than humans, too," Dave whispered to me.

"I just spent a month overseeing the building of an addition to Don's house to verify it met vampire standards," Pa said. "It would be nice to have a construction business we could trust to do it right."

Uncle Mack stared at Pa, shocked.

"Exactly," Angie said. "Don's an older vampire so he can afford to donate to us for our services, but we know the young ones can't. So if the businesses were paying us to get and stay certified, we could ensure the hominids got what they needed while we still got paid for it."

"It's something to think about," Ma said. "But we won't decide anything tonight."

"Well," Uncle Mack grumbled, "I don't like it. It sounds like a scam to me."

"You just don't like change," Pa said. "But times are changing."

Ma stood and tapped her glass with a fork. Silence settled through the room as all eyes settled on the head of the table. I held my breath; whatever Ma was about to announce could not be good. Why bring everyone to The Range and not tell Troy or me?

"Speaking of change, it's time to make our announcement. By unanimous vote, Kelley Mallard has been elected official Heir to the Venator family."

The family began clapping and all eyes settled on me.

"What?" I said, eyes widening. I stared around me, waiting for someone to start laughing, to say that it was just a joke.

"It's long past time that Pa and I start planning our retirement. We needed an Heir," Ma said.

"But I'm divorced. You do remember that Troy and I split?" I said, looking back and forth between Ma and Pa.

"Of course we do. But requiring the Heir to be married and have children is just so old-fashioned in this day and age," Ma answered.

"Says the woman who won't put in a driveway," Dave muttered from my right side.

"But what about Dave or Angie? They're older than I am," I said.

"You are the only one of our children to go into the family business," Pa answered, smiling at me.

"But I don't want to be Heir," I whined. I didn't want to run the Venator Hunters. I wanted to get my psychology degree. I had planned on helping people, not running a business.

Several people began talking at once, most of them trying to convince me I would change my mind. Why did older folks always think that they knew my mind better than I did? I had assumed Dave would take over someday; he was the oldest of us. Even Angie would be a better choice with her business degree. I just wanted to find my own niche in the hominid world and live in peace.

From behind me, I heard a cell phone ringing. Now who would dare risk Pa's rage by not putting their phone on vibrate?

I felt a hand on my shoulder. Turning, I saw Brent standing there, phone in hand, face pale and serious.

"That was the FBI," he said. "Snipers killed the Heirs of all the East Coast Families. They are still trying to get an accurate count of the casualties out West."

I felt the blood drain from my face. There were over fourteen Families in the East; I had met several of their Heirs. I could picture many of their faces. I had spent a summer with the Delamores back in middle school and their youngest son had been out here for a visit a couple of times. Who could kill them all?

"Peggy Delamore?" Dave asked in a choked voice. I stared for a moment before I remembered that Dave had dated the Heir of the Delamore family before she got married to another Hunter.

"I don't know all the names, but I did ask for a full list," Brent laid a hand on my brother's shoulder. "I assumed your family would want to know. I am so sorry."

"Does that mean Kelley's a target?" Angie asked. "Someone shot at her earlier."

"I don't know," Brent said. "We should assume she's still in danger."

"Ma, Pa!" Angie screamed. The room fell silent again. "Someone's killing Hunter Heirs!"

Chapter Seven

Brent had expected chaos to break out as the news spread. He knew his family would have panicked if someone announced a sniper might be after a MacKrae. To his surprise, the Venators became attentive and alert within minutes. Ma and Pa had the whole family ready to work within moments. Everyone turned to him, listening while he repeated what little he knew.

"Kelley, Troy, Dave, and Brent—in our office. We still have a mission to plan," Ma ordered as soon as Brent finished.

"Angie, head up the calls. I want contact made with every Family before dawn," Pa added as he and Ma left the room. Brent followed Dave out of the dining room as Angie's voice barked out orders to the others, dividing up the Families to be called. They walked through the industrial looking kitchen and into a small back hall lined with coat pegs, boots, and shoes. Ma opened a door at the far end, which Brent at first had assumed to be a closet.

They entered an office and Brent stared with envy. The two desks held the latest in computer equipment and a large screen TV displaying a map of Wyoming and Utah. Ma, in her white blouse and denim skirt, had struck Brent as a typical housewife, yet she had her computer up in moments. Pa, the typical rancher in jeans, cowboy boots, and plaid shirt, brought his online even quicker.

"Kelley, here's our map of the attacks in your case," Ma said as the map on the large display now showed red numbered dots. "We already ran the distance and time between each attack and this appears to be the path the attacker has been taking."

Kelley and Troy stepped closer to the screen, studying the white line that had appeared. The two looked at each other for a moment, then back over at Ma. Brent stepped closer and Kelley made space for him. The projected path appeared to wind around like a drunken snake.

"How did you figure out this path based on the limited data?" he asked, turning to face Ma.

"I programmed our computer with all the paths through the region; not just roads and maintained trails, but common hunting trails and animal paths," Pa answered. "It's rare for one of the hominids to break a new path. For one, a new path is easy for a Hunter to follow, and two, it's a slower way to travel. So, we assume the rogues will stick to some form of path. Our family has been keeping records on all these paths since we first came out West. It took a couple of years to get all that information loaded into the computer, but it's saved us a great deal of time."

"The BHA has nothing like this," Brent muttered.

"Oh, we are still negotiating with the BHA to purchase it. Most of the Families have something similar, but the BHA hasn't been willing to pay us a reasonable price," Ma answered.

"It's not our fault we don't have much of a budget," Brent said.

"It is what it is," Pa said.

"So where do you think the attacker is heading next?" Kelley asked, peering at the map.

Several dotted lines appeared on the screen, and both Troy and Kelley stared at them. The trails all seemed to be leading south and west, breaking away from each other and meeting back up. It looked like the drunken snake now danced with its friends.

"People," Troy said, pointing to one area of the map.

"You're right. The Lincoln County fair will be in Afton next week, and it will be crawling with people," Kelley said, looking over at Brent as she nodded to where Troy was pointing.

"The attacker won't get that far for at least four more days," Pa said as little hatch marks appeared along the paths.

"So we need to catch up with this creature in the next couple of days," Kelley said, leaning closer to the map as her ponytail slid over her shoulder.

"Here," Troy pointed to another area of the map where most of the paths either came together or paralleled near to each other. Brent wished he had studied the geography of Wyoming before he had come out here. Nothing on the map looked familiar, but he had a vague idea that Yellowstone might be in that region, or was that further north?

"Yes, I think you're right," Kelley said. "We can reach that area after we meet with the Patriarch tomorrow. If we spend the night near Merna, maybe in Daniel, we should be able to hike up there easily enough."

"What if you are still a target?" Brent asked. "Are you really going to continue on this case?"

"Safer," Troy said, looking Brent straight in the eye for the first time. Everything about Troy radiated a sense of controlled violence. Brent had to take a couple of breaths to calm his initial instinct to flee.

"Troy thinks I'll be safer on the Hunt. Hopefully, we'll know the terrain better than whoever is after me," Kelley said, pushing her ponytail back over her shoulder.

"I think Troy is right," Pa added.

"Well, I think we should wait for details from the other Families before we decide anything," Ma said, glaring at her husband and then at Troy.

"We need to talk about this threat," Dave said, looking over at Ma.

"Mission first," Troy said.

"I agree with Troy," Kelley added. "He and I have an assignment and we're going to do it. You guys can figure out what's going on while we do our job."

"You were shot at! Troy was wounded!" Ma said, turning to stare at her daughter.

Kelley looked away and walked to the back corner to sit on a couch Brent hadn't seen earlier. She stared at the floor for a long moment, her head in her hands. She looked up at Troy, the two locking gazes.

"Your call," Troy said, shoulders hunched.

"How's your shoulder?" Kelley asked, staring at his right side.

"Two stitches," Troy answered, shrugging the left shoulder.

"How much will it affect our Hunt?" she asked.

Troy just shrugged, using both shoulders this time.

Kelley sighed and looked over at Dave, who also shrugged.

"It's your assignment, kiddo, you have to make the call," Dave said in a soft voice.

"Troy and I can do this and you can stay here," Brent said. Everyone fell silent and stared at him. After a couple of breaths, they shifted their gaze to Troy.

"No," Troy said, scowling at Brent.

"Kelley and Troy are a team," Pa said. "They both go or they both stay."

"Am I missing something?" Brent asked Dave.

"They've trained together since they were kids," Dave said.

"Oh, don't try to be polite about it," Kelley cut in. "Troy's got a buttload of problems and doesn't work with anyone but me. Could you do this one alone?"

"No," Troy answered.

"Which reminds me," Kelley glowered at her parents. "What are you thinking, making me your Heir? If I have to start doing all the office work, Troy's wasted. Will you just send him out on solitary missions? Try to train someone else to work with him? You don't have enough Hunters to cover our area without Troy and me available."

"She sounds like an Heir to me," Ma said, giving Pa a fond smile.

"She sounds like you when you were younger," he answered with a matching grin.

"I'm serious!" Kelley said.

"Well, that will be one of the first tasks you take on as our Heir," Ma said, her voice gentle, as if trying not to scare away a young colt.

"No," Troy said, looking Ma in the eyes.

"No what?" Kelley barked.

"No decision," Troy said, turning toward her, their eyes locking for a long moment.

"No decision? Of course someone has to make a decision," Kelley muttered.

"Only you," Troy said.

"So my only option is to send you on solitaries?" Kelley asked, a low growl escaping as she finished.

"With you," Troy said.

"What?" Kelley said. "You won't even do solitaries? How will you earn a living without assignments?"

"Doesn't matter," Troy said.

"Whatever," Kelley said. "We are so not having this conversation right now. We have a murderer to find."

"So you're going to go?" Ma asked.

"I don't know," Kelley said, closing her eyes for a long moment. "Yes, I guess so. I'd rather be out there doing something I know than sitting around here waiting for someone else to shoot at me. And maybe it's over."

"Then I have dishes to do. Brent, why don't you help me in the kitchen." Ma said, getting to her feet. She stalked out of the room, refusing to meet anyone's eyes.

Brent followed Ma to the kitchen. The house had fallen silent and he wondered where everyone had gone. The kitchen counters were now covered with dirty dishes. Brent stared at the stacks with dismay, wondering where to start.

"You rinse, I'll load," Ma directed.

Brent grabbed the nearest pile and started working. The plates were caked with grease and left over food, each requiring more scrubbing than he wanted to do. Still, the simple motions gave him time to think. He had hoped this case would give him experience in the field. What was he going to do about the shootings? The FBI and Chief

Ellison expected him to provide some protection, but he had no idea how.

"Tell me the rest of what you know," Ma ordered as she placed the plate he handed her into the large dishwasher. Brent hesitated a moment, but then related to her what he'd learned about the hominid rights groups.

"Hominids for Equality started about thirty years ago," Brent said. "They primarily lobby Congress for legislation to ensure hominid groups have equal rights. They're suspected of a couple of threats against legislators, but nothing has been proven."

"I've heard of them," Ma said. "They seem more of a nuisance than a threat."

"The other group, People for Hominids, has only been active for about a decade," Brent said. "They originally fought against industries, arguing that the working conditions were unfair and unsafe for vampires. They took credit for bombing a couple of small automotive plants last year, and one of their members was behind the mass shooting at the Congregationalist church in Iowa last year."

"Idiots," Ma muttered when he had finished. "Some people always think they know best how other people should live their lives."

"I answered your question; now will you answer one of mine?" Brent asked.

"Maybe. What's your question?" Ma said.

"What's the deal with Troy?" Brent asked.

"Now that's a puzzle, all right," Ma said, shrugging as she motioned at him to keep rinsing. "Kelley brought him home from school one day as if she'd found a stray dog."

"When was that?" Brent asked.

"Oh, when they were about seven or so," Ma said. "He's been a part of our family ever since. His mother abused him badly but never objected to him being with us."

"So, it's all about the abuse?" Brent asked.

"I don't know about all that. Kelley's the one studying psychology," Ma said. "The school said he had a speech disorder and behavioral problems. After a few years, I just started schooling him here. He's a smart kid, but it all stays locked in his head."

Brent thought about his childhood best friend. He'd always known Timmy's dad beat him, but there never seemed to be much he could do to help. His family had been willing to take Timmy in when he needed a place to stay, but Timmy grew out of control by getting into drugs, alcohol, and possibly other things. He joined the Air Force to try to straighten out his life after high school. Brent hadn't seen Timmy since he'd gotten out of the military. He wondered if Troy hid in his head the way Timmy had hid in drugs.

"So he and Kelley were married?" Brent asked, handing Ma another plate.

"Yeah. They'd never dated anyone else," Ma said. "We were all heartbroken when they divorced."

"What happened?" Brent asked as he began working on a glass.

"That's Kelley's business. No more gossip now," Ma said, placing the cup into the dishwasher. "What about you? How much experience do you have?"

"Not much," Brent said. "I've had all the training. In fact, Dave was one of my instructors. This is my first case."

"Well, they may be young, but Kelley and Troy will show you the ropes," Ma answered.

Kelley and Dave came into the kitchen, looking around at the remaining stacks of dishes.

"I better help you with this, Ma. Brent needs to go get his kit together." Dave said as he shooed Brent away from the sink.

"Keep my daughter safe," Ma said to Brent as he left.

Chapter Eight

Brent followed Kelley from the kitchen and into the hall, feeling out of his depth. He'd heard stories and legends about the Families since he was a kid. He never imagined it involved talking tactics one minute and doing dishes the next. He wondered if all Family businesses were like this, a bizarre blend of family and professionalism.

"Dave said you might be a little unprepared for all of this," Kelley said as they headed down a staircase he didn't remember seeing before. The whole house seemed to be a warren of mystery doors and rooms.

"It's all a little new to me," Brent answered.

"That was a polite way of saying we're a crazy old family who seems too informal to know our business," Kelley laughed, shaking her head.

"Well, maybe a little," Brent admitted. He watched her, admiring her easy stride.

"I went on my first real Hunt when I was twelve, so that gives me eleven or so years of field experience," Kelley said. She shot a smile at him before opening the door at the end of the stairs.

They entered the basement, which doubled as a warehouse. Rows of shelves ran as far as he could see, all stacked with boxes and belongings. Kelley weaved her way through the obstacle course of supplies, turned to the left, and then down yet another row. Brent could see Troy pulling boxes off the shelves and tossing things into three army-green duffel bags at his feet.

"What pant size are you?" Kelley asked Brent as she yanked out a box of camouflage pants and tossed three pairs toward Troy. They disappeared into one of the bags, Troy not even glancing at them.

"32/34," Brent answered.

Kelley pulled out another box and dug out some pants.

"Hey, those are BDU pants!" Brent said, looking at the older style military gear.

"BDU?" Kelley asked as she tossed the pants into a duffel.

"Battle Dress Uniform. The old military style," Brent said.

"Well, that's a stupid name," Kelley said as she dragged out another box. "But yes; we buy a lot of old military gear."

"I didn't name them," he said.

"I didn't think you did," she said, smiling up at him over a box of brown T-shirts. "Grab a set and change; you won't want to be wearing that when we leave."

"What? Now?" Brent asked, but when he looked up he realized Kelley had already shucked off her jeans and had begun putting on a pair of BDU pants. He turned away, hurrying to do the same before she could look. When he turned back around, she had tucked a black T-shirt into her pants and begun to lace up a pair of black hiking boots.

With her gun holster on her hip and her hair back in a ponytail, she looked like an advertisement for a mercenary company.

"This time of year, we'll need warm and cold weather clothes." Kelley said. "Troy already has standard hiking and camping gear together. We'll go to the armory next."

"You have an armory?" Brent asked.

"Well, we've collected quite a selection of weapons over the year," Kelley said. "In fact, I think there are still some flintlock guns in there if you dig around."

"I'd love to see the collection, but I came well-armed." Brent said.

"Really." Kelley rolled her eyes at him.

"Of course," Brent said.

"So are you going to show me your guns?" Kelley purred.

Brent stopped and stared at her for a moment. It had been a while since a girl had flirted with him. Was she coming on to him? He could feel his cheeks heat up and knew they must be cherry red by now.

"Are you shy? Not willing to pull it out when a lady asks?" Kelley said. Her smile reminded him of the illustrations of the Cheshire cat he had seen as a kid. He wondered if this was flirting or harassment. He pulled his blazer back to reveal his Colt .45. Kelley stepped closer to him, looking him square in the eye. Her hand slid into his holster, and grasped his pistol firmly. She pulled it out and cradled it as she ran her hand along the barrel.

"Flirt," Troy growled.

Kelley laughed and broke eye contact to look at the weapon. She popped the clip out and removed a bullet. She shook her head and emptied his clip with practiced movements, dumping the bullets into an empty box on the shelf closest to her.

"He's going to need all new ammunition, but otherwise his pistol is sound," she called over to Troy.

"BHA idiots," Troy said.

"I know. No matter how often we try to tell them, they insist on buying ammunition from the lowest bidder," Kelley said, handing back Brent's gun.

"What's wrong with my ammunition?" Brent asked.

Kelley launched into a lengthy technical explanation as she continued along the shelves adding items to their two bags. Brent understood little of what she said, but did learn that a bullet needed the proper amount of pine to kill a vampire and the right quality of silver to kill a werewolf. In not-so-simple terms, they had to have the proper fast-acting poison administered in the proper dose for the hominid in question or the bullet would just make a nifty hole.

"Of course, cutting off heads works well too, but that requires a large sword and close contact," Kelley said, pausing to take a breath.

"Was I supposed to be taking notes?" Brent asked.

Kelley laughed, shaking her head as they reached Troy. Brent saw two duffel bags and several boxes stacked at Troy's feet. He wondered what they would do with all the gear; he couldn't imagine they would take it all with them as they hiked through the mountains.

"Most of this is just-in-case supplies," Kelley said. "If we end up in the mountains for a while, we'll want to set up a base camp."

Troy handed Kelley a vest that looked like the standard flak vest Brent had worn in the military.

"Do I have to?" Kelley whined, holding it up and staring at it.

"Shooter," Troy said, nodding. Kelley glared at him for a long moment before pulling it on.

"It's heavy," she whined, zipping it up anyway.

"Don't care," Troy said, handing her a helmet.

"Oh no," Kelley said, shaking her head and putting her hands behind her back. "No way am I wearing that thing."

Troy placed it on her head and grabbed the duffel bag from Kelley's shoulder, slinging it over his shoulder alongside his own bag. He walked out the door and Kelley pulled the helmet off her head, muttering something that sounded like "leach-brained loser" but he couldn't be certain.

Brent picked up the remaining bag and followed the other two into the armory. Looking around, he was amazed by what he saw. A row of high-powered rifles stood to his right, all with expensive scopes. Shotguns lined the left, as well-accessorized as the rifles. At the far end, he saw boxes of ammunition stacked and labeled in neat columns. He wandered down the row, pulling out some of the finer guns to look at, enjoying the feel of them in his hands. He came across guns that appeared to date back to the eighteen hundreds, but he knew he wasn't an expert. No two were the same; each one was beautiful and clean. They took good care of their weapons. Brent longed for more time to just look around.

By the time he had finished looking around, Kelley had linked her arm through his and led him back out again. She handed over two boxes of ammunition and he added them to his duffel bag.

"Can you think of anything else we need?" Kelley asked Troy.

"No," he answered, not looking back at them.

"All right; time to get on the road," Kelley said with a shrug.

"We're leaving now?" Brent asked, wishing for a few hours of sleep.

"We should be able to get out to the reservation in time to meet with the Patriarch," Kelley said.

"What about the sniper?" Brent asked.

"I'll wear the flak vest for now," Kelley said.

Noise enveloped them as they cleared the top stair back to the main floor. Brent followed Troy and Kelley through the halls, the sound of voices getting ever louder. They entered the living room and found everyone at The Range gathered together. Some sat with silent tears streaming down their cheeks. Others talked over each other, desperate to get their thoughts out into the open. Angie, tears rolling down her face, pulled Kelley into her arms.

"They're all dead," Dave said as he came to stand next to them.

"The Heirs?" Troy asked, eyes widening as he looked around the room.

"Yes, all the acknowledged Heirs in the U.S. were hit by snipers," Dave said. "The Canadian and Mexican Families weren't hit."

Kelley melted into her sister and Dave wrapped his arms around both of them. Brent could only watch as Kelley's shoulders shook with sobs. Other members of the family walked up, hugging everyone they passed. Tears flowed down each of the faces he could see as the noise dimmed to whispered condolences and messages of love. Kelley and Angie remained glued to each other as they made their rounds through the family.

He felt like a foreign visitor who had stumbled into a solemn ceremony he could appreciate but not understand. It had not occurred to him that the Families would be close to one another; he had thought of them more as branches of the government. The grief clogged the room with its weight, pushing him further to the outside. He took a step back, thinking he would wait outside when he caught Troy's eye.

"Load truck?" Troy said to him in a soft voice, gesturing for him to follow. Brent fell into step with Troy as they grabbed the bags, grateful to get away from the grief. The two of them made their way out of the house and into the cool of the night. Troy dumped the bags down and motioned for Brent to stay with him. They went back down to the warehouse and brought up the remaining boxes. Brent stared at the collected gear, wondering if they would have to walk all of it out to the parking area.

Troy disappeared around the corner of the porch and returned leading a pony, cart attached. Brent handed Troy boxes and gear from the porch and Troy settled them into the pony cart with deft movements. They had everything loaded in less time than Brent would have guessed. Troy pulled the pony to a walk toward the parking lot and did not look back to see if Brent followed.

#

They reached the truck as the moon dipped down below the horizon, taking most of the light with it. A Chevy pickup blinked its light as Troy pointed the key fob at it, unlocking the doors. Brent opened the passenger door and the back door, tossing his duffel into the backseat. Troy pushed him out of the way, pulling the duffel bag back out.

"No," Troy said.

"I don't want anything getting wet if we leave it in back," Brent said.

"Don't care," Troy snarled.

"Well, I care and it's my gear," Brent said, crossing his arms and glaring.

Troy ignored him and continued to load the back of the truck. Brent grabbed a box of food and set it down in the bed of the pickup. Troy growled, pulled the box back out, and sat it on the ground.

"I'm trying to help here," Brent snapped.

"Don't help," Troy said, placing a rifle case into the truck.

"I do know how to pack a truck," Brent said, picking up another rifle case.

"You're useless," Troy said, snatching the rifle from him.

"So why bring me out here?" Brent muttered as he backed away from the truck.

Troy shrugged and kept loading. He finished and walked the pony, cart trailing behind, into the barn. Brent could hear him clucking to the pony as he went.

"I know, it's totally crazy," Kelley's voice drifted through the dark. Brent could just make her out, a black shadow moving against a dark background.

"Yes, he's cute. Maybe I'll introduce you later," Kelley said. Was she talking about him?

"I should let you get back to sleep," her voice said. Brent thought sleep sounded like a good idea and wondered when he would get some.

"'Bye, Lisa," Kelley said as she stepped into the light. She tucked her cell phone back into her purse.

Brent opened his mouth to say something, but Kelley climbed into the backseat, leaving Brent to make his way to the passenger side. Troy strode over to the driver's side, straw clinging to his pants.

"I'm taking a nap," Kelley said as the truck pulled out. Troy said nothing as he kept his eyes on the road before them. With a shrug, Brent decided Kelley had the right idea, made himself more comfortable, and closed his eyes.

Chapter Nine

I woke up as the truck came to a stop. I rubbed my eyes and looked around; the nearby mountains glowed in the light of day, their distant peaks surrounding us in a massive hug. Troy opened my door and I slid out, blinking in the bright light. The heat had begun to creep up toward uncomfortable, and I felt a trickle of sweat slide down my back. The steady rhythm of the large farm's irrigation system gave a beat to the otherwise silent morning.

I tried to get my brain up and working, longing for a cup of coffee. It had been an eventful night and I'd had too little sleep. Troy looked as imperturbable as always, but Brent looked as rough as I felt. Looking at Brent's glazed eyes and slow movements, I felt a little better about my own exhaustion. As long as I stayed in better shape than the newbie, this mission had a chance of success.

Troy had parked in front of the main building on the Wyoming Werewolf Reservation, the largest reservation in the state, larger than even the Yellowstone Werewolf Reservation to the north. The huge log cabin in front of them sat tucked into a copse of trees. I climbed the steps to the porch, Brent trailing behind me. Troy, in the lead like always, held the door open. I stepped through, perking up as the rich smell of coffee wrapped itself around us. Troy followed his nose and I trailed Troy into the front room where a large, percolating pot of coffee sat on a folding table. I beat out the boys by a heartbeat to the steaming liquid. I added my normal obscene amount of sugar and creamer while watching the boys prepare their cups. Troy settled in to drink his black, but Brent added as much cream and sugar as I had. I loved a man who liked his sweets!

A few sips of coffee fooled my mind into a semblance of normalcy. I looked around to see that we seemed to have the large cabin to ourselves. I shook my head. How could I not have noticed earlier? The large fireplace took up the whole north wall, a variety of sofas and recliners strewn around the room in no real order. Where were they all? Usually a meeting with the Patriarch involved dealing with his normal entourage of at least ten fellow werewolves. Our visit hadn't been totally forgotten, or they wouldn't have had so much coffee ready.

Troy had already wandered off, coffee in hand, on whatever scouting mission he'd assigned himself. I decided to finish my coffee and wait for his return. I wanted at least two cups in me before I had to take over as leader of this mission. Brent had stationed himself at one of the windows, staring off at the fields as he sipped on his own coffee.

I went over to him, looking out the window at the familiar fields of the reservation. The backyard held the same swing set and slide I had played on as a child, looking a little more worn after years in the elements. Off to the left, three horses hung along the paddock's fence, staring up at the house as they snacked on whatever blades of green they could reach. Beyond the typical Western backyard, fields of wheat and hay could be seen to the right.

"Where is everyone?" Brent asked, glancing sideways at me.

"I don't know. Normally there are people here to greet us," I said, sipping my coffee.

"Does everyone live here?" he asked.

"No. There are cabins throughout the reservation," I said. "The Patriarch's cabin is about a quarter mile to the east."

"He doesn't live here?" he asked, turning to look around the room. It had a very homey feel to it, with paintings and wood carvings by werewolf artists on the wall and worn carpet over the hardwood floors.

"No, this is used only for business and official functions," I said, shaking my head.

"Sounds like you've been here often," he said.

"The local hominids help out with educating Hunters. I spent part of my summers on one of the reservations," I said. "This one was always a favorite of mine."

"Sounds like a fascinating childhood," Brent said, turning to stare back out the window at the swings.

"It's a tradition that goes back to the dawn of our histories, a way to ensure that we all work closely together," I said, turning to look at him. The sun played on his face, highlighting the lines from where he had been sleeping against the truck door.

"Pa says that before the scientists announced the existence of vampires and werewolves to the world, the Hunters were the only ones who knew where the local hominids lived. We often served as messengers and diplomats in addition to our role as law enforcement," I said, trying to distract myself from studying his strong cheekbones and patrician nose.

"I never understood why they didn't police themselves," Brent said.

"For predators, they are basically pacifists. The werewolves prefer spiritual pursuits to violence," I said as I swept my hand around to indicate the delicate carvings of the animals the werewolves communed with that decorated the walls.

"Vampires, on the other hand, can barely stand to be in the same city as another vampire," I said. "They seem to tolerate the presence of humans and werewolves a little better, but they prefer to stay isolated."

"And the Hunters, from the time before our oldest legends, have been kind enough to handle the barbaric necessities that allow us to maintain our way of life," said a deep voice from behind us. I jumped a little and turned to see Old Seth, with his entourage flowing in behind him. He leaned on the arm of Jim, his great-grandson. His cane dangled loosely in his other hand, and his steps were labored. His eyes sparkled with pleasure from beneath the weight of wrinkles that had taken over his face. He stepped forward, using his cane for balance, and held his free arm open. I stepped in for a quick hug, enjoying the smell of fall leaves that always emanated from him.

"Welcome to the reservation, young Kelley," he said as he pulled back.

"Patriarch Bullend, this is Agent MacKrae from the BHA," I motioned toward Brent.

"Welcome, Agent MacKrae," Seth said as he made his way with Jim's help toward the well-used recliner nearest the fireplace. I refilled my empty coffee cup and made myself comfortable on the sofa. Troy reappeared without a sound and sat beside me, leaving Brent to settle into the armchair across from Seth. The werewolves who had followed Seth in placed themselves along the wall where they would remain as silent witnesses during the meeting. Jim poured a cup of coffee and brought it to Seth before he too took his place along the wall.

Brent watched them, eyebrow raised in question. I shook my head; I'd explain it to him later. Werewolves had many strong beliefs, among them that an act must be witnessed to have happened.

Therefore, the Patriarch could not be left alone, to ensure that every moment of his life existed.

"Patriarch, we thank you for the coffee. It's been a long night and we all needed the caffeine," I said, taking another sip of the black liquid of life.

"I apologize for not being here to greet you," Seth said. "We had a birthing. Young Jim is the father of a little girl."

"Congratulations, Jim," I said with a smile. "Seth, you're a great-great grandfather!"

Jim grinned at me and nodded from his place by the wall. Seth smiled, glancing from me to Jim, before his face settled into a somber expression.

"We heard of the Hunters' losses this morning and grieve for you and all of yours," Seth said, bowing his head for a moment of silence. The werewolves along the wall bowed their heads as well.

"Thank you, sir. It was a shock," I said, after the moment of silence had passed.

"We sent three of our best Seekers on spirit walks to see if we could discover anything that would help make sense of this bloodshed," Seth said, glancing at Brent.

"I thought spirit walking just helped you travel," I said, looking over at Troy. He glanced at me and shrugged. I guess this was news to both of us.

"We normally use it to help others, allowing us to travel any distance in three days and find that which we seek without even knowing where it is," Seth said, his words slow and chosen with care, still eyeing Brent.

I knew the werewolves never talked of their talents among outsiders; even Hunters knew only the basics. As all Hunter children did, I had gone spirit walking with one of the Seekers as part of my coming-of-age ceremony among the werewolves. I had no idea if the spirit plane was real or a complex hallucination, but something extraordinary had happened there. After passing my three tests, I found myself stepping onto the porch at The Range three days later.

The Seeker who had been my guide was the only one who would ever know what had happened in there. I had long ago promised myself never to tell anyone. The entire experience had pushed me emotionally and mentally to places I never wanted to go again. I had learned secrets best left alone.

Troy had not done as well with the tests, and the trip had taken him six days. I could no more ask him what had happened than I could share my own trials. However, knowing Troy's past and his broken psyche, I knew it had to have been hard on him. The Seeker who had gone with him had recommended that Troy never try to spirit walk again, possibly out of concerns for his mental health. Of course, it was also possible that he felt Troy would not survive a second attempt.

"We can also use the spirit world to explore the deeper secrets of the universe and ourselves," Seth continued, thinking through how much to say.

"So, they may learn something that could help us understand why the Hunters were killed?" I asked.

"It is the least we can do for you," Seth said, meeting my eyes. "Other Patriarchs have sent their best out as well."

"Thank you, and please pass our gratitude on to the others," I said, following the formula.

The werewolves and the vampires had their own protocols and manners. To me they always seemed old-fashioned, but it never hurt to go through the verbal dances. The werewolves, in particular, expected gratitude for everything and no simple thanks would do. In this case, I was grateful and not just faking it. Whatever group had killed so many of the other Hunters needed to be stopped. The werewolves' offer to help meant we had allies with powers our enemy didn't know about. More than that, it meant we weren't alone.

"Do you still plan to Hunt?" Seth asked, looking from me to Troy.

"Yes, sir. This killer must be stopped," I said.

"I do not believe a werewolf responsible," Seth said, meeting my eyes with his own. I lost myself for a moment in the earth-brown eyes that had seen almost a century of life. Something of those experiences always lurked in his face; those eyes gave me a glimpse of the power of a life well lived. It was powerful and distracting.

Chapter Ten

I pulled myself out of Seth's eyes and back into the present.

"We did not think so, either," I answered. "The DNA didn't match a werewolf."

"I wanted to meet with you before you began. I wish to share what we do suspect might be responsible," Seth said, still looking into my eyes. In all the times I'd been out to the reservation, Seth had never tried a conversation with Troy. I think he found Troy unnerving.

"Anything you can offer will help," I said. "I don't have any ideas."

"I want to share with you a tale which might offer clues," Seth said.

"We would be honored to listen," I said, bowing my head in respect.

"There are tales from the tribes who once lived in this area and the early Europeans who traveled through it," Seth said. "They speak of a shy beast of the mountains, large but somewhat human in appearance, who could occasionally be spotted in the depth of night. These beasts surrounded themselves with an unpleasant scent which distinguished it from the other large beasts so common in those days. Some stories tell of a beast that helped those in need while others speak of dangerous beasts, harming those who crossed its path."

"You think there is truth in these old tales?" I asked.

"There are truths even in lies, child," he said, smiling. Trust a werewolf to go all philosophical if given a chance.

"No riddles," Troy said. I glanced at him in surprise; he always left the talking to me.

"I mean no riddles, Troy. I know no more than I speak and I can only hope that you will find the answers in the scent left from these tales," Seth said, his voice gentle. "Two of the tales stand out in my memory."

"We would be glad to hear them," I said, settling deeper into the couch. The soft cushions enclosed me and I tried not to relax into sleep.

"The first gives me hope," Seth said. "It speaks of a woman of one of the human tribes, living alone and forgotten by her people. One day she came across a wounded beast in the woods. She helped the creature and it thanked her kindly. The next morning, she came out and found meat and other gifts left for her. She thanked the unseen beast, speaking to the trees and the hills."

"So the beast could be kind," I whispered. Seth glanced at me but when I said nothing else, he continued.

"For many years the beast continued to leave her gifts, which allowed her to live comfortably without the constant fear of hunger. One year, her tribe suffered horribly from scanty hunting and a poor harvest. The woman, now old, shared all she had with the tribe. The tribe survived, and in gratitude they took care of the woman from then on out."

"A good deed is always rewarded," Brent said, more to himself than to the werewolf.

"True, young man," Seth answered with a smile. "I think all cultures have a similar tale, but it's the beast that concerns us—not the moral."

"One who recognizes a debt of kindness and had the resources to help," I said, thinking about the type of resources required to help a whole village.

"You mentioned another tale?" Brent said, leaning forward.

"A much darker tale, this one," he said. "From the earliest settlers comes the tale of a man who meets a strange, furry woman in the woods. She takes him in, cares for him, and has children with him. Eventually, he chooses to seek out his own people once again. She tries to prevent him, but he escapes anyway. As he walks away, she kills their children, leaving him with the memory of their screams."

"A beast that is close enough to human to interbreed?" Brent asked.

"It's possible," I said. I had heard tales of werewolves and humans mating, but it wasn't polite to bring it up in our current company. The children were viewed with horror by the werewolves— not that humans were welcoming to such half-breeds, either.

"Unknown hominid," Troy said.

"That is my fear," Seth said. "I thought we had discovered all that lived in this region and do not like the idea that we might be facing one so clever as to have evaded us over the centuries."

"So our Hunt may be more challenging than the others," I said. Great. My first time as lead Hunter, and I faced a complete unknown.

"This particular individual has broken their silence by killing so boldly," Seth said. "Like our own rogues, this killer has abandoned the norms of its species."

"Makes mistakes," Troy said, looking thoughtful.

"The rogues always make mistakes," I said, glancing at Troy.

"Mistakes happen when anyone steps out of the path of their familiar life, when they embrace the wild darkness within them," Seth said. "They do not have the experience to walk in violence unobserved."

"But still, a rogue from a species with skills at staying hidden," I said, wondering if my tracking skills would be enough. Troy was a better at it than I was, but it was traditional for the lead Hunter to track. Of course, I might have him do it anyway. If I could be an heir without a husband and kids, then Troy could track without being the lead.

"Female rogue," Troy said, looking at me.

"The story of the female killing her children?" I asked.

Troy nodded.

"Do you think she was a rogue for living with a human, or for killing her children?" I asked.

"With human," he said.

"That makes them a rogue?" Brent asked.

"It's a sign that they're abandoning their society's norms," I said, thinking of the rumors about Aunt Bertha. Family legend said she had had an affair with a vampire while Uncle Harold was in Europe during World War II. Though, I'd heard no tales of vampires and humans having children.

"Why don't hominids mate with each other?" Brent asked, leaning forward.

"We just don't find each other sexually attractive," I said. "At least, not normally."

"Pheromones," Troy added, looking at me with a challenge in his eyes.

"The biologists haven't proven that yet," I said, leaning forward, ready to argue my point.

"I think this rogue has passed the boundaries of their species so far as to be both extremely dangerous and easy enough to track," Seth said, interrupting before Troy and I could dive into a debate. He must have heard enough of those when we were children to recognize the signs.

"Can you offer us any other help?" I asked.

"I wish I could," Seth said. "You have your path to walk, and we will keep looking for any information that will protect you upon your return."

Old Seth struggled to his feet and Jim leaped forward to help him. They made their way out of the room, the rest of the werewolves trailing behind them. The three of us sat in silence, watching him disappear.

He had not said much, but he had left me thinking. An unknown hominid. It wasn't a new thought; both Troy and I had already considered it. However, it seemed so unlikely that any could have remained hidden in the modern world with all of our technology. The questions crowded themselves in my brain, vying for my attention, and I had no answer for any of them. What would they be like? How could they have hidden from us? How could we catch up with it, and if we did, would we be forced to kill it?

The old Aunts and Uncles still told stories of when the Hunts led to capture more often than kills. Those days disappeared when the human law enforcement system had gained the ability to arrest and hold rogue hominids. I'd never been on a Hunt that did not require a kill.

The rogues we were sent after now were those that had gotten so out of control, so dangerous, that the government could not handle it. The more kills Troy and I had, the more I wanted to give it up and work in a field where I could help people.

I could still remember my first Hunt as a kid; it had been a rogue werewolf from Seth's reservation. The werewolf had just lost his mate to cancer and something deep inside him had snapped. He'd killed a family of werewolves and we had been called in to deal with it. The werewolves still didn't like the BHA on their reservations and had bypassed them to come straight to us. Pa had been lead with Troy and me as his backup. It was supposed to be a simple case, an easy arrest. I'd tracked him to an abandoned cabin at the edge of the reservation and Pa had tried to talk to him, encouraged him to give himself up.

We had begun to move in for the arrest when flames consumed the cabin. Somehow, the werewolf had set a quick, burning fire and killed himself. I never did see the report on how the fire had started; Pa still thought I was too young for that.

They say you never forget your first case. I know I haven't. I still smell burning werewolf in my dreams sometimes. I walked away from that cabin determined to find a better way.

"Leave?" Troy asked.

"Are you okay to drive? You haven't had any sleep." I looked at him, studying him for signs of exhaustion.

"Fine," he said, running his hand through his hair.

"We could catch a couple of hours of sleep here, leave by noon," I said.

"I'm fine," he said, glaring at me.

"Really?" I snapped. "You were shot and you haven't had any sleep. Please explain how you are fine."

Troy shrugged.

"Don't blow me off," I shouted. "This isn't time for you to play Superman."

"I could drive for a while," Brent said.

We both turned to glare at him.

"No," Troy snapped.

"No one drives the truck but Troy," I said, shaking my head. "Even if he kills us all in the process."

"I'm fine," Troy said, squaring his shoulders and scowling at us.

"Fine, whatever," I said, throwing my hands up. "We should probably get on the road. We have a long drive ahead of us, but at least there will be beds on the other end."

Chapter Eleven

I found myself wedged between Troy and Brent in the front seat of the pickup as we headed back toward State Route 28. No more napping for me. The boys felt we needed to spend the drive planning. It wasn't that I disagreed with them—it was that I just didn't feel awake enough to think straight. The coffee could not replace a good eight hours of sleep.

I sent a quick text message to Ma, telling her about Jim's baby. The Family would need to send an appropriate gift; probably diapers, since that was the most traditional human-to-werewolf baby shower gift. Patriarch Bullend had embraced the disposable diapers for his tribe, to the great relief of the new mothers. Others still held that only cloth diapers resonated with the proper spirits to be allowed near a new life. The werewolves had strong protocols for gift-giving, viewing gifts as part of the sacred contract between sentient beings. A gift from friends, family, and partners was required and a gift from others was viewed as a new obligation or contract. It got complicated, and Ma kept track of who owed whom what.

"If it isn't a werewolf, what could it be?" Brent said, looking over at Troy and me.

I glanced over at him, way more aware of the warmth of his knee against mine than I wanted to be. He appeared unaffected by the contact and focused only on the case. His sandy-brown hair stood up at weird angles from his habit of running his hand through his hair as he talked. Part of me wanted to smooth it out for him, but another part just wanted to run my fingers through it to muss it up some more.

"Anything," Troy answered, keeping his eyes on the road.

"We really don't have much to go on," I said. "The hominid likely has some form of claws, judging by the damage to the victims."

"Tall," Troy said, changing lanes and gunning it to pass a large mobile home struggling to make it up the hill.

"Troy thinks the angle of the wounds indicates that the hominid was taller than a traditional human," I said, trying not to look out the windshield. I hated passing vehicles on these two-lane roads.

"Seven foot," Troy said, glancing over at me.

"So, at least seven feet tall, human in form, but with claws," I said, looking at Brent.

"The dismemberment didn't look as if it had been done by blades," Brent added.

"Torn," Troy said, looking back at the road.

"So, very strong on top of the rest," I said.

We fell silent. I tried picturing the possible hominid, and my mind slid away to thinking about how Brent smelled of coffee and aftershave. Did he take time to shave at some point? I glanced at him out of the corner of my eye and saw only smooth skin. Troy already looked pretty shaggy, his dark facial hair visible after going a day without a shave. I pulled my reluctant thoughts back to the case. What would be our best approach to track our unknown killer?

"How are we going to find it?" I asked as Troy's hand reached for the radio. At the sound of my voice, he dropped his hand.

"It would be easier to pick up the trail from the site of the last kill," Brent said.

"Too long," Troy said.

"How many others will it kill before we could find it? The killer's had too much of a head start. We know roughly where it's likely to be. We need to try to cut it off," I said. I hated making decisions, but I knew we couldn't afford to let it get another victim if we could stop it first. Following its trail would be the easier way to go, but we'd never catch up to it.

"So what do we look for to find its trail?" I asked, looking at Troy.

"Eliminate knowns," Troy said.

"I don't know if I'm good enough for that. I know what lives in that area and can probably eliminate most of the trails by the normal animals. But what about the game trails? Too many animals go through there for me to eliminate and narrow those down," I said.

"That's it," Troy said.

"What's it? You have an idea?" I asked, trying not to snap at him.

"Game trails," Troy said.

"You're right; that makes sense," I said as his meaning sunk in.

"What makes sense? What are you two thinking?" Brent asked.

"We'll follow the larger game trails, the ones capable of hiding the path of a seven-foot-tall hominid," I said. "We know they have to be smart or we would have stumbled across them before now. That means we can eliminate the smaller trails."

"Will it work?" Brent asked.

"It's our best chance. So, Mr. Agent Man, time to play get-to-know-you," I said, changing the subject to something much more fun.

Brent shot a surprised glanced at me. Gosh, it was so easy to get a reaction from him. It was like dangling a toy in front of a cat; I couldn't resist playing.

"Why, yes," I purred. "If I'm taking you into danger, I need to know what's under those agent clothes."

Brent's cheeks reddened as his eyes widened. Yep, I'd gotten him again. Troy growled, still annoyed by my bad habits. I couldn't help it. There was just something so sweet, so fun about a man who blushed like a virgin. He couldn't be a virgin, could he? Still, I should try to play nice or at least act somewhat professional. Some fool had put me in charge of this mission.

"What did you do before the BHA?" I asked. Troy's shoulders relaxed and Brent's tensed up.

"Air Force Intel for four years," he said.

"Did you deploy?" I asked. I had never met anyone who had been in the military before—well, I mean the modern military. Many of the vampires had been soldiers at some point in their long lives.

"Yes, I spent time in both Afghanistan and Iraq," Brent said, staring at the road ahead of us.

"Why'd you get out?" I asked. Troy rolled his eyes and shook his head. He always got irritated if he thought I was getting too personal.

"It's all a long story. I joined after high school because my best friend, Timmy, had joined. My parents were furious with me," Brent said, looking over at me.

"Why would they be furious? The military is a good option," I said.

"I was supposed to go to college and become a lawyer, a doctor, or an accountant—something that fit into their idea of the upper middle class," he said.

"So your family had some money?" I asked.

"Not rich or anything, but yeah, we did okay," he said, shrugging his shoulders.

"So you got out because they pressured you?" I asked.

"No. Timmy got wounded on his first tour of Iraq and was discharged," Brent said.

"Oh no," I said, putting my hand on his knee. "That's horrible."

"After that, well, I don't know. I never adjusted well to the military and just couldn't think of a reason to re-enlist." Brent said, staring back at the road.

"What's your family like? Do you have siblings? Nieces? Nephews?" I asked, changing the subject to what I hoped would be a happier one.

"My parents divorced when I was in high school. My dad remarried my senior year, but my mom still hasn't found anyone else. I have two sisters; the oldest got married a couple of years ago. And yes, I have one nephew," Brent said, grinning.

"So, girlfriend? Wife? Anyone special?" I asked, unable to meet his eyes.

"No," Brent said, staring at me so hard I finally looked up, losing myself in his green eyes.

"Kelley," Troy barked, warning me to back off.

"What? He's met all of our family. Shouldn't we know about him?" I asked.

"No," he said.

"Fine. What else are we supposed to talk about for the next gazillion hours on the road?" I said.

"Don't pout," Troy said.

"It's all right; I don't mind answering questions," Brent said.

"See? He doesn't mind." I said, sticking my tongue out at Troy. His chiding had taken the fun out of it. I loved learning all about new people, but not if Troy was going to be grumpy. He could hold onto a pout for longer than any man I had ever met.

"My turn to ask questions, then," Brent said, smiling at me.

"Go for it," I said, smiling right back.

"What's your favorite fairy tale?" he asked, cocking an eyebrow.

"What?" I said, looking at him. I hadn't guessed he would be the type of man to be into tales of princes and princesses. That had always struck me as a girl thing.

"Just answer the question," he said.

"Beauty and the Beast," I said.

"So you are attracted to the strong, moody, silent types," he said, looking at Troy.

"How'd you conclude that?" I asked.

"My sister always told me that a girl's favorite fairy tale showed what type of man she was attracted to," he said.

"And you think the Beast was moody and silent?" I asked.

"You don't?" he asked. "So how do you see him?"

"Of all the fairy-tale princes, he was the only one who talked to his princess and really listened to her," I said, thinking it through. I had never thought about why that particular story appealed to me, but I had always loved how the two had gotten to know each other despite being so different.

"I never thought about it that way," he said.

"I mean, what did Sleeping Beauty's prince do besides climb through some brambles and give her a kiss?" I asked, though it was not a question. Yep, he had stumbled into my secret addiction. I loved fairy tales—all of them. The little girl in me still wanted to be a princess with my very own happy ending.

"He does more in the Disney movie," Brent said.

"But that version does away with the one hundred years of enchanted sleep," I argued. "The older versions have her marrying some kid young enough to be a great-grandson."

"What? You study fairy tales?" Brent asked.

"No," I huffed.

"Yes," Troy said.

"Hey, who invited you into this conversation?" I said, elbowing him.

Troy shrugged.

The conversation drifted to other topics as the miles passed. I learned all about Brent's taste in music, books, movies, and TV shows. We liked the same classic rock bands, but that was about it. He defended his opinions well, though, and I enjoyed talking with a man who could explain why he liked or disliked something. Now that I had thought about it, I just liked talking to men who used full sentences!

Chapter Twelve

I listened to my stomach grumble and stared out the window. Where were we, and could we find food nearby?

"I need food," I told Troy.

Troy shrugged.

"No, really," I said, turning to face him. "You can drive until the truck runs out of gas, but the rest of us humans need to eat and use a bathroom."

"Not yet," Troy said.

"Seriously?" I said, leaning in to see the gas gauge. "You're already under a half tank. Can't we stop?"

"No."

"Please," I begged. "Please, please, please."

Troy stared at the road for a long moment before nodding. Of course, it took another twenty minutes to find a gas station and some fast food—not that Subway counted as fast food, but it was what we had on hand. Pinedale did not offer a lot of options, and Troy would not be willing to search further. Brent and I went for food while Troy gassed up. The teenager behind the counter gave me a funny look. I guess he didn't get women in flak vests ordering sub sandwiches that often.

Brent and I returned to the truck with bags of food for all. The seductive smell of fresh bread drifted straight from the bag to my stomach, which rumbled in anticipation. I had splurged and added cookies to my feast. My waistline would not thank me, but I felt a need for some good comfort food. I mean, if having someone try to kill you isn't an excuse for a cookie, what is?

I managed to devour my entire meal before Troy had time to start on my cookies. Brent ate with neat precision, not spilling anything. Troy kept glancing at Brent's remaining food, his eyes hungry and predatory. I rolled my eyes and dug in my purse for the candy bars I had bought while we had been stopped. I handed one to Troy and was awarded with one of his grins. The effect still startled me. Troy's most common expression was a blend of irritation and distaste but his rare smile melted knees (at least female knees, maybe a few men).

We neared the end of US 191 and the time for a decision. It was six in the evening, and we still had a couple hours of daylight left. Troy and I could manage the hike and make camp for the night with daylight to spare. I eyed Brent, contemplating his stamina. Being from back East, his body wouldn't be used to the altitude. Not to mention, Troy hadn't slept at all while Brent and I had managed a couple of catnaps. Real beds began singing a siren's song in my mind, calling me away from the mountains for the night.

"Hike?" Troy asked as he neared Daniel's Junction.

"No, I think a hotel for tonight. We'll all be better after a full night's rest." I said, knowing I was just being selfish.

"Sure?" he asked, glancing at me. I knew he'd have pressed on if he had been in the lead. A small burst of anger flared to life but died, extinguished by sheer exhaustion. I nodded.

He turned onto US 189, heading a bit out of our way. Daniels had a hotel and it was the last one in the area that I knew of, but this part of the world did not have many options. We pulled into Timberline Lodge and I smiled, remembering vacations here as a kid. The main lodge, a huge log building with a stone fireplace, looked like something out of an adventure brochure.

I walked into the lobby. The bright light from the windows reflected off the polished wood floors and various animal heads and pictures hung from the log walls. The whole place was empty. Peak season had passed, which meant we would not need reservations. I talked the guy at the desk into giving us a room, though he seemed determined to sell me on a cabin for the night.

Brent came in just as I turned to leave. I waved the keys as a sign of victory and we headed down the hall to find our suite. I opened the door and watched Brent's eyes widen as he saw the small apartment-like layout. We had a kitchen and living room—not to mention pine stairs leading up to the bedroom. I climbed up the steps, throwing myself onto one of the two queen-size beds.

"Who's sleeping where?" Brent asked.

I opened one eye to see him standing by the TV, staring at the two beds. I was too tired to take advantage of the wonderful opening he had given me to harass him some more.

"I don't care," I said. "There are the couches downstairs; I can take one of those and leave you boys up here."

"No," Troy said as he walked in. He held up a sleeping bag and pointed to the floor. I guess he planned to camp out up here.

"You haven't slept at all. You should have the bed," Brent said, standing up and gesturing toward the other bed.

"You two boys can argue it out from here," I said. "I'm taking a nap."

Sleep took me quickly. I drifted into the fuzzy world of dreams. I stood in the house Troy and I had lived in as a married couple, the background dissolving into swirls of purple, black, and red. Troy stood before me, silent with arms crossed. I looked at my hands, surprised to find a large baseball bat that had not been there a moment ago. No, no, no, I whimpered to myself. Not again. I raised the baseball bat, unable to control my hands. I swung it at Troy over and over. He raised an arm to block the blows. I heard the bat connect and then the horrible, gut-wrenching sound of bone breaking.

I woke up covered in sweat, gasping for breath. The vivid image of Troy's arm, broken bone poking through the skin, remained imprinted on my eyelids. I shuddered and curled myself into the fetal position, hugging my knees tightly against my chest.

"Nightmare?" Troy asked, his voice soft and gentle.

I nodded.

He moved to sit on the bed next to me, but I scrambled away. Visions of the bat in my hand, the horror of hurting him, lingered with me. Troy looked at me with big, hurt eyes and moved from my bed to his place on the floor. His puppy dog eyes never left me.

"I'm sorry. The dream with the bat," I said.

Troy nodded and dropped his head, breaking eye contact. I struggled to get my breathing back to normal, to slow my pulse. Breathe in, then breathe out. My head cleared, the dream fading, and I looked around. Brent stared at me from his bed across the room. I refused to meet his eyes, embarrassed that he had witnessed my weakness, my horror.

Brent shook his head and moved over to sit next to me on the bed. He reached out, moving slowly enough that I could avoid him, and took my hand. His warm fingers closed around mine and I looked up at him.

"Bad dreams happen," he said, his voice warm and gentle.

"I know," I mumbled.

"It wasn't real; just keep reminding yourself," he said.

I dropped my eyes and stared at our entwined hands. The dream was real, in some ways more solid than the waking world around me. I could remember the sights, the sound, even the smells. I wanted to close my eyes to shut out the image. I knew it waited for me—existing in my mind—something I could not avoid or run from.

I pulled away from him, standing up. I hated this, the dream and the reality. Everything that had happened over the past few days pressed in on me. I felt the anger rise. It wasn't fair. I just wanted a normal life. I kicked the bed, trying to release the fury. I was a good person! I slammed the wall with my fist. I didn't want to be responsible for Troy's pain. I hit the wall again. I didn't want people shooting at me. I kicked the wall. I didn't want to be Heir; too many lives would depend on me. I screamed, low and guttural.

Strong arms surrounded me, holding me still. I could smell Brent's aftershave as his body pressed against mine. I struggled for a moment, but his arms tightened, pulling me closer.

"Take a deep breath," he whispered into my hair. "It's all right, we're here."

I followed his advice, taking slow breaths, feeling my lungs fill up and then empty. With each breath, the anger seeped from me leaving only the pain beneath. I felt a tear slide down my cheek, and my body shuddered in a sob.

"I've got you," Brent said into my ear.

I began to sob, the uncontrollable pain of no longer having any control over my life or myself.

Brent turned me around, pulling me into a deep embrace. I cried on his shoulder until there was nothing left. No anger. No pain. Only emptiness. I pulled away from him slowly, giving Brent an embarrassed smile.

"I'm going downstairs," I muttered as I opened the door.

I walked down the steps and saw that one of the boys had set up his laptop on the rustic pine end table. I slid down onto the plush brown couch, sinking into the deep cushions. I pulled the laptop over, turning it on. I needed to clear my mind, to think about something outside my nightmare or my life. Homework always did the trick. It might be boring, but at least it wasn't trying to kill me.

I loved the idea of online courses and the freedom from lectures. I had decided to give them a try for the summer semester. The classes required more homework than I had imagined. I figured this Hunt should be over in a week, maybe two. Depending on how much time it took, I might be able to get the discussion board questions for two weeks answered. Sure, I didn't have my text books with me, but the class was History of Hominid Interactions. I should be able to ace it in my sleep. I took it for the easy credit more than anything. Though, I had been interested to see how the official history compared to the Family's history.

I logged in and scanned through the posts on this week's discussion board. I'd posted my own main response before this whole mess had begun, but still needed to respond to another student. I hated trying to find a student's response that I could answer. Most of the time, I just wanted to tell them they were idiots. Since the assignment required a thoughtful response, I had to scan for a post with something containing a little substance, if not intelligence.

I saw that Joe Smith had posted and read through his response, eager to see what he had written. Of all the students in my class, I found his take on hominid interactions the most fascinating. The others all seemed to get confused between the reality of hominids and the fiction of monsters we had inherited. No, vampires did not seduce young girls and drink their blood. No, werewolves did not infect their victims, should they survive. Joe seemed to understand that the hominids were completely different species.

Joe Smith had agreed with my own take, which reaffirmed my belief in his intelligence. No, hominids would not have revealed their existence if scientists hadn't figured it out. Back in the 1940s, doctors had begun to gather information showing that some of their patients had differences in their blood that made no sense. It took science another ten years to gather enough evidence to overcome the natural skepticism, proving that at least two other branches of hominids had evolved and survived to the modern age. They gave the two new species fancy names, but popular culture called them simply werewolves and vampires.

I replied to Joe's post and commented that I felt that humans would have reacted with violence if the hominids had revealed themselves. Centuries of legends and fairy tales had taught humans that these beings were dangerous monsters, and no reassurances that they made would have stopped the slaughter. However, since it was human science which revealed them, people by and large trusted the doctors and biologists to present the truth. It had taken a while for humans to adapt to the idea, but they had done so with a minimum of violence. In fact, the hardest part of the adjustment had been getting people to believe their old myths were real.

With my response to Joe done, I turned my attention to the discussion board question for next week. Why did human laws extend to hominid species? I remember listening to that debate at the dinner table growing up. The vampires had always lived among humans and avoided each other. They had very little in the way of laws or tradition. I still could not understand how a species evolved to dislike members of its own kind. What would Darwin make of that? Anyway, it had made sense to wrap them into the already-existing framework of human law and society.

The werewolves, however, had a long history of intricate laws that governed every aspect of their behaviors. This had been one of the reasons they had applied to the federal government to be given reservations on the same terms the American Indians had been given. While this followed already-existing precedence, it allowed the werewolves to maintain their own traditions for the most part.

The practical reality was that the humans outnumbered the other two species and had ready-made complex laws that fit the needs of the hominids in most circumstances. It hadn't been getting the laws to fit that caused a problem; it was getting the punishments to fit. Life in prison for a vampire could span hundreds of years. While it was possible, it didn't seem fair or practical. The end result had been adjustments that, when possible, applied to all species. So sentences were now handed down in years. Humans now got a hundred or more years of prison time instead of life. Each species was provided prison cells that accounted for their species' needs, and we continued to try to figure out how to adapt as new hominids joined society.

I submitted my response and stared at the screen for a moment. I wasn't ready to go back to the bedroom. I decided to log on to the Families' site and see if anyone had learned anything new about the shootings. Yes, the Families had adapted to the modern age and had their own Internet site to allow for easier communication with the global community. I scanned through the comments.

Most of them were expressions of sympathy from Europe, Canada, and Mexico. Some of the American Families had posted eulogies for their lost Heirs. The stance of the American Families seemed to be that none of them would declare a new Heir until we knew what was happening. The most interesting part? I had a new title: The Last Heir. Delightful. I didn't want to be an Heir at all, and I certainly didn't want to be the last one in the country.

I sighed and logged off. I had better get back to the room and try for a good night's sleep. I climbed the stairs and opened the door to the bedroom. I stepped forward and found myself falling backward, sliding down the stairs. The night echoed with the sound of breaking glass as I tried to wrap my mind around what had happened. Brent and Troy appeared at my side, grabbing my arms to pull me the rest of the way down the stairs. They each had their guns out, scanning the living room in both directions. They pulled me to a corner well out of sight of the windows.

I sat up, moving with caution, and looked down. I could see where the bullet had hit the flak vest. It had been a clear shot to the heart. I felt my hands start to shake as the adrenaline reaction set in. I had faced death before, been in battles with hominids willing to kill me rather than be killed themselves. I had been the Hunter then, the one in control of the encounter. I had never been the one hunted before and I did not like it. I found myself gasping for breath as the fear pressed around me. I closed my eyes and lay back down, trusting the boys to watch over me until I could get myself together.

Chapter Thirteen

Brent closed his eyes, forcing his breaths in and out in a steady movement. Don't flash back now, he told himself. When he trusted himself again, he pulled out his cell phone as soon as he felt the danger had passed. He listened to the ringing on the other line, waiting for someone to pick up. Finally, a voice answered.

"This is Agent MacKrae, BHA. A sniper attempted to kill Heir Venator," he said, trying to sound calm and professional.

"She's alive, then," the voice said, flat and expressionless.

"Yes. The bullet hit her flak vest," Brent said.

"We want you to bring her in. We have a safe house ready," the voice said.

"I'll let her know," he said.

"Call me back and I'll give you the details," the voice said before hanging up.

"Who was that?" Kelley asked, her voice still shaky.

"My FBI contact. He wants me to take you to a safe house," Brent said, running his hand through his hair.

"I don't know," Kelley said, staring at the ceiling.

The sound of police sirens echoed in the night. The three of them looked at each other in silence as the sirens got closer.

"What do we tell them?" Kelley asked.

"The truth," Brent said. "But I better let the FBI know. I'm not sure how they'll want to handle this."

Brent called his contact back.

"The police are heading here. Any instructions for dealing with them?" he asked.

"I'll make calls from my end. They can offer you protection en route to the safe house," the voice told him.

"If the shooter is still nearby, won't that be a little obvious?" Brent asked.

"We know how to handle these matters," the voice responded before hanging up.

"Leave now," Troy said, staring down at Kelley.

"You don't trust the FBI?" Brent asked.

"We protect," Troy said, thrusting his shoulders back.

"The shooter has to know what your truck looks like," Brent pointed out.

"I protect," Troy said, standing up and stepping toward Brent.

"Do you think the safe house would really be safe?" Kelley asked, sounding like a lost little girl. Brent looked down at her. Her face in the moonlight looked scared and tired. He wanted to take her in his arms, comfort and protect her.

"I don't know. We still don't know who's behind this or how good they are," Brent said, trying to ignore Troy's stare.

"So I'll either be a sitting duck or safe," Kelley said.

Brent just nodded. He wished he could offer more reassurance, but he had his own hesitations. His gut told him to pack Kelley up and take her far away from all of this. As much as he hated to admit it, he agreed with Troy. They should leave.

"Let's get out of here," Kelley said, getting to her feet and ignoring both of their offers to help.

They headed toward the balcony door to their suite with Troy in the lead. They hugged the walls, guns at the ready. Troy opened the door and slid out to the patio, scanning the area. He motioned Kelley to his side, crouching beside the hot tub. Brent joined them a moment later, staring into the night. He could see the trees in the moonlight and smell the pine. The mountains rose in the distance, tall guardians in the night.

He could see two forms approaching. He aimed his gun, waiting to make a clear identification. As they came closer, Brent could make out the police uniforms. Troy and Kelley broke into smiles at the sight of them.

"Don," Kelley said, walking toward one of the officers and bowing with a graceful nod of her head.

"Mr. and Mrs. Mallard," the officer returned with a slight nod of his head.

"Don't you keep up on gossip, Don?" Kelley asked with a smile. "We're divorced now."

"My condolences," the officer said, lowering his head in a moment of respectful silence.

"What happened here?" the other officer asked.

"Someone's been taking out Family Heirs. I'm the only one left," Kelley said with a shrug. Brent stared at her, surprised by her sudden calm.

"Miss Venator, you were made the Venator's Heir?" Don asked.

"Yeah, and I'm not happy about it," Kelley said.

"Miss Venator and Mr. Mallard are Hunters from the Venator Family," Don told his partner.

"So this was an assassination attempt?" the other officer asked.

"We think so," Brent said, stepping forward.

"And you are?" Don asked.

"Sorry. I'm Agent MacKrae of the BHA," Brent said, pulling his badge out of his pocket.

"Then you are on a Hunt," Don said to Kelley, who nodded.

Another officer came running around the corner of the lodge and grabbed Don's partner for a private discussion. Kelley watched him as he disappeared from sight while Don stared at Brent.

"Yes; an unknown hominid has been killing humans," Kelley said, looking back to Don.

"And the FBI wishes to provide Kelley with a safe house," Brent added.

"By the bonds set forth long ago between our people, you have but to ask," Don said, staring into the night, refusing to make eye contact.

Kelley and Troy shared another one of their long glances. Brent looked away and studied Don. The officer looked no older than twenty-five. He was at least six foot tall, and very pale. His black hair made his white skin look almost translucent. His body language confused Brent; he stood still, moving in practiced gestures when speaking. Brent had no idea what to make of this strange acquaintance of Kelley and Troy's. His gut told him this Don did not want to be involved, no matter what he might say.

"I, Kelley of the Venators, request sanctuary for myself and my team," Kelley said, looking back at Don.

"As it has always been, so shall it be now," Don said, bending his body in half in formal obeisance. "I am not set up for guests."

"I know," Kelley said. "If I had a better option, I'd never ask this of you."

"I do my duties," Don said, shoulders pulled back.

"Thank you," Troy said.

Don's partner returned at that moment, eyeing them all with suspicion.

"I have been instructed to take you all to a more protected location," he said.

"Yes, my partner," Don said. "I will ensure their safety."

"Those weren't my instructions," his partner said, eyes narrowing as he looked at Kelley.

"James, this is not a human matter any longer," Don said, staring at his partner without blinking.

"It sounded like humans trying to kill humans to me," James said, returning Don's stare.

"This has become a matter of the Families and of vampires," Don said.

"Fine," James said. "Agent MacKrae, you agree with this plan?"

Brent just nodded. Don was a vampire? This night kept getting stranger and stranger.

"All right, then," James said with a shrug. "I'll assume MacKrae's the ranking federal agent and we'll do it your way."

Brent and Kelley made their way back inside and up to the bedroom to grab their things while Don and Troy went to grab the rest of the gear from the truck.

"How do you know Don?" Brent asked.

"He's one of the vampires my Family assists," Kelley said.

"A vampire police officer?" Brent asked. His idea of vampires still had a lot to do with Dracula. No matter what he had learned in the BHA academy, he could not imagine Dracula being a police officer.

"Sure; he got bored and thought police work would be interesting for a few decades," Kelley said, tossing her things back into her bag.

"And this place of safety?" Brent asked.

"Don's the oldest vampire in Wyoming," Kelley said, exhaustion making her words slur a little.

"And that means?" Brent asked, tossing his things into his bag.

"The older ones tend to get a little paranoid, so his house is more like a fortress," Kelley said. "Nothing will be able to get us there."

"Is he someone you spent summers with?" Brent asked, watching as Kelley packed up Troy's belongings.

"Oh no! He's too paranoid to let kids go running around his place," Kelley giggled. "And we spent winter break with the vampires; more hours of night to spend with our hosts."

"But you trust him?" Brent asked.

"Sure. He may be a little odd, even for a vampire," Kelley said. "But he believes in the old ways, the sacred duty of vampires to protect their Families in a time of need."

"Do you know every hominid in Wyoming?" Brent muttered.

"Of course. It's part of the job," Kelley answered, shooting him a smile as she picked up her purse.

On the way back through the living room, Brent grabbed his laptop and tossed it into his bag. He'd have to pack it better later, but he did not want to take the time. Kelley struggled out the door ahead of him, carrying both her own duffel bag and Troy's. Brent reached over and grabbed them both.

They made their way back to Troy and Don, who stood in the parking lot, lost in private silences. James stood with them, talking with animated gestures, until he spotted Brent and Kelley. He turned toward them.

"We'll leave your truck parked at the station," James said.

"What?" Kelley said, looking from James to Troy.

"Safer," Troy said, shrugging his left shoulder.

"All right, let's go," Kelley said.

Don held open the back door of the patrol car as James slid into the driver's seat. Brent and Kelley crawled in.

"Troy?" Kelley asked, turning to peer out the door.

"He'll follow us," Don said, shutting the door.

"Will he be safe?" Kelley asked as Don slid into the passenger side.

"His choice," Don said. "Now lie on the floor and keep your head down and out of view."

Kelley lay on the floor, her legs draped over Brent's feet. For safety's sake, Brent slouched low as the car pulled out of the parking lot. His heart pounded so loudly he wondered if Kelley could hear it. His breathing became ragged. The fear beat at him and he closed his eyes, trying to slow his breath, to calm himself. He felt Kelley's hand wrap around his calf, patting him.

"We'll be okay," she said, keeping her voice down.

"Aren't I supposed to be comforting you?" Brent asked, opening his eyes to look at her.

"Well," she said, eyes twinkling, "you weren't doing a good job at it. I thought I'd show you how it's done."

"I'll take notes, then," he said, choking a little on the laugh that threatened to escape.

They pulled to a stop and Don opened the back door. They were in a parking lot behind a squat brick building he assumed must be the police station. He stood and looked around, seeing Troy's truck pulling up beside them. Kelley crawled out and Brent stepped away to give her room. Don gestured for them to follow him, and soon they had piled into his tiny Toyota Corolla.

They pulled out onto the road and Brent closed his eyes. He could hear the others breathing, but no one said a word. The gentle rhythm of the car's wheels against the road and the hum of the engine lulled him to sleep as exhaustion beat out fear.

Chapter Fourteen

Brent opened his eyes again in surprise as the car came to a halt. Looking up, he saw only a garage and a blue Ford pickup next to them.

"Where are we?" he asked as he rubbed the sleep from his eyes.

"Don's place in Merna," Kelley said, crawling out of the backseat and heading for the stairs. She reached the door to the house and turned. Brent blinked and Don stood beside Kelley, unlocking the door and turning off an alarm system.

"Permission to enter your home," Kelley said.

"Enter," Don said. He moved slower this time, staying in sight, as he went to help Troy get the gear from the trunk.

Kelley opened the door and motioned for Brent to follow. He looked back at Troy, thinking he should help, but exhaustion won out. He followed Kelley up the stairs and into the house. He heard the trunk slam shut. He turned to see Troy and Don walking toward the door, duffel bags slung over their shoulders.

Don's house was a small ranch-style built of cement several inches thick. The interior looked as if an antique store tornado had hit it. Furniture and decorations from historical periods Brent couldn't even guess at covered the house in a patternless sprawl. A strange scent, something like decaying roses and rosemary, covered everything.

They all settled into chairs in the living room. Kelley filled Don in on everything they knew about the shootings and their case. Troy sat in his usual silence, studying Kelley as she talked. Brent listened with part of his mind as he tried to think of what to do next. It seemed clear that the shooter still wanted Kelley dead, and he had no idea how to protect her. He supposed she could stay in the vampire's home until the FBI figured out who was responsible and put an end to it. Only, they also had another killer to catch.

He had no idea what he could offer to solve either problem. Kelley and Troy may not have the professional sheen of his fellow agents, but they knew the terrain and the local hominids. They knew their jobs—whereas he struggled to remember BHA regulations and policies. He had military intelligence training, but that was useless without access to all the government intelligence data. He was an analyst and not a real operative. He felt like extra baggage drug along just in case he was needed. He'd pack up and head back to Washington, D.C., where he could at least help from an intel gathering standpoint, but that would mean conceding he couldn't be the agent that he wanted to be.

"Well, that's about it," Kelley finished.

"So you need to remain alive and you need to catch this killer," Don said.

"Catching the killer seems much easier right now," Kelley said.

"Then that should be where you focus your energy," Don said.

"And my safety?" Kelley asked.

"I am required to offer you sanctuary; it remains yours if you ask," Don said, arms crossed.

"But when would it be over? Who's going to stop this guy?" Kelley asked.

"The FBI has that job," Brent said, forcing himself into the conversation.

"So I would need to stay here until they found the shooter?" Kelley asked.

"Yes," Brent said. If she would just agree to stay here, Troy would refuse to work with him and he would be free to go back to his computer systems. He might be able to find who was after her and help the FBI solve the case.

"Do they even have anyone in Wyoming yet?" Kelley asked.

"Not that I know of," Brent said. He wished his contact had given him more information. For that matter, he wished he knew about the FBI. Did they even have agents in Wyoming? Where would their nearest offices be? Maybe he should have listened closer to Jan's stories.

"So, do my job and possibly get shot at, or stay here for ages?" Kelley asked.

No one answered.

"Troy?" Kelley asked, looking over at him.

"We hunt," he answered.

Kelley fell silent, her unfocused gaze fixated on the carpet. Brent longed to say something to comfort her, to help her make this decision. He could not think of anything useful. She had the lead; he would follow her directions.

"We should all get some sleep, then. We have a long day tomorrow," she said, after the silence seemed to have stretched on for an hour.

"We hunt?" Troy asked.

"Yes," Kelley said, shoulders slumped. "We do our job."

"I protect," Troy said, laying his hand on her shoulder.

"I know you'll try," she said, patting his hand.

Don led them to their separate bedrooms. Brent entered his and saw a rusted army cot in a room full of wooden crates and cardboard boxes. He must have been given the room with the warehouse motif. Brent sat on the cot, lost in thought. He made a decision, pulling out his cell phone and dialing.

"Hi, Chris," he said when a voice answered.

"Brent? What's up?" Chris's voice came through the line, clear and welcome.

"I have an odd favor to ask. Do you guys do anything with domestic terrorism?" Brent asked.

"Technically, the NSA focuses on international terrorism," Chris answered.

"Have you heard of the hominid-rights group taking out Family Heirs?" Brent asked.

"Are you involved with that? I thought BHA just focused on hominids," Chris said.

"I'm working a case with one of the Heirs out here in Wyoming," Brent said. "She's been shot at twice now."

"And you thought I might be willing to look into it?" Chris asked.

"I was thinking I have no idea what to do, and you taught me everything I knew back in Iraq," Brent said.

"I can't promise anything, but I'll ask if I can work on it for you," Chris said.

"Thanks. I appreciate anything you can do. I'm out of my depth here," Brent said.

"Hey, you were the best young analyst I ever worked with and I can't imagine you aren't up to this," Chris said.

"It's just a different world out here," Brent said.

"You chose the BHA after seeing the atrocities the werewolves had suffered in Iraq," Chris said. "Never forget why you are doing this."

"The Families there were devastated by their inability to protect the hominids when the chaos started," Brent said, his voice soft as memories took him back to a time he preferred to forget. He could still see the pictures of the bodies, tortured and killed. The Iraqi insurgents had killed whole werewolf families, believing them to be allied with American forces. It had been one of his cases as an analyst: to try to locate the insurgents responsible. He remembered the young Heir of the Baghdad family begging the Air Force for help and how the young man had cried as he told Brent all he knew.

"The hominids there were never accepted into society," Chris said. "If you've run into a new form of hominid, you have a chance to help them and give them all the Iraqi hominids never had."

"But to risk the life of a young civilian to do it?" Brent asked, getting to the heart of what kept bothering him.

"You're a civilian, too, these days," Chris said. "You have to stop thinking like you're still in uniform. She's a Hunter, doing her job. You wouldn't stop doing your job just because your life was in danger."

"I know, but…" Brent had no idea how to finish that sentence. He knew Kelley could do her job, but that didn't mean he shouldn't protect her.

"Do you like her?" Chris asked.

"What's that got to do with it?" Brent asked.

"I think your knight-in-shining-armor complex is interfering with your good sense," Chris answered.

"You don't think I can be attracted to a woman and still respect her enough to let her do her job?" Brent asked.

"You haven't yet," Chris answered with a laugh. "I promise that I'll do what I can to figure out who's after your damsel in distress."

"I appreciate it," Brent said before hanging up.

He lay down and tried to get to sleep. His mind ran through the events of the day, teasing him with all the moments he had failed to act, all the times he had offered nothing. I can offer information, he told himself. They may know everyone in the hominid community, but he had contacts in the government. He still had ways to find things out.

Chapter Fifteen

My cell phone alarm chimed. It was one of the most annoying sounds possible. I woke up in a strange bed, my heart pounding. I stared at the walls covered in mismatched tapestries and paintings. Memories trickled back, disconnected and out of order. I was at Don's. Someone had shot at me. I was Heir. I was Hunting. I closed my eyes again, longing to go back to sleep and wake up three days ago. The dang phone kept going off.

I shut off the alarm and thumbed through my messages. I had lots of them for someone who had been asleep for just a few hours: one from Ma, one from Dr. Lyman, and plenty from Lisa. First, I listened to the voice mail from Dr. Lyman, enjoying the authoritative sound of his voice. He assured me I would have a job when I came back and told me to stay safe. Then, the message from Ma told me to stay safe. Really? Why was everyone telling me to stay safe? I wasn't asking to be shot at! I texted Ma back that I was alive, at Don's, and would head out Hunting soon. I called Lisa back; it was quicker to talk to her than to text.

"You aren't going to believe what my mom did now," Lisa started straight in without even a hello. "She just showed up at the door, demanding to stay here while you were gone. I still had a boy here!"

"So is your mom sleeping in my room?" I asked, smiling at the image of Lisa's religious and conservative mom waking up to the vision of my naked Apollo poster. There was nothing like a classic and oh-so-gorgeous Greek god to start the day. Maybe a good look would help her mom loosen up?

"Oh no, I sent her packing," Lisa said. "She left willingly enough when she saw my date."

"Will she forgive you?" I asked.

"Eventually," Lisa snickered. "Now she knows you led me to the ways of the devil!"

"Hey," I laughed. "I thought you were corrupting me."

"I keep trying, but you won't let me!" Lisa said. "I'll never get why she's so hung up on the werewolves being pagan. They seem a lot more peace-loving than her church is."

"Never argue with religion, my Ma always said. It's like trying to figure out the Buddhists. People have a hard time understanding all of the werewolf teachings. I've been around them my entire life and don't get their spiritual practices."

"Oh, don't get started on that," Lisa whined. "You make my head hurt when you try to explain."

"We're heading into the mountains today," I said, shifting conversational gears.

"So I won't hear from you again until you're done," Lisa said.

"Yeah," I said.

"Well, don't let anyone shoot you," Lisa said, her voice serious. At least she didn't tell me to be safe. Well, at least not in so many words.

"I'll take care. Promise," I said.

"Love ya and miss ya, girl," she said, hanging up.

I smiled as I tossed the phone onto my bag. Talking to Lisa always gave me the courage to face my day. I swung my legs out of bed and dug through the duffel for clean clothes. The ones I had on passed dirty and had hit ripe sometime last night. Old army pants, T-shirt, sweatshirt, undies, bra, socks, bathroom kit, and my .45 Colt revolver. It made for quite an armful, but I stumbled out into the hallway in search of a shower and a towel. The delightful smell of coffee and bacon hit my nose the moment I opened the door.

I hesitated a moment, tempted by breakfast, but opened the bathroom door instead. I wanted one last long, good shower before we hit the mountains. I may not be a Barbie-doll type girl like Angie or Lisa, but I hated getting dirty—at least, the type of dirty that involved grime under the fingernails and greasy hair. The hot water hit me, washing away the remaining stress. I took my time cleaning up, making sure to shave as well as possible (who knew when I'd get to do that again) and taking extra time with my hair. I stared at myself in the mirror, pleased enough with what I saw. I wondered if Brent would notice; it wasn't often that I managed a French braid. I shook my head to clear the thought. Work first, think about men later.

Once I felt clean, I hurried to dress and finish the morning routine. Gathering up my dirty clothes and wet towels, I darted back to my room to toss everything in my bag, eager to get to the kitchen. I managed to get back to the kitchen before the boys had finished off all the food. I dug into the piles of bacon, eggs, and waffles with a good appetite before my brain kicked in. Don even had French vanilla creamer for my coffee. My morning was perfect.

"You know how to cook?" I asked Don.

"All this new technology intrigued me. I wanted to know how to use my kitchen," Don said.

"Well, my stomach thanks your curiosity! This is wonderful!" I said.

"I am glad it came out well. You are the first humans I've had over to taste test it for me," Don said, nodding his head toward me.

"Nesting," Troy mumbled around a mouthful of eggs.

"Are you?" I asked Don.

"Yes."

"Hey, Annabella just moved here and she's nesting, too," I said.

"I know," he said.

"Oh!" I said, my brain catching up. "She moved here for you?" Vampires never stayed with their mates. Once the hormones shifted, they couldn't stand their mates and would return to their solitary lives. However, some pairings worked well and the vampires would seek each other out again the next time they went into heat rather than mate with a stranger.

"We've mated in the past," he said.

"That's so sweet," I said.

Don just stared at me.

"Sorry," I mumbled. I knew better than to expect romance from a vampire.

"I will, of course, be asking your Ma and Pa to do the negotiations for me," Don said.

"They will be delighted," I said, trying to get my tired brain back into vampire formality-gear. I should never try conversation with a vampire without at least two cups of coffee or a good night's sleep. "If you are both open to company, my sister and I would be honored to attend."

"I will remember," Don said. It wasn't a promise, but it was a start. Maybe Angie and I would get to see a vampire mating.

"Thank you again, for everything. We'll try to be out of here before you need to get to bed," I said.

"I've got another hour or so before the sun rises high enough to force me to sleep," Don said. He stood and poured himself another cup of coffee. He brought the pot over and topped off all of our cups.

"I didn't know vampires drank coffee," Brent said.

"We can drink nearly anything, but it offers us little nourishment. Of course, coffee does not provide nourishment to humans, either," Don said as he sat back down.

"True, but many of us need the pick-me-up in the morning," Brent said.

"I, too, like the feel of the stimulant. This century's soda pop has been another treat for me," Don said. I smiled over at Brent. He was doing a good job charming the vampire.

"But you don't eat?" Brent asked.

"No. The vampire digestion system can only handle liquids. Animal blood provides all of our required nutrients, though the last few decades have offered us a wide number of options."

"The training classes don't really get much into the everyday details," Brent said. "Would you mind answering a few more questions?"

"If I can. I know the basics of my life, but truthfully, Miss Venator and Mr. Mallard probably know more about my species," Don said, nodding toward Troy and me.

"Why is that?" Brent asked.

"Vampires are solitary," Don said. "I have not seen another vampire in nearly a century, and that meeting was a brief biologically-required encounter. With Annabella, in fact."

Brent looked confused and glanced over at me. I smiled at him and mouthed the word mating to him. His cheeks flushed to their most charming pink, and he stared into his coffee cup for a moment.

"Pa said you had an addition built?" I said, giving Brent time to collect himself.

"Yes," Don said. "I am grateful for your Pa's assistance."

"Is there anything else we can do for you?" I asked.

"Not at this time," Don said. "Your Ma e-mails me regularly to ensure my welfare."

"Shower," Troy said as he stood up and took his dishes to the sink. He disappeared down the hallway.

"How are you enjoying police work?" I asked.

"It is a pleasant physical challenge," Don said. "It has been a while since I used my full speed or strength. Plus, you humans do the oddest things."

"We sure do!" I said.

"It had been a few centuries since I interacted this much with your species," Don said. "I find much has changed since then."

"Yes; the whole world seems to have changed, according to my old Aunties," I said.

"They are right. I can barely comprehend a world where stealing an identity garners more riches than breaking and entering."

Brent took his dishes to the sink and I followed. As Brent sat back down, I began running the water to clean the dishes. Don may have adjusted well to the modern world, but I had yet to meet a vampire who had adjusted to modern roles of women—even when they knew the times had changed. He would freak out if one of the boys offered to help with the cleanup. It was a miracle he had even been willing to cook.

"I gather the Families do a lot more for you than just acting as law enforcement," Brent said as he sat back down.

"Yes. For vampires they have been essential intermediaries between us," Don said. "We do not mind human company; some of us even enjoy it. So we rely on humans for any social needs and to help us with others of our own kind."

"Are these matters things you would trust to the BHA?" Brent asked.

"The older we get, the more we resist or just ignore change," Don said. "The BHA has made huge strides in the last few decades, but it would take centuries before vampires trust them the way we do our local Families."

"The Families have served the hominids for as long as the history of all three species records," I told Brent. "We meet different needs for both vampires and werewolves. Law enforcement has always been a small part of our role."

"I believe the werewolves are more independent of you than the vampires," Don said.

"In some ways," I said. "The werewolves still depend on us as negotiators between different reservations and with the vampires."

"Education," Troy said as he reentered the kitchen. His hair was dripping water down the side of his face and his clothes were damp. He never did take the time to dry off all the way after a shower. His facial hair remained untouched; he had decided against shaving in favor of speed. He handed me the flak vest I had left in my room.

"I am not wearing this into the mountains," I snapped.

"Yes," Troy said, stepping forward to loom over me.

"No," I said, crossing my arms, anger burning through me like acid.

"Put on," he said.

"Don't boss me," I snarled, shoving him. I pulled my fist back to hit him but stopped, staring at my closed hand hanging in the air. I closed my eyes, counted to twenty. I opened them to see him standing there, round eyes gazing at me with a mixture of hurt and love. Dang, the kicked puppy look.

I put the vest on, feeling trapped as I zipped it up. I turned away from him, unwilling to meet his eyes. The weight of it made my shoulders ache; and to think the day had not yet begun. I shoved my discomfort away. Time to get back on track. I tried to remember where the conversation had left off—werewolves and education.

"Yes, the werewolves do not like being around humans, so we often provide them with whatever advanced education they desire," I said.

"Well, I better shower so we can get going," Brent said as he got up from the table.

Troy joined me by the sink, taking the dry dishes and finding homes for them in Don's cabinets. I heard Don sigh at Troy's participation in the kitchen. I motioned for Troy to sit back down, but he shook his head and kept putting the plates away. Troy and I worked together in silence, finishing cleaning the kitchen in record time. Our host had closed his eyes, taking on the stillness that often preceded vampire sleep. I had just finished sweeping the tile floors when Brent reappeared.

"I think we're ready," I told Don. He took several seconds to reopen his eyes.

"Here are the keys to my pickup," he said, holding out a set of keys.

"We truly appreciate all your help," Brent said.

"I fulfilled my obligations. You must now fulfill yours." Don turned and walked back toward his bedroom.

We nodded our acknowledgement to his departing back and loaded our gear into Don's Ford pickup with as much speed as we could manage. It was a bit smaller than Troy's truck, but we made it all fit. The sun had just begun to make an appearance as we pulled out of the driveway. Troy, as usual, drove as we headed away from Merna toward the Bridger-Teton National Forest and the trailhead closest to our target search area.

Chapter Sixteen

We all settled into Don's pickup, and once again I got the center seat. The drive itself took less than twenty minutes. It took us at least another twenty minutes to sort out our gear. In the end, I carried a small backpack holding just my ammo, a hoodie, and a rain jacket— plus a SOCOM 16 rifle. I tucked a couple of bottles of water into my thigh pockets, wet wipes into the right hip pocket, and a couple of protein bars into the left hip pocket.

Troy had sorted through all the boxes, selecting enough supplies to keep the three of us comfortable for at least a day and tossed them into an empty duffel bag while his personal gear and most of mine went into a backpack. Troy shouldered the bulk of our supplies as well as his own gear. At my insistence, Brent pulled out a change of clothes, some food, and water to put in a backpack, leaving his duffel in the truck.

We headed up the trail, walking on one of the paths maintained for tourists.

"Do you really act as matchmakers for the vampires?" Brent asked as we walked.

"Are you interested in vampire sex?" I asked. Sure enough, bright pink spread across his cheeks. He was just too easy.

"It's not so much matchmaking as it is negotiating," I said. "Vampires only come into heat once a century or so, and it's hard for them to woo a mate when they avoid each other. For the most part, we keep good records of who might be coming into heat at the same time and let our vampires know who their options might be. After that, we negotiate between the two to determine when and where. More importantly, we negotiate the fate of any offspring. Most vampire matings don't result in kids, but when they do vampires rarely want to raise them."

"Dare I ask what happens to the kids?" Brent said.

"Most of the time," I said, "one of the Families will raise them until they're ready to launch. Occasionally a vampire wants to raise a kid and we negotiate an adoption."

"I feel a little like Alice," Brent said.

"The reality of the hominids doesn't match the books and movies," I said.

"Not sexy," Troy said.

"Nor scary," Brent added. "Why isn't any of this in my training?"

"No one felt it pertinent to law enforcement," I said. Ma often ranted about how stubborn the BHA was; they held myopic views about what their agents needed to know about hominids. How could you enforce laws when you didn't know the society or the biology?

"What happens if a vampire doesn't find a mate?" Brent asked.

"Go rogue," Troy said.

"Most vampire crimes occur when they are in heat and haven't found an outlet for those urges," I said.

"What happens to those in prison?" Brent asked.

"We successfully petitioned to get vampires conjugal visits, but none of them will be in heat anytime soon,"

"You seem so much older than you are," Brent said.

"It's not age, it's experience," I said. "I grew up with all this, an apprenticeship that started at birth. I know more about vampire and werewolf cultures than I know about humans."

"So you can tell me about vampire mating but not human mating?" Brent asked with a shy grin. I blushed. I didn't even know I could get embarrassed.

"Umm, I was married, you know," I half stuttered. Brent laughed.

Troy gestured for silence as we slowed down. We left the main trail and had begun following one of the larger game trails. I kept my eye out for anything out of place along the right side of the path, trusting that Troy had the other side covered. I moved as quietly as possible. Of course, Troy moved more silently than I did; he had a unique gift for it. Brent managed to do well for someone not used to our wilds; he was a little louder than I was, but not enough to startle our target.

The trees shaded the trail, the undergrowth reaching out to snag or trip us as we moved. The branches offered handholds for balance as I fought my way up and down along the path, often clinging to a branch to keep from sliding onto my butt. The steady buzz of flies, sounding more like bomber aircrafts than tiny insects, broke the silence. The wind rustled the trees and caressed my face as we walked. My arms itched from scratches left behind by the overgrowth. I pulled the hoodie on, knowing it would be too hot but needing something to protect my skin.

The path began to angle upward. The going roughened. I found the extra weight of the flak vest dragged me down. The boys began to get ahead of me as I began to struggle, feeling the burn in my leg muscles. My chest and shoulders ached with the additional exertion and my lungs strained for air. I kept the boys in sight and began debating ditching the vest.

To my annoyance, my morning coffee made a call of nature necessary and I began glancing around for a good place to pee. The boys had glanced back, but I waved at them to keep going while I found a clump of trees capable of sheltering me from view. An awkward stance and a few more moments took care of my bodily needs. The wet wipes kept me sanitary, or at least that's what I told myself. As I made my way back to the path, I saw the boys in heavy competition to scale a rock pile.

The rocks lay piled like discarded children's toys. Moss had begun to grow on many of them, giving them greenish tones. Troy and Brent elbowed at each other as they pulled themselves up rocks standing taller than either of them. They had made it about halfway up, managing to stay even with each other. From where I stood, I had a nice view of straining butt, arm, and back muscles. Now that was a view! I told my hormones to behave and contemplated how best to make my own way up the stone.

I headed their way, bemused by the need of boys of all ages to compete. As I reached the rock pile, I heard a noise off to the left. I froze, listening hard. The boys had reached the top, but again I waved at them to go on. Troy stared down at me and I glared back. I put my hands on my hips and tapped my foot. There was no way I'd let Brent watch my awkward crawl up the rocks. Troy nodded and headed down the path. Brent followed and they disappeared from sight.

I heard the sound again, but it didn't sound like a deer or an elk. Whatever was moving out there was big, though. Maybe a bear or a moose. Or maybe our killer. I pulled the rifle off my shoulder and held it at the ready. Moving with careful steps I made my way toward the sound, making as little noise as possible. The path narrowed and the long grass whipped me in the face.

Up ahead, I saw it. Standing over seven feet tall, it stood with its back to me. The chocolate-brown fur held swirls of beige, guaranteeing it wasn't a bear or any other creature I knew. Sure enough, it looked like a big, hairy person. The wind blew against my face, hitting me with an odor I could not describe—maybe a blend of decaying fish and skunk. I fought not to gag as the smell intensified.

Oh. My. God. I'd found Bigfoot! I couldn't think of anything else to call it, as images from children's books flitted through my head. But was it our killer? Just because it happened to be an unknown hominid, in the area we thought the killer would be, did not mean it was the killer. Okay, it would be a huge coincidence if it wasn't the creature we sought. Still, I didn't just want to shoot on an assumption.

I followed the creature as it made its way along the path, reaching for my cell phone. A quick search of my pockets convinced me I had left it in my purse back in the cab of the truck. Well, there was a slim chance that I'd even have a signal. I wondered if the boys had noticed I wasn't behind them yet. I'd be more confident with Troy here. I might be a better shot than he was, but I'd feel better with some backup.

I couldn't just kill it but I couldn't just follow it forever, either. I needed some way to determine whether it was the killer. What had Old Seth said of the tales? A creature that helped those in need, but could be dangerous. That was it. Could I play wounded? If it attacked I could kill it, but if it ran away could I conclude it was innocent? For that matter, would I be quick enough to kill it if I was faking hurt?

I wished the boys would hurry up and find me. If I was playing bait, I'd rather not have to defend myself, too. There had to be a better plan. I continued to follow the beast as I thought it through. The creature did not appear to be moving with a purpose but moving at a

119

sedate pace along the path. It kept looking around and sniffing the air. Was it even intelligent, or was I dealing with a big animal?

A deer darted across our path and the Bigfoot took off in a blur of fur, breaking the deer's neck. I stopped dead. That creature was fast and strong—even faster than a vampire. I wouldn't have a chance if it attacked me. All I could do was watch as it disemboweled the deer and began eating. From what I could see of the deer's corpse, I was pretty sure it was the same type of damage done to the murdered humans. So probably the correct species, though it told me nothing about whether or not I had my killer. Dang, I hated this. Where was Troy? He always made these decisions.

I settled into the brush, deciding to let the possible hominid continue on its way. I needed to find the boys and track it when I had backup. I wasn't going to chance killing an innocent creature. I didn't want to risk my life, either.

The wind shifted, and I felt it against the back of my neck. The Bigfoot turned and gazed at me with copper eyes. We both froze, staring at one another for a couple of heartbeats. Then, a low howl issued from the creature as it eyed me for a long moment. It began to move in a blur of speed, leaping. Right at me.

Chapter Seventeen

I pulled my rifle up, hoping to get a shot. The creature flew at me, faster than my reaction time, and I landed on my back with Bigfoot on top of me. The sheer weight of the beast made it difficult to breathe. The rifle lay trapped across my chest, but my fingers brushed the gun at my belt. I stretched my fingers, unsnapping the holster.

Bigfoot roared at me, the stench of rotten fish and skunk wrapping around me. Working my hand a little further over, I managed to wrap my fingers around the pistol grip. I pulled it out an inch at a time, straining against my own weight. I released the safety and twisted my wrist at an awkward angle. The creature reared up. I saw claws, like a handful of sharp kitchen knives, heading toward my head.

I pulled the trigger. The beast fell back a little. I kept pulling the trigger until I heard the click telling me that the clip was empty. My ears rang from the noise of the gun and I lay dazed, trying to gather my thoughts. The creature had fallen across my legs, unmoving, the horrendous smell dissipating. I stared at it for a long moment, waiting for any sign of movement. Nothing. I had killed Bigfoot. I closed my eyes and shuddered. I had a dead body lying on my legs.

I fought to get my legs free, twisting every way I could. Primal panic pushed me hard; I needed to get away from this dead thing, this creature I had killed. I heard my own breath, more a whimper than a breath, as I tried to kick my legs. No luck. I couldn't move my legs at all. Fear of being trapped teamed up with horror at touching a dead body, shoving me over the edge into unthinking terror. My whimpers became muted screams as tears rolled down my face.

My legs came free as the weight disappeared without warning. I scrambled back into a crouch, rifle clutched in both hands as I stared. A second Bigfoot, this one had cinnamon fur blended with pumpkin orange, stood to almost twice my height—ten feet tall at least. He carried the Bigfoot I had killed and arranged the body with gentle hands. Oh crap! I had killed his friend. I clicked the safety off and aimed the rifle. I was going to be ready this time.

He turned toward me, moving in slow, deliberate motions. Startling purple eyes, tinged with blue, met mine. Despite the terror, I could not help appreciate the beauty of the creature before me. He studied me for a long moment before sitting down on the path, several feet away.

"You killed Sincha," the beast said in English.

"I was attacked," I said, arms shaking as I clung to the rifle.

"That is irrelevant," the beast said. "It is a crime to kill a fertile female."

We sat staring at each other. I could end this right here, pull the trigger and run to find Brent and Troy. The creature did not move, did not appear at all aggressive. He sat still and calm, like a statue of a Bigfoot. I took my finger away from the trigger. I could not kill in cold blood.

"So what happens now?" I asked.

"I arrest you and take you back for trial," the Bigfoot said, still not moving.

"I'm under arrest?" I asked. The absurdity of it hit me and I found myself giggling despite my efforts to control myself. I had spent a lifetime training to arrest or kill hominids and here I was, the one under arrest.

"Are you okay?" the beast asked.

"Yes," I gasped, trying to control my laughter. It had to be nerves. The situation was not at all funny. I tried to pull myself together, but the hysterical giggles kept pouring out.

"What is that sound you are making?" he asked.

"Laughter. Humans make that noise because we are amused or nervous or just losing our minds," I answered. I suspected mine was the latter. I was nuts. Here I was, discussing the meaning of laughter with a creature out of legend. A creature who was going to arrest me! Of course nerves ran a close second to insanity. I hadn't been this nervous since the first time I'd had to give a speech in school.

"And which were you?" the beast asked.

"I'm not sure; can I get back to you on that?" I asked. I sat up and took inventory of the damage.

My sweatshirt had been torn to shreds, though the flak vest underneath seemed fine. I guess this was the second time in two days I owed the awful vest for saving my life. I stared at the hoodie and its shreds. I'd liked that shirt; Lisa had bought it for my last birthday. I should know better than to wear something nice on a Hunt. However, outside of the shirt, everything seemed intact. Well, everything seemed to be covered in blood and mud but since most of the blood wasn't mine, I'd live with it.

I flicked the safety back to the on position and slung the rifle over my shoulder. Since I wasn't going to shoot this guy, I might as well free up my hands. Bigfoot stood, his movements slow and steady, giving me plenty of time to react. I watched him, ready to run if he leaped. He walked over to me and held out a hand or paw or whatever you wanted to call five fingers with scary claws.

I reached out and took the extended extremity, watching as my entire hand disappeared in its grip. He pulled, not enough to hurt, but enough to get me back on me feet. My body felt a hundred times heavier than it had this morning.

"I am called Domel," the beast said once I was standing.

"Hi, I'm Kelley," I said, smiling. Maybe charm could get me out of this. "I'm one of the Venator Hunters, if you've heard of us."

"I have heard of your Family," Domel said. "I did not know they had a Kelley."

Ouch. That was a blow to the old ego.

"I usually go by my married name, Kelley Mallard. Though, I guess now that I am divorced, I should go back to the Family name." Great. I was babbling. That was never a good sign.

"Kelley Mallard of the Venators, I place you under arrest for the killing of Sincha," Domel said.

"Umm, do I have a choice?" I asked.

"No," he said. "Do you offer options to the hominids you arrest?"

"Good point," I said, shrugging. "Can't blame a girl for trying. So, how's this work?"

"You shall accompany me back to my people and then stand trial for your crime," he said.

I nodded and picked up my backpack. Two more Bigfoot appeared from the woods and gathered up Sincha's body. They disappeared into the trees before I could react. I stared after them, thinking of the woman I had killed. It had been easier to deal with not knowing her name, not knowing the Bigfoot could talk.

"Did you know her well?" I asked.

"There are few of us; we all know each other well." Domel said.

"I am so sorry. I didn't want it to end like this," I said. There had been so much death. The other Heirs, and now poor Sincha. Even if she had been a killer, I didn't feel good about pulling the trigger. Now that the adrenaline had deserted me, I felt the guilt settle in.

Domel gestured for me to follow and I did. Every part of me ached and each step increased the pain. I realized that I still had both the handgun and my shotgun. I could try blasting my way to freedom. The boys couldn't be far behind; they had to have heard me when I killed Sincha. I could get out of this mess.

No, my gut told me that was not the answer. Domel had done no wrong, nothing to earn the death penalty. The fact that he had not killed me already indicated that whatever legal process they had, it might yet give me a fair chance to prove my innocence. Besides, no one knew of the existence of Bigfoot. Heh, what was the plural? Bigfoots or Bigfeet? I must have lost it if I was contemplating grammar.

Anyway, the end result: I was the only human with conclusive proof that Bigfoot was real. Perhaps I could convince them to become one of the hominids the Families protected. It would be better for them if they came into contact with the larger hominid community.

"Would you like my weapons?" I asked Domel.

"You can keep your guns until we reach the settlement," he said. "I do not believe you will shoot me, and your restraint will help your legal defense."

"So how come you speak English? Do you have your own language?" I asked.

"We had our own language once," Domel said, "but it died out as we all grew addicted to your radio and TV programs."

"You have radios, TVs, electricity?" I asked.

"Of course. We are quite civilized." His lips twitched upwards and I hoped they smiled the same way humans did.

"How is that even possible?" I asked.

"Generators," Domel said.

"So how come no one knows about you?" I asked.

"We have not chosen to be known," Domel said. "We have talked about it since your government recognized vampires and werewolves, but we look so different from you that we did not think we would be accepted."

"There are many hominids that have chosen not to let their existence be public knowledge, but they let the Families help them." I said.

"Yes, I know," Domel said. "Do you believe that gives you and yours the right to act as law enforcement even on those you know nothing about?"

"I believe it is my job to protect all the species that have accepted the help of the Families," I said. "If that means occasionally being at odds with a species we do not have formal contact with to save the lives of those who look to us for protection, then yes."

"You speak like a lawyer," Domel said.

"I talk like a Hunter, trained from birth to the responsibilities before me."

"But you kill without regret," Domel said.

"No, I always regret killing," I said. "I wish I never encountered a situation that required the death of another being."

"Truly?" Domel asked.

"Yes," I said.

"Why do you do it, then?" Domel asked.

"I want to become a psychologist, to help hominids as a healer of minds," I said. "At least, I did before I was named Heir. Now, well, I guess I Hunt because I'd rather a Hunter dislike death than have those who embrace it take over."

"And now you are a philosopher," Domel said. I smiled up at him, surprised at the teasing.

"I guess my college classes are paying off," I said.

We hit a steep incline and I had to give up on conversation in favor of gasping for air. Domel took several steps, outpacing me, before seeing my struggles. He came back to my side, walking slower to keep from leaving me behind again.

"Is there anything I can do to assist?" he asked as we reached the top of the slope and I stopped to rest a moment. I shook my head, still too out of breath to speak. My lungs stopped burning and my heart eased to a more tolerable beat.

"I'm okay" I said, still gasping a bit for air. "I'm just not used to hiking like I used to be. And I'm certainly not used to wearing this vest."

"I could carry you," Domel said.

"I'd rather stay on my own two feet," I said.

"Then may I carry some of your gear?" he asked.

I handed him my backpack and the shotgun. I pulled out one of the protein bars to eat as we walked. We continued along the trail in silence. I wondered if the boys were looking for me. If they were, I wondered what would happen if they found me. Could I calm Troy down before he escalated the situation? How would Brent respond? He was an unknown factor in the equation. I wanted rescue, but no more corpses.

Chapter Eighteen

We walked until close to sundown, taking breaks for me to rest as often as I needed. The Bigfoots ahead of us came to what appeared to be an abandoned mine shaft and disappeared into its darkness. Domel and I entered and soon came to a dead end with a hole leading to who-knows-what with a ladder descending into darkness. Studying the ladder, I realized that there was no way I could reach from rung to rung. Domel saw the problem the same time I did.

"You'll have to let me carry you down," he said.

I nodded and crawled on to his back. I hadn't ridden piggyback since I was five or six. It was an odd feeling to be carried as if I weighed no more than a backpack. Domel began the descent and I clung to his back. The darkness left me nothing to look at; in fact, I could tell no difference between having my eyes open or closed. I considered keeping my eyes closed, but I worried I might fall asleep.

After what felt like an eternity, I saw light beneath us. A few heartbeats later, we stepped down onto what appeared to be a subway station platform. The other two Bigfoots stood by Sincha's body as far from us as possible. A few minutes after we arrived, a subway pulled up. The other Bigfoots took Sincha's body and boarded first. Domel motioned for me to follow. The seats were way too large for a human, but I climbed up on one and curled up like a little kid on a couch. The subway began moving and I stared around. The small car held about twenty seats, ten to each side. Domel sat across from me while the others sat on the far side of the car, guarding the corpse laid out on the floor between them, careful not to bump it against the seats along the way. There were no windows, but a large map on the wall of the car seemed to show where we were. I watched the little light that I thought represented our subway as it moved along bit by bit.

"We should be to the settlement in about an hour," Domel said.

"Do you really have subways under the Rocky Mountains?" I asked.

"It took us several decades to build them," he said.

"And no one noticed?" I asked. Had the Bigfoots evolved to be the stealthiest of the hominids, or the most ruthless?

"Are you wondering if we killed any witnesses?" he asked.

"No, that hadn't crossed my mind. Did you?" I asked.

"We have simply been gifted with an ability to avoid detection," he said.

"Then how did I find Sincha?" I asked.

"She had lost herself," Domel said. "A hunter accidentally shot her daughter and she lost control. We tried to restrain her, prevent her from hurting anyone, but she managed to get away."

"I'm sorry," I said. "I cannot imagine her pain." Great. I had killed a grieving mother.

"You mentioned an interest in psychology earlier," Domel said.

"Yes, that's my major," I said.

"Do you think human and hominid psychology are the same?" he asked.

"No, I think each species thinks and feels differently. I wanted to discover those differences and find a way to help," I answered.

"After watching Sincha's mind crumble before our eyes, I have to agree. We need some study of how our brains work," he said.

"You could go to school and get a degree in psychology," I said.

"I haven't decided on my major yet," he said.

"You go to school?" I asked.

"Online classes," he said. "I have just been taking a class at a college and then transferring because I am worried I might expose my people."

"Online classes are pretty anonymous; I can't imagine them catching on," I said.

"It's hard to set up the required bank accounts and IDs to allow me freedom of the internet and online classes," Domel said. "I keep changing them so no one will trace them."

"That sounds like a lot of work," I said. "Do you have any assistance from others?"

"No," he said. "We have a few homesteads established so that we have addresses for mail delivery."

"The Families could make it much easier for you," I said. Did I sound like a diplomat or a used cars salesman?

"You can make that case while you are with us," Domel said. "If the Council finds you innocent of killing, they may even listen to you."

"What will I need to do to prove my innocence?" I asked.

"When we arrive, I will find someone to act as your speaker," he said. "That's something like one of your lawyers. They'll help you prepare your case."

"I would feel better if you helped, too," I said.

"Then I shall help," he said, giving me another smile. "Do you cook?"

"A little," I said. "Why?" Was I going to end up as a servant for them when this was all over? Did I have any chance of seeing my people again? I wished Troy and Brent had caught up to us before I ended up on a subway to who-knows-where. They would never be able to track me now.

"I've seen so many TV commercials for pizza. I'd love to try some," he said.

"Well, if we can get the ingredients, I can do pizza," I said. "It's even easier if we get a frozen one."

"You would make many friends with a dinner like that," he said.

"Speaking of dinner, I don't suppose I can get anything to eat?" I asked.

"Tell me what you will need, and I will make sure you are taken care of," he said.

"Cooked meat would be preferable; and bread and vegetables, if you have it," I said, trying to think of how to explain what I needed to someone who had never had a pizza. "Also, I'll need water to drink. I don't suppose you have coffee?"

"No coffee, but I think I'd like to try some," he said.

"I would be happy to show you how to make it if we can get a coffee pot and some grounds," I said.

"And you can watch TV with us and explain the many things we don't understand," he said.

"I'll try," I said. "I'm not sure I'll understand them all, either, depending on what you watch."

The subway slowed to a stop and Domel stood up. I slid off my seat and followed him out of the car. The door slid open and all I could see was yet another subway station. We climbed a set of steps up to the next floor. I lost track of the other Bigfoots and Sincha's body as we climbed. The spacing of the steps made it awkward to get up them, but I managed. The next floor up held a ton of steps. I guessed they all led down to different platforms, but my curiosity was sidetracked by the smell of roasting meat.

"The next floor up has food stalls. I'll get you whatever looks edible to you," Domel said.

I followed him up another set of stairs, eager to find food. I found myself surrounded by Bigfoots manning stalls selling things I couldn't identify. Domel led me over to one counter, but I was too short to see over it. Domel placed his hands on my hips and lifted me so that I could see. Tray after tray of meat on wood skewers greeted my eyes. I had no idea what the meat was, but it all looked good. I pointed to a skewer of dark meat and Domel set me down.

"We'll take three of those," Domel told the Bigfoot behind the stall. He handed me one of the skewers and we continued walking. I gnawed on the meat and decided it tasted most like elk. I soon finished the first one and Domel handed me a second as we passed into a larger hall. Bigfoots moved up and down the hall, entering and leaving from the numerous doors along both sides, each of them with places to go and things to do.

After walking halfway down the hall, Domel opened one of the doors and we entered the jail, complete with barred doors. The Bigfoot at the front desk was a mountain of smoky gray fur.

"Menit, this human has been charged with killing Sincha," Domel said.

"We don't have any human-size cells, but I could put her in the child cell," Menit said.

"That should work," Domel said. "And these are her personal belongings."

He handed over the backpack and the shotgun. I took that as my hint and handed over the handgun as well. Menit took it all without comment and entered notes on a pad of paper in front of him.

"Do you take responsibility for her care?" Menit asked.

"Yes," Domel said before turning to me. "I'll be responsible for bringing you meals, clothes, and anything else you need."

"Thank you," I answered.

Menit used a key to open a large door and led the way down a shadowy hall. He stopped and unlocked a door at the end of the hall. He turned on the light, using a light switch near my eye level. The room held a large bed, a desk, and a set of drawers. The walls were bright blue with a variety of young animals playing in a large forest painted in great detail.

"I will be back with water and some more supplies for you," Domel said. Menit closed and locked the door behind me. I took off the flak vest and boots and crawled into the bed. It was more comfortable than it looked, and I felt sleep creep up on me. Unwilling to fight it, I drifted off into a dreamless sleep.

Chapter Nineteen

Brent struggled to hide how out of breath he was as he followed Troy. His lungs burned as he made each step. His thighs ached along the scar from the surgery back in Iraq after he had been hit by a small piece of shrapnel from a shoulder-fired missile. He didn't even have a good war story to go with the wound; he had been hit on his way to the chow hall, one of several airmen looking for breakfast. He considered himself lucky that no one could see the scar unless he wore a Speedo to the beach. Since he never intended on wearing anything shorter than boxers, he should be okay. Of course, Kelley might want to see it someday and be impressed with his war injury.

He pulled himself up another embankment, trailing Troy by several feet. He gasped for breath as he reached the top and paused for a moment to suck in more air. Kelley had warned him about the effects of the altitude, but he hadn't listened. After all, he ran five miles most mornings before work; he could handle walking in the mountains. The race up the rockslide had pushed him over the endurance edge, and now he tried to keep stumbling along. He grabbed a tree branch and used it to help pull himself up another incline.

He had been able to see the game trail earlier, but whatever path Troy had followed now was invisible to him. The underbrush had become nothing but spiked vines all determined to destroy him, forcing him to fight for each step forward. His hands and arms bore bleeding scratches, battle wounds that proved the weeds were winning. He glanced behind him, hoping to see that Kelley had caught up, but saw nothing. Only the bugs seemed to keep pace with them; he swore the same bee had been buzzing around his head for over a mile. He struggled to move a little faster, trying to keep Troy in sight. It would be just perfect if he lost both of the Hunters on his first day in the wild.

Troy came to a halt in the first area that appeared to be clear of man-eating vegetation and sat on a rock. Brent copied his motions, choosing a rock that looked comfortable—if that could even be said about a rock. He pulled his boots off, grateful for a chance to stretch his toes and rearrange his socks, which had twisted painfully during the hike. He concentrated on his breathing, trying to slow it down to normal. Troy pulled out protein bars from one of the packs he was carrying and tossed one to Brent.

"Are we going to wait for Kelley to catch up to us?" Brent asked, opening the wrapper and taking a bite of the protein bar.

Troy nodded, proceeding to dig through his duffel bag. His hand emerged, gripping two bottles of water. Again he tossed one over to Brent, who missed the catch and had to chase after the rolling bottle.

"Should we backtrack a little in case she got lost?" Brent asked, sitting back down.

"Not lost," Troy answered, taking a drink from his water.

"How can you possibly be sure?" Brent asked, eyebrows creeping down over his eyes. How could Troy be so arrogant? Brent hadn't seen anything yet to impress him about Troy's abilities.

"I know," Troy said, his mouth tightening.

"You know what?" Brent asked, nose flaring and voice tight.

"Kelley," Troy said, meeting his eyes, muscles tensing.

Brent gave up questioning Troy before he lost his temper. He took several breaths to calm back down. He had known some characters during his time in the Air Force, but Troy outdid them all. Brent finished his protein bar and water, tucking the trash into his backpack.

He wanted to understand what they were looking for and how they were going to find the killer. He'd be content just knowing that they had a plan and that the plan made sense. He did not have the patience to play twenty questions with Troy to get the information. How did Kelley stand it?

Troy took his time finishing his ad hoc lunch while Brent watched. Once he had put his trash away, Troy stood facing the direction they had come from and Brent followed suit. They began to head back down the path. The sound of a gunshot echoed through the mountains, followed by another and another.

Troy's head came up, scanning the forest. In a flash, he took off at a run despite the amount of gear he had on his back. Brent followed, doing his best to keep up. He thought the gunshots had come from the other direction, but Troy seemed confident in exactly where to go.

Fear pulsed through him as he ran, giving him the extra energy needed to keep Troy in sight. Had Kelley fired the gun or been fired at? The Chief had told him to protect her and he would not fail on his first assignment. He needed to get to her, to make sure she was safe. He pushed himself harder, fighting gravity, the weeds, and his own aching lungs to move a little farther, a little faster.

They slowed down as they reached the rock pile. Gravity tried to pull them down the fast way, but safety required time. Brent stared down the length of his body, looking for a place to put his foot, then another foot. Going up had seemed so much easier. He felt his grip slip and clung tighter with his other hand, searching for a toehold with his foot. He managed to steady himself, glancing down. Almost there. He managed the last few feet and looked up to find Troy.

Troy already stood on flat ground, looking around at the game trail running along the side of the rockfall. After a long moment, he chose a direction and the two of them set off again, this time at a fast-paced walk. Troy kept scanning the environment, on alert for something.

Brent stared around but saw nothing more than the same trees and weeds they had been walking through all day. The grass came up to his waist in places, and the aspens ahead chattered to each other in the wind. Occasional flowers broke the dull greens and browns up with splashes of purple, yellow, and white. He could see storm clouds over a nearby peak, and lightning streaking toward the rocks. He saw no sign of Kelley or a possible killer.

The sun began its descent, casting long shadows across their path. A deer carcass lay in the shadow of the brush, crows feasting on the flesh. At first glance, Brent thought it looked as if it had been disemboweled by the same creature they were Hunting. He had studied those pictures enough to recognize the wounds when he saw them. Troy studied the animal for a long moment before pulling the crime scene photos from his pack. He looked back and forth between the two before handing the crime scene photos to Brent.

"Same," Troy said, pointing to the long claw marks along the deer's haunches.

Brent studied the photos and the animal. He thought they looked the same too, but he wouldn't have been confident enough to testify in court.

"You're sure?" he asked, staring at the photos.

Troy stood and looked over Brent's shoulder at the pictures. He pointed to the wounds along the belly of the woman in the photo and then to the deer. Brent looked closer at the picture where Troy had pointed to, trying to see what Troy had seen.

"I'm not sure," Brent said.

"Angles," Troy said.

Brent tried to study the angles but saw nothing that helped. He shrugged. He would have to accept Troy's judgment for now.

"So our killer did this, but where's Kelley?" he asked, looking around for any sign to tell him what had happened.

Troy had already walked a little way off, studying the ground. Brent stayed out of his way and watched. He could see the dark clouds moving closer, flashes of lightning dancing toward the ground. The temperature had begun to drop and he shivered, wondering if he should dig through his bag for one of the sweatshirts Kelley had packed. He had heard the weather could change quickly in the mountains, but he had never imagined a storm moving so fast.

"Four," Troy said, standing and pointing at the game trail.

"Four of what?" Brent asked, eyebrows burrowing down. He stared at the ground, trying to figure out what Troy was talking about, trying to see what had attracted the other man's attention.

"Creatures," Troy said, scanning the game trails nearby. Brent could see at least three different trails branching out from the small clearing. He looked for prints, fur, or any other sign of animal life but saw nothing.

"There were four creatures of the same type as our killer?" Brent asked, looking at Troy.

Troy nodded, staring at the ground.

"Are you sure?" Brent asked.

"Big feet," Troy said, pointing to the footprints along the brush. He crossed his arms and faced Brent, nostrils flaring.

Brent knelt to study them, wishing he had spent more time hunting with his uncle. For all he knew, these could be bear tracks. They did look human-like, but larger than any human footprint he had ever seen, and they seemed to have claws on the end of the toes. If he had to guess, he'd say they were made by creatures that topped eight feet in height.

"Kelley?" Brent asked. Now that they had found plenty of signs of their possible killer, would they have to go after the beasts or would they look for Kelley? Brent would prefer to look for Kelley. He couldn't imagine leaving her alone with multiple unknown beasts in the area.

Troy shrugged and kept looking. Brent felt the stirring of fear. Could Kelley have encountered four of these beasts all alone? He could imagine how scared she must have been. How could she possibly have protected herself? He knew she was armed, but one against four weren't good odds. Was she dead?

"Not dead," Troy said. Brent realized he had said the last part of his thoughts out loud.

"Was she even here?" Brent asked, thinking of the gunshot they had heard. There would have been a body or blood, he was sure of that much.

"Yes," Troy pointed to an area of wet dirt. Brent went to look closer at it, realizing as he bent down it was blood. He looked around the area, searching for signs of Kelley, and saw a .45 shell casing. He picked it up, looking closely at it. Troy grabbed it from his hands, sniffing it.

"Kelley's," Troy said, tossing the casing back to the ground.

"You can smell that?" Brent said, one corner of his mouth quirking up as he snorted.

"I know," Troy said, nodding once.

"If you say so," Brent muttered. He stared at the bloody ground, hoping none of it was Kelley's. He just wanted to find her, to know that she was safe. He stared at the clearing, trying to imagine what might have happened. If Kelley had come across these four, what would she have done? There had been a fight and gunshots, and someone had gotten hurt. Had Kelley killed one? Then where was the body? It was possible that the other creatures had taken the body away. Had they killed Kelley? He refused to believe that; he needed to see her again if only to decide what he felt for her. If they had killed her, why had they removed the body? The killer had left all the other bodies to be found. Was there any way she could have survived such a fight?

"I'd know," Troy said, looking at him.

"What?" Brent said, standing to face Troy.

"Not dead," Troy said, looking off at the trails around them.

"Kelley's not dead. What, are you psychically connected?" Brent asked, crossing his arms and leaning forward.

"Yes," Troy said, matching his posture.

Brent shook his head but kept quiet. Never argue with crazy people; at least, that's what his dad had always said. He didn't want to argue with an insane person who stood taller than he and was better muscled.

"Believe," Troy said, thrusting his jaw forward.

"Sure, whatever," Brent said, backing down. He knelt back down to study the prints, trying to imprint them in his memory.

"Werewolves," Troy said, moving back to his duffel bags.

"What? Werewolves were here, too?" Brent asked, startled.

"No," Troy said, shaking his head.

"Then werewolves what?" Brent asked, irritation making his voice sharp.

"Help us," Troy said, waving his hand to encompass the clearing.

"How are the werewolves going to help?" Brent asked. "They're a day's drive from here."

"Spirit walk," Troy said.

"But we're right here. Kelley couldn't have gotten far. You can track her." Brent said, unwilling to leave the area, to leave one of his team behind. Kelley had to be here somewhere, possibly hurt, needing rescue.

"Too big," Troy said, gesturing around him.

"You know Kelley well; which way would she have gone?" Brent asked. The sun disappeared behind the clouds and the wind picked up. Brent stared around at the trees bowing before the approaching storm. They had to find Kelley before the storm hit.

Troy studied the area. He walked a little down a couple of different paths before coming back to Brent. Each time, he shook his head. Rain began to fall, solitary drops hitting the leaves.

"Don't know," Troy said, coming back to stand in front of Brent.

"You don't know which way she might have gone?" Brent asked. Raindrops landed on his head and streamed down his face. He brushed off the drops before they reached his eyes.

"Gone," Troy said, running his hands through his hair.

"She's gone and you're just going to sit here and do nothing," Brent said, facing Troy with his hands on his hips. "She's going to be caught in this storm and you have all of her gear."

"No, werewolves," Troy said, turning to face Brent, legs apart, and hands on his gun belt.

"We are not leaving Kelley behind just so you can go get some mystical help," Brent said, raising his voice to a near shout. The rain began to pour, drenching them both. Kelley had no food, no clothes, no camping gear. What would she do out here alone?

"No choice," Troy snarled.

"Do you want her to die? I know you two are divorced, but I thought you still cared," Brent said, shoving Troy.

"Do care," Troy growled, shoving back.

"Then why are you suggesting abandoning her before we even try searching?" Brent asked, balling his hands into fists. Lightning flashed across the sky and thunder crashed.

"Need Kelley," Troy mumbled, his shoulders slumping.

"Then we should keep looking," Brent snarled.

"Don't understand," Troy snapped.

"What don't you understand?" Brent snapped back.

"No. You." Troy muttered.

"I don't understand?" Brent asked, voice rising. "You're right. I don't understand. I don't get why you are willing to leave. I don't see how the werewolves can help. I don't believe Kelley can survive out here by herself."

"Kelley survive," Troy said, shaking his head.

"What? Just because you two are Hunters?" Brent asked. He was getting tired of the Hunters and all their odd ways. They were human, just like him; not some mystical creature like the werewolves with their weird powers.

"Yes."

"That doesn't make you some sort of superhero," Brent said.

"No."

"How does anyone ever understand you? Say something, an entire sentence. Explain this to me," Brent shouted.

"I need," Troy said. Brent just stared at him.

"Kelley to."Troy's face tightened with concentration.

"Translate." Troy stood looking at him, breathing hard as if he had run a marathon.

Brent looked at him, seeing the pain and effort that simple sentence had taken. He thought of the last couple of days, the way Kelley had always seemed to understand him and would explain to others what he had said. He could picture the number of times the two of them had seemed to communicate by look alone. He remembered Ma telling him that they had grown up together.

"Kelley has always been there for you. You don't know how to get by without her," Brent said. Troy nodded.

"You trust that Kelley can survive until we get to her, and you really believe the werewolves are our best chance of finding her," Brent continued. Troy nodded again.

"I believe you will do what you have to do to get Kelley back. Let's go back to the werewolves," Brent said.

Troy's body sagged as the tension drained from his body. He began heading down a path and Brent followed.

Chapter Twenty

Back in the truck, Troy gunned the engine and got them back to the main roads. Brent stared at the window, wishing he had something to contribute to this mission. He had been little more than baggage to the Hunters since he had arrived. What was the point of the BHA if the best they could do was handle easy cases? How could he make a difference when he didn't understand the world he had fallen into?

Troy pulled into Pinedale, soon coming to a stop outside of a grocery. Brent looked at him, but Troy got out of the truck without saying anything. He followed Troy into the store, wondering what strange mission they were on now. They wandered up an aisle filled with baby supplies, and Troy stared at the rows of diapers.

"What are we doing?" Brent asked.

"Baby gift," Troy said.

"We're buying gifts? Now?" Brent asked. Had Troy lost his mind? They needed to get to Kelley.

"For Jim," Troy said.

Brent stared, trying to remember where he had heard that name. Troy grabbed a bag of diapers from the shelf and walked away. Jim. Brent remembered. He was the werewolf that had just had a baby.

"Why are we taking the time to buy a gift for Jim's new baby?" Brent asked.

"Best Seeker," Troy said.

"Who's the best Seeker?" Brent asked.

"Jim," Troy said, grabbing a bottle with dancing teddy bears on it off the shelf.

"And we need a Seeker?" Brent asked.

Yes," Troy said, heading down a new aisle.

"And giving him a gift will get his help?" Brent asked.

"Yes," Troy said, studying rows of gift bags.

"Is this a werewolf thing?" Brent asked, handing Troy a pink bag with multicolored balloons on it.

"Yes."

They checked out and returned to the truck. Troy handed Brent the bag and pulled back onto the road. Brent arranged the gifts in the bag and sat it down on the floorboard. He longed to send the head of the BHA academy an e-mail explaining how much they had left out of their training. When the mission ended, he wanted to spend a month with Ma and Pa learning about vampire and werewolf cultures.

His cell phone rang. Brent stared at it in shock, surprised he had a signal.

"Brent," Chris's voice said as soon as he answered. "I've got bad news, more bad news, and a small bit of good."

"What happened?" Brent asked.

"There were bombings in Rock Springs yesterday," Chris said, his voice thick with exhaustion. "Kelley Mallard's apartment building and the office where she worked."

"Casualties?" Brent asked.

"Nearly thirty-five people died," Chris answered. "We're still awaiting identification of the bodies."

"Terrorism?" Brent asked, leaning his face against the window. How did this escalate from searching for a hominid killer to getting caught up in a terrorist plot?

"Yes," Chris said. "The NSA has been tasked with helping the FBI investigation, and my boss agreed to put me on it when I told him about your call last night."

"Have you found anything yet?" Brent asked.

"We're just beginning to look, but I wanted to get some more information from you," Chris said.

"Ask away."

"How long has Kelley known Lisa?" Chris asked.

Brent repeated the question to Troy, who looked at him with curiosity in his eyes.

"Two years."

"How did they meet?" Chris asked, and again Brent relayed it to Troy.

"College class," Troy said, staring into the rain.

"Did you know Lisa's mother attends one of the radical Christian churches advocating that humans need to remain pure from contamination from other races?" Chris asked.

"No," Brent said. Could Lisa be involved in this somehow? Or had her own church set bombed her for betraying their beliefs?

"Did you know that Kelley was arrested for domestic assault and battery?" Chris asked. "The charges were dropped by her husband, though."

"No, I hadn't known that," Brent said, trying not to stare at Troy.

"Do you think her husband might be involved?"

"No; he has been with us the entire time."

"What?" Chris asked, shocked.

"They are the Hunter team I'm working with."

"Could he have hired someone?"

"From what I've seen, I can't imagine anything more unlikely," Brent said. He knew they would have to investigate Troy. So often, the husband, ex-husband, or boyfriend of a victim turned out to be the killer. Brent knew Troy had problems, but he couldn't imagine that Troy would hurt Kelley.

"You know it's normally family," Chris said.

"I know, but that doesn't account for all the other Heirs that were killed."

"I'll let you know if we find anything. Just keep her safe," Chris said before hanging up.

Brent stared at the road. Yes, he had been doing a great job of keeping Kelley safe.

"What said?" Troy asked, looking over at him.

"That was a friend of mine at the NSA," Brent said. "Kelley's apartment and workplace were bombed last night."

"Dr. Lyman?" Troy asked.

"Presumed dead." He wondered why Troy had asked about Kelley's boss and not her roommate but decided not to ask. It would take too long to get an answer.

"Why?" Troy asked.

"I have no idea why they bombed those buildings," Brent said. "They had to know Kelley wasn't there."

"To hurt?" Troy asked, gripping the steering wheel, his knuckles whitening.

"To hurt whom?"

"Kelley."

"Maybe, but what would that get them?" Brent asked. He knew Kelley well enough to know this would hurt her, but she wasn't the type to kill herself over it. Did the killers have a personal grudge against her? That was the single reason he could think of for a move directed at causing her pain.

"Flush out?" Troy said.

"If Kelley were still with us and had gotten the news, do you think she would go rushing back?" Brent asked. "Or do you think whoever is behind this will think that?"

"Yes."

"You might be right," Brent said, thinking that that would make sense. If the killer had lost them back in Daniel, then they would need a way to try to find her again. "Would Kelley have gone back? Even knowing it might be a trap?" Brent asked.

"Yes."

"Would you have been able to talk her out of it?"

"No."

"Then we had better hope Kelley doesn't find out about this anytime soon," Brent said. How would he protect her if Kelley had found out and went rushing back to Rock Springs without them?

Troy pointed to Kelley's purse on the floor by Brent's feet.

"Cell phone?" Troy asked.

Brent picked up the purse, feeling as if he was violating Kelley by going through it. The tiny purse held a small wallet, some loose change, lipstick, a tiny .22 pistol, and the cell phone. He held the phone up for Troy to see. He tried to open it to see if she had been contacted, but Kelley had a password on it.

Troy grabbed the cell phone, typed in the password, and passed the phone back. Brent looked at the unlocked phone. Kelley had several missed calls and text messages. Lisa had called once last night and had texted several times. Dr. Lyman had called once. Both Angie and Ma had called her this morning. Otherwise, nothing unusual appeared. Nothing from any phone numbers not already programmed into Kelley's contacts. No text messages threatening her or telling her about the bombings.

"Just Lisa, Dr. Lyman, Angie, and Ma," Brent said.

"Call back," Troy said, glancing at the phone.

"Call back who?" Brent asked. Since two were presumed dead, he assumed Troy meant Angie or Ma Venator.

"Ma."

"And tell her what, that we lost her daughter?" Brent asked. Now that was a call he did not want to make.

"Tell all."

"Why?" Brent asked. He could not imagine why Kelley's family needed to be worried. He and Troy would find Kelley and all would be fine.

"Venator head."

"Yeah, and?"

"The mission."

"Oh, they need to be updated on how our mission is going? I forget that Hunting is a business," Brent said.

"And family."

Brent pulled out his own cell phone, preferring to call from it rather than Kelley's. It seemed more respectful that way. He started to dial before realizing he no longer had cell phone reception. He checked Kelley's phone and found the same thing.

"No signal," he said. "We'll call when we get to the reservation. That way, we can tell Ma what the plan is."

Chapter Twenty-one

I sat up with slow, unsteady movements. My mind fought its forced return to consciousness. The cell I woke up in looked just as surreal after a good night's sleep as it had the day before. I gazed groggily at the paintings along the wall. Each one depicted a mother and its child. A doe with her fawn grazed, while a mama bear and her cub played in a stream nearby. On the opposite wall, a she-wolf gave suckle to a wolf puppy and little lambs played around them while an ewe lay in the shade of a tree. It was all too sweet; I needed an insulin shot.

I stood up, feeling the protest from the muscles I had abused yesterday. Between hiking with the heavy vest and wrestling with a Bigfoot, I hurt everywhere. In fact, even the backs of my knees ached as if I had strained a muscle. I was pretty sure I didn't have muscles back there. Maybe I needed to take a biology class next term. More than that, I needed a cup of coffee! What was I doing trying to figure out muscle groups while being held prisoner by Bigfoot?

I stood up and worked my way through the standard stretches mixed with a handful of yoga poses Angie had taught me. She had become a huge fan of yoga just after moving to Salt Lake City and had been preaching the many benefits to me for the past couple of years. I'd gone with her a couple of times and had found it boring. But I was the first to admit that some of those pretzel-like poses stretched muscles that normal athletic warm-ups didn't touch. By the time my muscles had been stretched and warmed up, I felt more like a human being.

I sat back down on the bed and looked around for something to do. No computer, cell phone, TV, radio, or even a book in sight. Well, when was the last time I had nothing to do? I couldn't even remember. It sounds wonderful, when you're busy, to have nothing on your schedule. The reality was not so much fun. In fact, it was boring. Mind numbing, need to get up and pace sort of boring.

I wondered what Troy and Brent were doing. If I knew Troy, he would have searched for me as long as possible. He might still be searching if he had found even a hint of a trail to follow. How good was he? Could he have found our trail to the mine? Even if he did find the mine shaft, he would have to give up there; that ladder had not looked possible to scale down. At some point, he would have to make his way back to the reservation and spirit walk.

Hunters always worked in pairs; it was the safest way to handle the unknowns we faced on every mission. A few missions could be handled alone, but those did not appear often and only involved safe and quick problems. Ma and Pa had taught us that if we got separated for longer than twenty-four hours we had two choices: finish the mission if we were close to an end or return to the nearest reservation. Not only was it a meeting point we could all find; it also allowed us the option of spirit walking. Granted, a spirit walk took three days at a minimum, but it guaranteed reuniting the two partners. The first rule of Hunting was that partners always took care of each other and never left one another in danger.

I remembered when Uncle Mack got separated from his partner back when I was in middle school. He had gone to the nearest reservation but had refused to spirit walk, having failed at it as an adolescent. I didn't blame him. Spirit walking was the scariest thing I had ever done—and that included fighting off an enraged werewolf. Uncle Mack had called Pa, asking Pa to go looking for his partner. Of course Pa went and brought Mack's partner back, but Uncle Mack was never allowed to Hunt again. No one would trust him to be a partner.

I figured it would take the boys a day to get to the reservation and then the minimum three days to spirit walk. So I had four days to stay alive. More importantly, I had four days to see if I could talk the Bigfoots into accepting Family help and joining the wider hominid community. If I couldn't do that and the boys suddenly appeared...well, who knew what would happen. This could just as easily turn into a trap for the boys—or a bloodbath. Oh yeah; I also needed to prove myself innocent. How was I to do that? It may have been in self-defense, but I did kill Sincha. I had no idea what Bigfoot law had to say on the topic.

My stomach rumbled; it was empty and making sure I knew about it. I tried to remember what I had had yesterday: breakfast at Don's, a couple of protein bars, and some of meat skewers. No wonder I felt as if I could eat a whole cow.

"Hello," I called out as I pounded on the door. Maybe someone could be convinced to feed me. "Hello, anyone there?"

I heard a key in the door and stepped back like a good prisoner. I mean, seriously, what threat could I be to one of these guys? The door opened and a Bigfoot I hadn't met yet appeared.

"Yes, human?" it said, staring down at me.

"Hi, I'm Kelley. I'm not sure how things work around here, but are there any chances of getting some food?" I asked, trying to look as harmless and pathetic as possible.

"Domel's responsible for you, mother-killer," the guard said before shutting the door in my face.

That had worked well.

I sat back down on the bed, trying to ignore the various bodily functions fighting for my attention. I needed to eat. I needed to drink. I needed to pee. Great. Dang body needed to be quiet. I searched the room for anything that looked as if it could be used as a toilet. Even Bigfoots must need to use the bathroom. Okay, the vampires didn't. But the hominid rule of thumb seemed to be that whatever went in had to come back out in some form. Vampires seemed to sweat it out, but the others I knew of had processes similar to humans.

I spotted a pipe standing about five inches above the floor. The diameter seemed large enough to handle the bodily waste of even a Bigfoot. I stared at it for a long moment, contemplating the option. No way. I was not going to squat over some pipe. What if it was an air vent? I'd have to smell it for the rest of time I was here!

I gave up and sat back on the bed. Domel would be along soon. He wouldn't have forgotten about me, would he? I just needed to learn to wait. Dr. Lyman had been telling me to learn patience since I had started working for him, but that hadn't helped. How do you learn it? I'm sure someone had published a book on it, but I never believed that self-help stuff. Sitting and waiting just made me mad, not patient. I growled at the room. I hated feeling helpless.

I stood up to beat on the door again, but it opened. Domel entered, carrying two bags. I sat back down on the bed as my nose recognized the smell of meat. Domel handed me one of the bags, a quick peek showing me some more of the meat on sticks and something that looked like a potato. I ate the meat, then downed the potato. Without butter or salt it tasted like dirt, but I choked it down anyway.

When I had finished, Domel handed me the other bag. I dumped it on the bed. It held something I guessed was meant to be clothing. They resembled sweats in a sewn-together-without-a-pattern sort of way. Under the clothes, I found a full canteen. I took a couple of sips just to wet my mouth. I really wanted a toothbrush and some toothpaste. Morning mouth, yuck!

"I'm sorry the clothes aren't very good," Domel said. "We don't wear such things and I had to ask a friend to make you something."

"Thank your friend for me," I said, trying to keep it polite instead of sarcastic. I did appreciate the thought, even if I did not like the clothes themselves.

"Um, does this place have a bathroom?" I asked, looking up.

"I will try to get you permission to use the bath pools later today," Domel said.

"How about other bodily functions?" I asked.

"What do you mean?" Domel said.

"How do I pee or poop?" I asked, blushing. Gee, I sounded like a kindergartner.

"Oh," Domel said, the room filling with the scent of scorched popcorn. What was that smell and where was it coming from?

"The hole over there will take your waste away." He pointed to the pipe I had noticed earlier. Wonderful; I'd have to squat and aim.

"I will give you privacy to change and do what you need," he said. "I'll be back in a short while. Then we need to start preparing for your trial. We have only a short time and many are advocating for your immediate execution. They do not believe you should be treated with the same courtesy as a Sasquatch."

Chapter Twenty-two

Alone again I used the pipe, trying to be both quick and accurate; I did not want to pee on myself. I used the wet wipes, glad I still had them with me. The clothes took a little more time figuring out. The shirt had three equal-size holes, but after trying a few combinations I found where to put my head and arms. The pants were a little easier, and I used a strip of fabric as a belt to hold them up. They wouldn't win any fashion prizes but they weren't uncomfortable, either. Best yet, they were clean. I wouldn't complain, I promised myself.

I piled my dirty, bloody clothing on the floor. It felt good to be in something not drenched in Sincha's blood. I stared at my socks and boots; they were caked in mud, blood, and prickers from the mountains. I left them sitting on the floor, not able to bring myself to put them back on. I sat back on the bed, still feeling naked without my gun or socks.

Domel came back a few moments after boredom had set in again. This time he held an armful of books. Now, this looked more promising. He sat the pile on the desk and brought a couple of the books plus a notepad over to the bed. He sat on one end, his huge frame taking up way too much bed. I managed to arrange myself on what space was left, trying to look ready for whatever came next.

"I was assigned to be your advocate, and Neller will be your speaker," Domel said.

"So, what does an advocate do?" I asked.

"Prepares your case, puts all the information together."

"Then what does the speaker do?"

"Speaks before the Council of Matriarchs on your behalf," Domel said. "You will not be allowed to speak unless one of the Matriarchs asks a direct question."

"So I don't get to testify or anything?"

"No. Neller will act as your voice, speak your case, and say your words," Domel said. "I, too, will be there and will be allowed to speak if it should be needed."

"Do you have any training for this?"

"All of us learn how to advocate in school," Domel said. "Trust me; I will do a good job."

Nice. I got an advocate with no experience and faced a legal system I didn't understand. Maybe I should change my major to law, become a lawyer? If hominids were going to start arresting me for doing my job, it might become a good skill to have.

"Then where do we start?" I asked.

"Tell me everything about your encounter with Sincha," he said, bending over his notepad.

I started to tell him about the encounter itself, the memory of Sincha leaping at me, captured in my memory like a photograph. That didn't seem like much. I had better go back and explain about the case itself. Troy had the case folder with the pictures so I couldn't show him the evidence itself, but I related what I remembered as best I could. I talked until my throat hurt while Domel took pages of notes.

"So you had been assigned to kill whomever or whatever had killed those humans?" Domel asked when I ran out of words.

"It doesn't work like that," I said. "We were authorized to use lethal force if we had to, but the best outcome would have been an arrest."

"How do you decide when an arrest can be made?" Domel asked, continuing to make notes.

"If the killer had been a hominid that we could restrain, one who would not die as a result of being kept in jail, we would have tried to bring them in to let the courts decide."

"How often does it work out that way?" Domel asked.

"Less often than I want it to," I said. "We usually don't get called in on cases that can be resolved peacefully, but I always try."

"And what was your plan once you saw Sincha?" Domel asked.

"I hadn't formed a plan. I had no proof that Sincha was the killer," I said. If I'd had any common sense, I would have gone back to find Troy and Brent the minute I had spotted a Bigfoot. I had been an idiot for thinking I could handle it alone.

"But you thought she was?" Domel asked.

"I actually didn't have any proof that Sincha had more intelligence then a bear," I said. "I had originally planned on just following her until my partners caught up to me."

"So why didn't you do that?" he asked.

"She saw me and attacked," I said, looking down. I could still remember the feel of her weight bearing down on me, the fear that had filled me as I scrambled for my gun.

"Do you believe Sincha killed those people?" Domel asked.

"I still don't know. I'm pretty sure one of your people did based on what Sincha did to the deer," I said. "A BHA or FBI forensic lab would be able to tell for sure if they had a sample of Sincha's DNA to match to what was found on the victims. Do you think she killed them?"

"We're pretty sure," he said, looking up from his notes.

"What happens if I am found guilty?" I asked, getting up and pacing around the small cell.

"The Council will determine your punishment," he said, and the small cell began to smell like wood ash.

"Would I survive that punishment?" I asked.

"I don't know," Domel said. "The usual punishment for murder is death."

I guess I should get used to people threatening to kill me. I'd seen enough attempts in the past couple of days. What had I ever done to deserve this? I paced back and forth, trying to find a happier thought as fear pulsed through me, distracting me.

"If I'm found innocent, will you let me go back to my people?" I asked.

"The Council will decide that, too."

"What do you think my chances are?"

"We've never had a case like this. I really don't know."

"That is not comforting," I muttered. Pa had said the most difficult part of learning about new hominids had been trying to decide what made for intelligent life, sentient life. Humans had struggled to determine ways of separating species that deserved equal rights from those who didn't. If a werewolf was equal to a human, should the great apes be considered equal as well? All the hominids had adopted an evolutionary standard; those species on the hominid part of the family tree were considered sentient. Where did Bigfoots fit into that? How did the Bigfoots view the rest of us?

"I'm sorry," Domel said. "I will do the best I can for you."

I sat back on the bed, feeling defeated. I couldn't think of any way I'd convince the Bigfoots that killing one of their own had been necessary. They didn't know me, and they knew little about humans. I was going to be executed for murder.

"What do we do now?" I asked, looking up at Domel.

"We go through these books on previous cases and see if we can find cases similar to yours to base your defense on," he said.

"How long do we have to prepare?"

"Three days."

Not enough time. Unless Troy and Brent had left for the reservation the moment they realized I was missing, they would never get here in time. Even if they had left right away, the timing would be close. They still might not be able to get here before my execution.

He handed me the book he had brought over to write on and went over to the desk. After great thought, he selected one of the books and settled back on the bed. I cracked open the book he had handed me, grateful to see it was in English, and began to read. The introduction told me that I was holding a summary of case law related to necessary homicide. Huh, now that was a category I hadn't heard of before; what was necessary homicide? I turned to the first chapter and began reading. It appeared that the Bigfoots recognized that killing was the only option in cases where a higher ranking Bigfoot's life was in danger, or if a Bigfoot had been found guilty of murder or crimes against their species. I saw nothing to define ranks among Bigfoots or what crimes against another species might be. However, it appeared the punishment for murder was death—either a slow death or a fast death.

I didn't want to die here; no one would ever know what had happened to me. My poor Ma and Pa. Troy would never stop looking, never know it was hopeless. He would ruin his life searching. He and Brent had to get here on time and save me from Bigfoot justice.

From the descriptions, it sounded as if one of the senior Bigfoots would present the case against me. On my side, Neller would speak for me and Domel would present any additional evidence. The final decision would be made by the Council of Matriarchs.

"Who is the Council of Matriarchs?" I asked, looking up.

"Our ruling body," Domel explained. "The Matriarch of each clan and the elected Chief of the tribe form the Council."

I began to wonder if my best option might be to try to go out with guns blazing. Assuming I could get my guns back. Why had I given them up so easily? Oh yeah, I had trusted Domel for no rational reason whatsoever. Great. I wondered if I could find another way to escape. I forced my mind back to the book.

I made it word for word through three cases before the redundancy numbed my brain. I began to skim through the others. This felt as if I were doing a school assignment. How could I get held captive by an unknown species and then get forced to do homework? Geesh, could this be considered cruel and unusual punishment? Okay, not as cruel as having my claws ripped out (I winced as a read the description of the Council's judgment) or being blinded with a hot poker.

I sat up straight and began to stretch my neck. I had no idea how long I had been bent over the books, but my eyes hurt and my neck had tightened into knots. Domel looked up and put his book and notes aside.

"It's not pleasant reading."

"No, it's going to give me nightmares."

"I shall be right back," he said as he stood. He pounded on the door twice and was let out. I sighed and stood, pacing back and forth across the small room just to get my blood flowing. The door opened again and Domel gestured me through it.

"I shall take you for your daily exercise now," he said as I joined him in the small hallway of the jail.

"I get exercise?"

"Of course. We do not want anyone to suffer from their confinement."

"At least until I'm executed," I muttered.

"Don't give up hope yet."

"So where are we going? Some jail gym?" I asked. I tried to picture running on a Bigfoot-size treadmill. I would look like a Chihuahua trying to exercise at a human gym.

"No, out into the settlement," he said.

"You can do that? Just walk out of here with me?" I asked.

"I am confident I could prevent an escape attempt if I had to," he said with one of those odd smiles.

"I don't doubt that, and it's not like I have any place to go."

"Exactly! So let me show you some more of my home."

Chapter Twenty-three

Brent stared at the endless road, thinking over the past couple of days and trying to make sense of it all. Here he was, alone with a Hunter who did not speak, heading to ask the werewolves to do something he didn't understand. All this to get back to the girl who was supposed to be leading this mission. The worse part of the situation was that he offered nothing; all he could do was trail behind Troy and hope for the best.

He did have a better understanding of terrorist groups than either of the Hunters. Granted, his experience had been overseas and domestic terrorism operated a little differently, though it used many of the same principles. He thought he might be better equipped than Troy to help figure out who was after Kelley and how to stop them from his office and a secure computer. So while he may be ill-equipped to Hunt, maybe he could offer something.

He pictured Kelley's smile, her laugh, and the twinkle in her eyes when she teased him. Daydreaming like a lovesick puppy would do nothing to keep her safe. He knew that, but his thoughts kept circling back like a cat after its tail. He wondered what she would say if he asked her out. Stop that, he chided himself. Deal with it when she was safe, when she was back with them.

The Chief had said the domestic terrorists wanted the BHA to handle all cases with the Families out of the picture. Many terrorist groups tried to manipulate public opinion and public policy through fear, such as some of the anti-abortion or animal rights groups. Killing the Heirs made a strong statement, not just by attacking the young but also by damaging the Families' leadership. It wouldn't stop the Families, and the government had a policy never to give in to the demands of terrorists.

Still, the hits had been successful; all targets had been killed except Kelley. Had the extremist groups hired professional hitmen or were they using their own members? He suspected they were dealing with professionals or at least some of the snipers would have been caught. What he'd read about the Hominid Equality Movement and People for Hominids indicated both groups had managed small plots without leaving enough proof to get caught, so they either had professionals as part of the organization, were quick studies, or knew how to hire the good ones.

It took practice to kill without being caught, and Chris would have said if there had been strong leads on any of the cases. How did the terrorist know Kelley had been named Heir when she hadn't even known it the first time they shot at her?

The wet pavement glowed in the headlights beams. They hadn't seen another car in hours; the road was devoid both of traffic and signs of habitation. Troy had turned the radio on miles ago, and the sounds of country music filled the truck with tales of angst and loss. Brent kept checking his cell phone but he never got a signal for more than a mile or two, enough to tell him he had messages without letting him check them. A streak of light across the horizon signaled the coming morning; they had driven all night.

The truck pulled back into the reservation as sunrise burst across the sky. This time Troy did not pull into a parking spot before the large lodge, but turned onto a small dirt path that wound off to the side. Brent could make out a series of smaller log cabins ahead. People began wandering toward the road at their approach, making Brent nervous with their serious expressions. Troy pulled to a stop in front one of the log cabins and Brent slid out, eager to stretch. They had barely stopped in the twelve hour drive, and he had begun to stiffen up after traipsing through the mountains.

Troy got out, leaning back into the truck to grab the pink bag. He held it before him as if he were an old woman with a clutch purse, moving uncertainly toward the crowd. The pink bag stood out garishly against the commando attire he wore.

"Troy," a voice called out, a young man stepping apart from the crowd. His dark hair was pulled back in a ponytail, his face was matted with sweat, and his jeans were covered in dust. Did they really start work at the crack of dawn here?

"Jim," Troy said, nodding his head in greeting. He held the bag out toward Jim, letting it swing awkwardly between them. Jim raised an eyebrow and took the small bag. He glanced inside and smiled.

"Hunter Troy has gifted my new child," he told the crowd. The werewolves broke into smiles. A few sighed while others looked thoughtful.

"Thank you," Jim said.

"You're welcome," Troy said, looking at his feet.

"Where's Kelley?" Jim asked, looking back and forth between Brent and Troy.

"Lost," Troy said, shoulders slumped.

"She didn't make it back here," Jim said gently.

"I know."

"You aren't thinking of spirit walking?" Jim asked, eyebrow raised.

"Have to," Troy said, looking Jim in the eye.

"You were pretty bad at it when we took you a few years ago," Jim said.

"I remember," Troy said, lips drooping.

"You could end up in the spirit world for a month. That's not going to help Kelley any," Jim said.

"What do you mean a month?" Brent interrupted. He thought this would take three days. They needed to get to Kelley before she found out about the bombings.

"To spirit walk, you must pass three tests. If you pass them all, you spend only three days in the spirit world. If you fail, you can spend much longer."

"Must try."

"And if you fail?"

"Brent."

"Me, what?" Brent asked.

"Find Kelley."

"It's a risk, Troy. He's never been spirit walking before; there's no guarantee he'll be able to do it. He may end up with his mom or in his bed for all we know," Jim said.

"Can't someone else go, someone with experience, just long enough to see where she is and come back to tell us where to go?" Brent asked.

"We can go with you as a guide but we cannot exit the spirit world, not the way humans do," Jim said, shaking his head.

"Troy, can't one of the other Hunters come out and help us, then?" Brent asked.

Troy looked at him for a long moment, and Brent had been around him long enough to see thoughts fighting to find a way to express themselves. He wished he could just read Troy's mind.

"They backup," Troy finally said.

Brent thought that through, biting his tongue to keep from peppering Troy with more questions. He didn't want to start yelling at Troy in front of an audience—especially in front of people who had known Troy for years. Troy wanted the Venators to hold back and be backup in case they failed. Was it just his pride or that he didn't want to admit he couldn't save Kelley? Or was there some other reason, some weird Family thing Brent just didn't know about?

"Does this involve some Hunter thing no one's told me about yet?" Brent asked.

Troy nodded.

"Can it be bent or broken under the circumstances?" Brent asked.

Troy shook his head.

"So you want me to trust you, trust that you know what you are doing?"

Troy nodded.

"I don't trust easily."

"Me, either," Troy said.

"But you ask me to trust you anyway."

"Trust you," Troy said.

Brent stared at him, shocked. This odd and somewhat scary man trusted him. Should he be honored or horrified?

"Let's do this, then," Brent said.

"For gifting my daughter, I owe you the chance," Jim said, holding the pink bag up. "I'll go ask the Patriarch for his blessing."

Troy nodded and went back to the truck. The other werewolves went back to wherever they had come from, leaving them alone. Troy dug through the back, dumping out the contents of his bags and reloading them with new gear. Brent wondered if he should do the same thing but had no idea what to expect from the spirit world. Troy emerged with two duffel bags, so Brent hoped he had packed enough for both of them. Troy settled down on the steps, leaned against the post, and closed his eyes.

Brent stared around, not really seeing anything. He pulled his cell phone out and checked his messages. Mike had called. That was odd; Mike had done nothing but harass him since he had started at the BHA. Brent called him back, trying to remember the time difference between Wyoming and the East Coast.

"Agent Poliski," Mike's voice answered.

"Mike, it's Brent."

"Chief wanted to let you know that that FBI contact he gave you—don't use it," Mike said.

"Why?"

"He got arrested last night for being part of the terrorist plot."

"He's one of the People for Hominids?"

"Yep," Mike said. "And I hear you got shot at."

"They weren't shooting at me."

"You ready to come home? Let a real agent take over?" Mike sneered.

"I'm fine," Brent said. "Did you have any other news for me?"

"Yeah, you might want to buy some diapers. It's gonna be scary out there," Mike laughed.

"We already did that," Brent muttered, thinking of the pink gift bag. He hung up, wondering at what age hazing finally stopped. He had put up with it in high school, in the Air Force, and now at the BHA.

He stared at the phone and realized he had better call Ma and Pa. He took a deep breath, dreading the conversation. He looked the number up on Kelley's cell but dialed from his own. The last thing he wanted was to give Ma and Pa false hope.

"This is the Venators," a woman's voice answered.

"Can I talk to Ma or Pa?" he asked.

"This is Ma," the voice said.

Brent quickly filled her in on everything from losing Kelley to the bombings. Ma listened and did not interrupt, giving him no idea what she was thinking or feeling. How could she be calm about it all? These Hunters were even more stoic than the special forces guys he had met in Iraq.

"We'll take action to protect our own," Ma responded without offering details. "Just find Kelley and keep her safe."

"Before you told Kelley she was Heir, did you tell anyone else?" Brent asked.

"Well, the family here knew," Ma said, "and I posted it on the Family board."

"When did you post it?" he asked.

"After Troy texted me to say he had located Kelley," Ma said. "I knew she wouldn't have a chance to look at the boards after that, and I wanted it to be a surprise."

"Who has access to the board?"

"Mostly just other Families, but sometimes our friends as well," Ma said. "I know Kelley signed Lisa and Dr. Lyman up for the board because they were so curious about what we did."

Brent hung up and stared into space, thinking. So someone had to have had access to the board to read the announcement that Kelley had been made Heir. Then they would have to know where she was going and be close enough to do something about it. Lisa or Dr. Lyman would have been close enough, but did either of them know where she was going?

"Did you tell Lisa or Dr. Lyman that you had a Hunt?" Brent asked Troy.

Troy opened his eyes and looked at Brent for a long moment.

"Dr. Lyman."

"You called Dr. Lyman?" Brent asked, sighing. He wished he knew a quicker way to get information from Troy. This could take forever.

"At office."

"You went to Dr. Lyman's office?" Brent asked.

"Looking Kelley."

"You went looking for Kelley at Dr. Lyman's office and ran into him there," Brent said. "You told him why you were looking for Kelley."

Troy nodded. Brent tried to imagine how that conversation had gone. Dr. Lyman must know Troy well enough to decipher his odd utterances.

"Did you tell Lisa? Go by her apartment when looking for Kelley?"

"Hated Lisa," Troy said, shaking his head. Brent stared at Troy for a moment before shifting his gaze.

Brent fell silent and Troy closed his eyes again. Dr. Lyman would have known Kelley had been heading out to The Range. He probably knew the most likely route there. He had access to the board, and he could have known Kelley was the Heir. Did he have connections with any of the hominid rights groups? No, that did not make sense. If he had done this, why would his own group have killed him when they bombed the office?

Brent looked up and spotted two werewolves walking toward them. He recognized Jim and Patriarch Bullend long before they had come into easy conversation range. Jim supported the old man, helping him cross the uneven ground. Brent resisted the urge to rush things along, throw the Patriarch over his shoulder if needed to get this process moving.

"Young Troy," Patriarch Bullend said as he reached them. "You remember the last time you spirit walked?"

"I remember," Troy said, looking the Patriarch in the eyes.

"Are you sure this is the way for you?" the Patriarch asked Troy.

"Only way," Troy said, shrugging his shoulders.

"Then I give permission for you two to enter the spirit world," Patriarch Bullend said. "Jim shall be your Seeker on this trip; we recognize your right to his services in return for your gift. Hold true to your need and all will work out."

"Thank you," Troy said, nodding his head.

"Before you leave, I have news from my spirit walkers," Patriarch Bullend looked at them both. "Kelley walks in a darkness none of them can penetrate. The danger deepens. The next week will see it through to the end, possibly her end. They still seek for more."

"That sounds more like prophecy than fact," Brent said softly.

"It's shit," Troy said.

"Kelley has gone where the spirit world does not touch. The danger from the human hunting her is nothing compared to the current situation," the Patriarch said, ignoring Troy and looking at Brent.

"Can you tell us anything else?" Brent asked.

"Very little," the Patriarch said. "The walkers see only that the danger has two faces. One danger comes from the force of an ideal and the other from a person Kelley trusts, with strangers pulling the strings. We won't stop looking, though."

Brent stared at the Patriarch in shock. Maybe Dr. Lyman or Lisa had been the shooter and then had some falling out with their group? The evidence all seemed to point in that direction. Maybe they had been killed in retaliation for failing at their assignment or covering up the plot? He still had too many questions and not enough information. He pulled out his cell phone and sent a quick text message to Chris, summarizing what he'd just learned.

"Go now?" Troy asked.

Patriarch Bullend nodded. He reached out and lay a hand on Troy's shoulder before turning to walk away.

Chapter Twenty-four

Jim stepped forward and gestured for them to enter the log cabin. Troy led the way, disappearing through the cabin door. Brent walked up the steps and entered the cabin, the smell of sage and cinnamon so strong he almost stepped back outside.

The interior had been decorated in painted symbols that Brent could not begin to identify. He thought some of them might be Celtic, but others looked Native American. A symbol in the corner looked like some of the odder symbols he had seen in Iraq. On the floor, a circle had been painted surrounded by writing that looked a little like Arabic. Confused, he looked back at Jim.

"Werewolves have always been among you," Jim said. "Many human religions have drawn upon our ways."

"So all this started with you?" Brent asked, gesturing to the symbols.

Jim nodded and motioned for them to step into the circle. Troy stepped forward and Brent followed.

"The two of you have chosen to walk the paths of the spirit world," Jim intoned in a chant. "You shall enter there in body, thus what happens to you there will be as real as what happens here. Any wounds you earn in the spirit world will be wounds to your body. Any healing you earn in the spirit world will be healing to your body. Any food you eat in the spirit world will nourish you and any poison you consume will sicken you. Do you agree to these dangers?"

"I do," Troy said.

"I do," Brent echoed.

"You will face three tests. You will face your greatest fear, your greatest hope, and your greatest secret," Jim said.

"What do you mean 'face'?" Brent asked.

"It cannot be explained, only experienced," Jim said, giving him a slight smile.

"Spiritual shit," Troy muttered.

Brent nodded. He completely agreed with the sentiment.

"Upon completing each challenge, the guardian will present you with a token denoting the number of days you will spend in the spirit world," Jim continued, ignoring Troy's comment. "At the end of the final challenge, you will exit the spirit world to your destination."

"What do you mean?" Brent asked.

"You will concentrate on where you want to be—in this case, with Kelley. When you step out of the spirit world, you will be with her, wherever she is," Jim said. "Time will pass differently there than here. If you have three days of tokens, you will exit three days from now. If you have twenty days of tokens, you will exit twenty days from now. Are there any more questions?"

Troy shook his head. Jim looked to Brent, who could only shake his head. He knew he should ask more questions, but for the life of him he couldn't think of a single one.

"I shall begin, then," Jim said. His body began to blur, Brent's eyes unable to interrupt what he saw before him. In moments, a large brown wolf stood before them. The wolf stepped forward and touched a paw to one of the symbols. The air shimmered and Brent found himself standing in a grassy meadow, dandelions sprinkling it with yellow. The wolf that had been Jim took off across the field, occasionally stopping to snap at a passing butterfly.

Troy and Brent walked side by side. No sound greeted them from any direction and Brent realized he could not smell anything, either. The grass and dandelions bent beneath a wind he could not feel. A forest appeared in front of them. Literally. One minute Brent could see nothing but grass, and the next breath he found himself staring into a dark forest. He looked closely at the trees but could not tell what kind they were, as if all identifying features had been blurred into the generic idea of a tree.

"Know Plato?" Troy asked.

Brent shook his head. He had managed to finish his bachelor's in business while in the Air Force, but he had never been much for reading. He preferred practical knowledge, something he could see and apply, like business or science. He hated all that abstract stuff, sitting and thinking about things no one could know or measure. It had been why he had avoided philosophy and literature courses.

"Ideal tree," Troy said.

"I'm not sure I understand."

"Our tree," Troy made a gesture, indicating back the way they had come.

"Trees back in our world?" Brent asked.

Troy nodded and gave him a partial smile. "They image."

"They're an image," Brent nodded, not sure he understood.

"These real."

"What we see in the spirit world is real and our world is an image?" Brent asked, sure he did not have it exactly right. The world he lived in had to be the real world; this entire spirit world had to be nothing but an illusion if it wasn't a hallucination.

"These archetypes."

"So, these are the real trees in the sense that they contain all tree-ness?" Brent said, confusing himself as he spoke.

"Philosophy," Troy said as he shrugged.

"Did Plato know of the spirit world?" Brent asked.

Troy shook his head.

"But you read it and liked how it applied to this place?" Brent asked.

Troy nodded.

"I did not have you pictured as someone who read old Greek philosophers," Brent said. In fact, Brent was a little surprised Troy could read. He had pictured Troy as the dumb jock type rather than the intellectual type.

Troy shrugged.

They entered the forest, the darkness pressing around them. Brent found himself walking closer to Troy than he would normally get to another man as the trail narrowed. He started to fall a bit behind but it felt as if the forest began to squeeze him, separating him from the others. He sped up and fell back into step with Troy.

Jim, the wolf, stayed a few feet in front of them but always within sight. The path before them continually branched in many directions, but the wolf seemed confident of which way to go. Brent tried peering down the other paths as they passed, but could see nothing but more trees.

A light broke through the trees up ahead. Jim led them unerringly into the clearing. A large circle on a wooden platform stood before them, and a giant of a man sat on a tree stump.

"Welcome to your first trial," the giant rumbled.

Chapter Twenty-five

I looked around me with amazement as we strode down the main hall of the settlement. Bigfoots of all possible colors walked down the hall; some entered through various doors, while others exited. Some of the Bigfoots looked at me curiously, but none came up to us as we walked. Part of me kept waiting for someone to come up and scream at us, and force me back to my cell. Domel made a conscious effort to keep to a pace I could keep up with. His long legs gave him a distinct advantage.

"Do we have an itinerary for this trip, or are we just wondering aimlessly?" I asked, trying to keep pace with him.

"I do have a plan," Domel answered, slowing a little so I could keep up.

"Are you going to tell me what it is?" I asked, giving him my best pleading look.

"No," he said, giving me a small smile.

I sighed. I should be used to men telling me little. Domel paused and opened a door, holding it for me to pass through. We entered a new hallway, with doors along both sides. The hall was lined with pictures of foliage, detailed paintings of trees and flowers as far as the eye could see. I sensed a theme of the settlement, a maze of halls and doors. I'd go insane living in a place like this. I began to study the doors, looking for numbers or markers to tell them apart. I saw nothing that distinguished them from each other. I wondered if the Bigfoots simply counted the doors as they walked down each hall. How confusing!

We paused at another door and again Domel held it open for me. I entered a huge living room. It had a large TV on the wall and a variety of seating, so I assumed it was the Bigfoot equivalent of a living room. A shelf lined the walls with a variety of figurines and other knickknacks. Two wooden chairs sat on either side of a bench, all of them drenched with pillows, looking as if a rainbow had thrown up on them.

"These are my rooms," Domel said. "Find a seat and make yourself comfortable."

"Didn't your mom ever tell you it's bad manners to invite a girl to your room on the first date?" I asked, smiling over my shoulder at him as I went to check out the TV. It was high definition and at least ninety inches. I wondered how it had gotten here and how they could afford it.

"My mom would be delighted if I dated," Domel said, closing the door behind him.

"Is she nagging you for grandkids?" I asked, looking over my shoulder at him.

"Yes," he said. "Ever since I was declared an adult."

"My Ma's the same way," I said.

I crawled onto the large bench and rearranged pillows until I had made myself a human-size nest. Dormel puttered around a back room for a moment before returning with a platter of sliced cheese and sausage. He turned on the TV and began flipping through the stations. Typical man! Offering finger foods and watching TV, thinking it was a good time. He stopped on a football game and I rolled my eyes. Men were the same, regardless of species.

"Can you explain this game to me?" he asked, glancing over at me.

"Each team of men tries to get that small ball to the opposite end of the field," I said.

"Why?" he asked.

I laughed. I had never understood, either. How to explain humans' preoccupation with sports? He waited patiently for an answer, so I tried to calm my giggles.

"They get points for doing so, and whoever has the most points wins," I said.

"It's a competition of physical prowess?" he asked.

"Something like that," I said.

"Does it help them to mate?" he said, looking intently at the screen.

"Well, I have never heard of a football player having trouble getting a date, so I guess it does," I said.

"Human females must be attracted to men with lots of stamina," he said as he peered at the screen. I dissolved into giggles again and he looked over at me.

"I'm sorry," I managed before the laughter escaped again. "Lots of stamina, oh yeah. I like a man with stamina."

"This sound, amusement or embarrassment?" he asked.

"Amusement this time," I said.

"Do women watch this sport to select a man?" Domel asked, looking from me to the TV.

"No," I said, not sure how to explain.

"Then how do women select their mates?" Domel asked, abandoning TV watching to look at me.

"Well, men ask us out on dates," I said. "If we like them, then we agree to go. If the date goes well and they ask us again, we go for another date. That keeps up until the man asks us to marry him."

"So you don't get to select the man," he said. "You just get to accept or refuse whoever presents themselves to you."

"Essentially," I said, shrugging. "Sometimes a girl asks a guy out, but that's not the most common method."

"It's the opposite among us," Domel said. "The women chose their mates and the men only have the right to refuse."

"And no one's selected you yet?" I asked. He seemed like a nice Bigfoot to me; I couldn't imagine the girls avoiding him. Unless Bigfoot girls looked for something different than human women did.

"One did, but I had to refuse," Domel said, shaking his head.

"Why?" I asked.

"She smelled like ambition, not love," he said.

"'Smelled'?" I asked. I had heard the expression that someone smelled like ambition, but Domel said it as if it was his reality and not just a saying.

"Yes. We communicate a lot by our smells," he said.

"So, love has a smell?" I asked.

"Oh, yes. Romantic love smells like roses and vanilla," he said, smiling.

"Do all emotions have smells?" I asked. I wondered what it would be like to smell everyone's emotion. I would never have to wonder if a guy was attracted to me. Of course, that meant the guys would be able to smell when I was attracted to them. Now that could get embarrassing!

"Of course," he said. "You confuse me because I cannot smell your mood. How do humans communicate emotions?"

"With our facial expressions," I said.

"What does that mean?" he asked.

"Give me the remote and I'll show you," I said. He handed me the remote and I flipped the channels until I came to a daytime soap. We watched it until the commercial break and I explained each facial expression we saw; smiles for happiness, frowns for sadness, and on it went.

"My turn," I said. "What's the smell of happiness?"

"What do I smell like now?" he asked.

I sniffed the air, trying to identify the scent.

"Um, oranges and cinnamon," I said.

"That's happy," he said.

"So you are happy now?" I asked. I could grow to like this; what an easy way to read emotions.

"I enjoy talking to you," he said. "Are you happy?"

"I enjoy talking to you, too," I said. "I'm happy when I forget that I might be killed in a few days."

"I'm sorry," he said. I noticed the smell of iron and ash.

"What are you feeling?" I asked.

"Regret and sadness," he said. "I do not want you to die."

"Let's think happier thoughts, then," I said. I eyed Domel. I had finally met a male who could name more emotions than "feeling good" and "feeling bad." I wondered if Brent knew the difference between sadness and regret. Maybe growing up with Troy had given me a cynical view of men's skills in the emotion department.

"Okay," he said. "What do you do for fun?"

"Between work and school, I don't get a lot of time for fun," I said. "I guess I mostly hang out with my friends."

"What do you do with your friends?" he asked.

"Talk, eat, go to a movie," I said, realizing I sounded boring. Didn't I have any hobbies? As a kid at The Range, I had always had some new activity that obsessed me: horseback riding, archery, drawing, and even crocheting for a brief time. When had playtime given way to responsibilities?

"What about you?" I asked, distracting myself from my internal analysis.

"I like to make things," he said, the smell of oranges and cinnamon growing stronger.

"What do you make?" I asked.

He got up and went over to the shelf on the wall. He pulled down one of the wooden figurines and handed it to me. The wood had been polished smooth and gleamed in the light from the lamp overhead. The deer looked as if it might leap from my hand at any moment.

"It's beautiful," I breathed.

"It's just a hobby," he said.

"Well, humans would pay a lot of money for something like this," I said. I had seen worse carvings than this sell out at local tourist traps during the season.

"Are you suggesting trade with the human world?" he asked.

"It's a possibility," I said.

"We sell the ore from the mines to get money to buy what we want from your world," Domel said.

"How do you keep your secret?" I asked, wondering how a large screen TV got delivered. I could just imagine the delivery truck pulling up to an abandoned mine shaft and leaving the box on the ground.

"It took us a while to find a solution," he said. "We ended up setting up a legal company. The office building, warehouse, and a couple of houses are on land right above us."

"You own the land?" I asked.

"Well," Domel said with a shrug, "The Sasquatch Mining Company owns the land. We hire people to pick up the ore and take it to be sold, then the money gets deposited in our account."

"And you order TVs?" I asked.

"We order whatever we can't make here," he said. "It all gets delivered to one of the houses up above."

It made sense. The front of a mining company would explain most of what humans would detect in this region and keep anyone from getting curious. I didn't know much about what satellites would pick up but guessed it could all be explained by a mining operation.

"No one ever insists on meeting you?" I asked.

"That's caused some trouble in the past," he said. "But we've managed to work around it."

"How?" I asked. "Humans are really curious."

"I have to keep some of our secrets," Domel said, smiling at me.

I looked down at the deer in my hand, wondering how such big hands could create such tiny details. I held the deer up to Domel and he took it gently. I stared at his hands, watching how carefully he handled the figurine. He placed the deer on the shelf, giant fingers gentle and nimble. He looked at me for a long moment.

"What do you do with your friends?" I asked, trying to fill the silence.

"We go hunting or watch TV," he said, shrugging. Well, that sounded like most of the men I knew.

He looked around the apartment, then looked back to me. The silence stretched awkwardly between us. I became aware that I sat in the presence of an unknown species, completely separated from my life. It's not that I had forgotten, exactly. It was just so easy to talk to Domel; he seemed so much like one of the boys at college.

Chapter Twenty-six

Brent stared at the wooden circular platform before him. It did not look much larger than a high school wrestling mat. The top of the platform had been painted a bright yellow, which glowed in the sunlight. Brent wondered how the trial would work. Troy sat down his duffel bags and guns, moving forward to meet the giant.

"You choose to go first," the giant said, staring down at Troy.

Troy nodded.

"Step forward onto the platform and face your deepest fear," the giant said.

Troy nodded again and stepped forward. He took the single step up onto the platform only to be surrounded by a rainbow fog. When the fog drifted away, Brent could see Troy facing a man six times his size, bearing his face. The giant Troy held a leather whip with a wooden handle in one hand and a large whiskey bottle in the other. He raised a long, leather lash and swung it forward. The tip landed square across Troy's face. A large welt appeared in its wake. The giant took a drink from the bottle before drawing back his arm again. It shot forward, and again Troy just stood there. Blow after blow Troy stood still, staring into his own face on the giant body.

Brent moved forward but found Jim blocking his path. He couldn't just stand and watch Troy get beaten; they were partners. He looked down at the large wolf and saw it shaking its head. Jim pushed against Brent's legs, driving him back a couple of steps. When Jim stopped pushing, Brent looked back toward the platform.

Troy stood there dripping with blood, his clothes ripped. The giant finished the bottle and threw it to the floor. The shards flew everywhere, hitting both Troy and the giant. Another bottle appeared in the giant's hand and it took another long drink. He looked at Troy and pulled the whip back again. The lash flew forward. This time Troy reached out, catching the leather switch along his forearm and wrapping his fingers around it. He wound it around his arms a couple of times, arms straining. He pulled back with his whole body, the wood handle beginning to slide from the giant's grasp. The giant grabbed it with his other hand, nearly pulling Troy off his feet as he stepped away.

The giant and Troy wrestled for control of the whip in what looked like a violent game of tug-of-war. Troy knelt, bracing himself, and leapt backward. It slipped free from the giant's hands and Troy fell back a step. He brought his arm all the way back, then forward, the lash flying out with a crack. The edge of the leather cut into the giant's face, leaving a trail of blood behind.

Troy pulled back again, taking another swing. The whip leapt forward, cutting the giant beneath the eye. Troy swung it over and over. The snap of the whip took on a steady rhythm as it was drawn back and flew forward. The tip of the lash connected with the giant over and over. Blood flew with every strike. Throughout it all, Troy's face never changed; it continued to hold the same calm it had held when he had been the one being beat.

The giant fell to the ground and lay motionless, Troy still beating him. The giant let out a final bellow of pain mixed with rage and remained still. Troy swung the whip several more times before dropping it. He picked up the giant's full bottle, sniffed it, and dumped it out. He stepped down from the platform and glanced over at Brent. The deadness in Troy's eyes made Brent take a step back.

"You have passed," the giant said, handing Troy a token. Troy glanced at it and walked to Brent's side.

"It is your turn," the giant said, looking at Brent.

Brent walked forward, dreading what he would find in the circle. He stepped gingerly up onto the wooden circle and the rainbow fog surrounded him, caressing him with a silken touch. When it faded, he stood back in Iraq, hearing the squeal of mortars flying through the air. He dove down and curled in on himself. He could smell the dust and sweat that had permeated everything. He felt the heat of a sun set to broil all day, every day. He could feel the weight of all his battle gear holding him down, making movement seem impossible.

Not again. He was not going to relive this again. He felt his thigh up to his crotch, but the pants lay smooth and whole. He looked down: no blood, no wound, no shrapnel. He closed his eyes. He wasn't really back there; this was all part of the trial.

He heard a scream and looked up to see an airman less than six feet from him. A long piece of shrapnel glinted in the bright sun, embedded deep in the boy's back. The young man's dark brown eyes locked on him, his face twisted in pain.

"Help me," the airman cried out, stretching out his hand.

Brent shook his head. It was too dangerous. He would be safe if he stayed right where he was, stayed under cover. His legs ached, echoes of past agony making him curl in upon himself. He could recall seeing his own blood pooling in the sand beneath him, remembered the pain immobilizing him. He looked up again, staring at the boy. He knew the enemy had horrible aim; they probably wouldn't hit the base again. Only, what if they did? He could hear another mortar in the air, another shoulder-fired missile heading toward the camp. His entire body shuddered.

He could not move; the terror held him close. He tried to close his eyes but they remained open, staring in horror as the boy bled into the sand. He could hear his own breathing, fast and ragged. He could feel his heart beating so hard that he thought it might come out of his chest at any moment.

"Please help me," the airman cried out again.

"I can't, I can't," Brent chanted over and over to himself. He began to rock back and forth. Back and forth.

I must help, Brent thought as he began to understand. I am supposed to face my greatest fear. This is it, the moment that haunts me. I failed to act, to save that boy. He forced his limbs to straighten, his heart pounding so frantically he knew it would explode any minute. He did manage to stand, though, panting with the effort. Slowly, he put one foot in front of the other. Tears streamed down his face, blending with the sweat as he forced himself to ignore the fear consuming him.

Another two steps took him to the side of the young man. He knelt, checking for a pulse. He could feel the reassuring thump-thump against his fingertip. He grabbed the airman under the shoulders and dragged him away. He managed two more steps backward before the young boy began to dissolve. Brent looked around frantically to see himself back on the stage in the forest.

He sank to his knees and let himself cry. He cried for the young man who had bled to death while he had cowered in fear. He cried for himself, for the guilt that had been eating at him every waking moment. He cried because he knew he was a coward, not the hero he had dreamed of being.

Jim nuzzled him with his snout, offering him the comfort of a canine. Brent looked into his eyes and saw human understanding and compassion. He wiped the tears from his face, hoping Troy had not seen his breakdown. Burying his hand in the werewolf's fur, he stepped slowly off the stage and went to meet the giant.

"You have passed," the giant said, handing him a coin. Brent looked down to see the number one emblazoned on the red coin. For an instant, he wanted to toss it away. All that anguish for a simple token! When he looked up, the giant and the stage had disappeared. The glade now held daisies and buttercups, butterflies dancing from flower to flower.

Brent walked slowly over to Troy and sank down into the grass. Troy looked up at him with blank eyes before staring at the grass once more. Jim lay down between them, resting his head on Troy's lap. Troy opened one of the duffel bags and pulled out two waters, handing one to Brent.

They drank in silence, letting the reality of the trial fade into a dream. Brent tried to understand what had just happened, how the whole trial worked. This was the trial to face their fear. Was that moment in time his biggest fear or did it just represent his fear, his cowardice? He guessed it did not matter; he had moved despite his fear. He had saved the boy this time. So what did Troy's test mean? Killing the giant had been the way Troy had faced his fear. Did he fear killing? Brent remembered the look in Troy's eyes after the trial. No, the killing hadn't scared him. Did he fear what the giant had represented?

"Don't think," Troy said, reaching over Jim to nudge Brent's knee with his water bottle.

"I don't understand what happened or what it meant," Brent said, rubbing his temple.

"Time helps," Troy said.

"As in time heals all wounds?" Brent asked, raising his eyebrow.

"No," Troy said, shaking his head.

"Time helps it make sense?" Brent asked, brow wrinkled as he tried to understand. He wasn't sure he wanted to know. There were some things best left unexamined, some mysteries left unexplained.

"Yes," Troy said with a slight smile.

"Do you understand your trial?" Brent asked, studying his companion's blank face.

"Yes," Troy said, looking away.

"Can you explain it to me?" Brent asked, cocking his head to one side.

"No," Troy said, scratching Jim behind one ear.

"Is it the same as the last time you were here?" Brent asked, taking a drink of water.

Troy shook his head.

"Does that mean your greatest fear has changed?" Brent asked.

"No," Troy said, putting his empty bottle into one of his duffel bags.

"The next trial is our hope?" Brent asked, thinking back to what Jim had said before they had started.

Troy nodded.

"How can seeing our hope be a challenge?" Brent asked. Hope was a good emotion, one of his favorites.

"You'll see," Troy said, shrugging one shoulder.

"Does it hurt as badly as this one did?" Brent asked, finishing his water and handing the empty bottle to Troy.

"More," Troy said as he dumped Brent's bottle in the duffle bag.

192

Family Heir

Brent looked at Troy for a long moment. Bright red gashes crisscrossed Troy's skin. Blood still trickled from some of the deeper wounds. The dark brown of drying blood crusted the rips of his torn T-shirt, forming macabre stripes. How badly hurt was he?

Chapter Twenty-seven

"Would you like to see the rest of my place?" Domel asked.

I nodded and slid out of my nest of pillows. He led me to a room along the back. It opened to what I assumed was a kitchen. An oak table sat in the center with two large chairs made from the same wood. Cupboards lined one wall, painted white, and a counter ran below them.

The other wall held a large stove from the frontier era; it was one of those old fire-type stoves you see in Westerns. I had never seen one in person and went over to check it out. Sure enough, there was a stack of logs tucked into it, unlit. I didn't smell any signs of fire.

"I don't actually cook," he said.

"Neither does Troy," I said.

"Who is Troy?" Domel asked.

"My Hunting partner and my ex-husband," I said.

"Why do you humans get divorced so often? I see it on TV all the time," he said.

"We don't make good decisions about who to marry, I guess."

"We mate for life," he said. "We take our place in society from our wives' ranks."

"Does that mean you don't have a place right now?"

"My mother is Matriarch of the Sasquatch Clan," he said, "so I have a place under her rank, but it's not much."

"What does that mean for you?"

"Well, I do what my mother tells me to and people accept that I do it with her voice."

"And if you get married?"

"I will learn the trade of my wife's family," he said. "I'd like to marry a woman from a family of Makers so I could learn to make the things we need to survive."

"You don't want to marry a Matriarch?"

"Oh no. Men in a Matriarch's family don't get to do much."

He led the way back out into the living room and opened a door I had not even noticed. Stepping through, I found myself in an office. A large desk held a computer with a printer. The walls were lined with shelves of books. I walked over to look at the book titles. Shakespeare, Aristotle, Plato, and Caesar were all clustered together. I stepped over a little and found an amazing collection of murder mysteries and legal thrillers. A little further and I found a large collection of American history, followed by text books (biology, algebra, English, and public speaking).

He motioned me through another door and I found myself in an underground garden. I looked up and saw several long tunnels with angled mirrors. It appeared that the light truly did come from outside (wherever that was). The garden held a variety of flowers, spices, and vegetables with no discerning order to them. The overall effect was oddly pleasing.

"This is amazing," I told him.

"Another little hobby of mine," he said, smelling of oregano and parsley.

"What feeling am I smelling?" I asked.

"Pride," he said, hanging his head. Now I smelled burnt popcorn.

"And now?"

"Embarrassment."

"Why would you be embarrassed of being proud of this?" I waved my arm to indicate the garden.

"Pride is discouraged," he said.

"Well, I don't mind a little pride over an accomplishment," I told him.

He motioned for me to follow him to the next room, which was his bedroom. It looked like any bedroom I had ever seen, if you ignored the oversize furniture. The bed could have easily held a family of six or a good-size orgy. I looked around the room and realized that it did not have a dresser or a closet. I guess that made sense; I hadn't seen a Bigfoot wear clothing. So if they didn't wear clothing, how did they hide their private parts? I tried to study Domel's crotch as we walked. All I could see was fur, not even a bulge to indicate male genitalia. Maybe they had them in a different place? Or maybe they kept them internally, like some sort of kangaroo pouch?

He pointed to an archway that led to another room, and I went over to look in. It held a small pool fed by running water on one side, which drained out a small pipe on the other.

"I am supposed to take you to the public bath, but I have never seen humans bathe publicly on TV," he said. "I thought you might be more comfortable with some privacy."

"Is this a perk of being a Matriarch's son?"

"The whole place is hers."

"Well, thank you for sharing," I said. I eyed the water dubiously. It did not look warm. Still, it was private and I was filthy.

"Shall I leave you to bathe?"

"Yes, please."

He disappeared and left me to my own devices. I dipped a finger in to discover the water was warm, though cooler than I liked. I stripped down and settled in. Glancing around, I found a bar of what I assumed to be soap. Testing it on my hands showed I had no allergic reaction to it, and it seemed to remove the grime. I washed as quickly as I could but made sure to get the blood and mud off. The water swirled red, brown, and white as it passed me, curling down the pipe. I watched it, entranced by watching my troubles of yesterday disappear from sight. I shook my head to clear it and got out, dripping all over the floor. I looked around for a towel and found nothing that would come close to serving that purpose.

I glanced through the doorway to the bedroom, but all I saw were the blankets on the bed. I thought about using a small corner of blanket, but Domel was being such a good host and I didn't want to be rude. I snarled to myself as I tiptoed to the door of the bedroom.

"Domel," I called out.

"Yes," he called back.

"Do you have anything I can use to dry off with?"

I heard movement and scurried back to the bathroom. I heard him digging around his bedroom and after a moment a large, fluffy object landed on the floor. I picked it up and saw Domel watching me from the bedroom. I blushed and dove away from the door while trying to cover myself with the towel. The linen completely covered me, making me wonder if it was a large towel or a small blanket. Deciding it didn't matter, I quickly dried off and slid back into my donated clothing.

I made my way back to the living room, stopping only momentarily to eye the books in the office. Domel sat in his chair, watching TV. He glanced up as I came in the room, which was filled with the scent of oranges and cinnamon. It was a rather nice way of knowing a guy was happy to see me.

"I'm afraid your exercise time for the day is nearly over."

I sighed at the reminder that I still had to return to my cell and prepare for trial.

"If you'd like to borrow a book, you may," he said.

I smiled at him as I nodded.

"That facial expression means happy?" he asked.

"Yes, it does," I said as I headed back to his office. I randomly grabbed one of the mysteries because I didn't feel up to anything more tasking when I had a desk full of legal books waiting for me. I returned to Domel and we made our way back to the main hallway.

"I will come back later this evening with food," Domel said as we turned onto the large main hall. I nodded at him.

"I have a few friends I want to talk to about your case this afternoon," he said. "Maybe I can build some curiosity and support for your cause."

"I appreciate everything you are doing for me."

"I am not the only one who has become fascinated with humans and their culture," he said. "You may yet find you have more friends here than just me."

With that optimistic note, we reached my cell and I found myself once again staring at four walls. I sat on the bed, thinking of Brent and Troy. Had they made it to the werewolves yet? How would Brent do in the spirit world? The werewolves explained so little about spirit walking. Ma and Pa had told me what to expect before I went. Poor Brent had no one to tell him; Troy wouldn't even think to try. Would Troy at least warn Brent about the dangers? The trials themselves left emotional and physical damage behind. Then there were the wogs, the shadows that lurked in the forest attacking travelers. They seemed to be attracted to emotional pain, hunting those who struggled with the trials. Ma had said they killed one of my Great-Aunts. I could still remember running from their dark shapes, terrified during my own trial.

I had to trust that they would be all right. I had to believe that they would rescue me before the Bigfoots killed me. I liked Domel, but I did not trust him to get me out of this mess. I needed heroes with guns or a way to convince the Matriarchs that I was an intelligence species, someone to be dealt with as an equal. I had to show them that I had a right to kill Sincha, and I had no idea how to do any of that.

Chapter Twenty-eight

Brent stared at Troy's chest. The ripped and bloody shirt clung to the wounds beneath.

"Do you have bandages in there? I could clean up your face, your chest?" he asked.

Troy dug in the duffel bag and pulled out a first-aid kit. He pulled off his T-shirt, tossing it into his bag. Brent set to work cleaning the facial wounds and putting band-aids on them.

The cuts on the chest were longer but not as deep. His right arm hung limply. Brent had forgotten Troy had been shot and he took a moment to make sure the stitches held. The skin around the stitches on Troy's right arm had turned bright red from the exertion. He rinsed the whip wounds with peroxide but didn't bandage them. They should heal fine on their own. He studied his handy work and decided it was good enough. He sat back and Troy dug in the bag until he pulled out another T-shirt. He pulled the clean shirt over his head, readjusting it until it sat loosely over his wounds.

"Thank you," he said.

Brent nodded.

Jim stood and walked to the edge of the glade. Brent reluctantly stood as well and went to join the wolf. A blue jay sat on the tree, watching them. After a moment, Troy grabbed his things and they started out again through the woods. The blue jay flew above their heads, disappearing into the depths of the forest.

"Do you enjoy killing?" Brent asked as they reentered the thick forest.

"Sometimes," Troy said, studying the forest around them.

"Does it scare you that you enjoy it?" Brent asked, glancing from Troy to the forest and back again.

"Sometimes," Troy said, looking over at Brent.

"Why didn't you stop the beating at first?" Brent asked.

Troy shrugged.

"Was your fear getting beat?" Brent asked, remembering that Ma had said Troy had been abused as a child.

Troy shook his head.

Brent pictured the giant with Troy's face, the whiskey bottle in hand. He remembered Timmy's struggle with drugs and alcohol.

"Do you fear that will be you?" Brent asked.

Troy shrugged.

"I'd get more answers from the wolf," Brent muttered.

Jim yipped.

Troy smiled.

Giving up on conversation, Brent walked on, following the others along the path. The trees, which had struck him as being a bit surreal earlier, had begun to look sinister. He wondered if they might leap out at him if he looked away for a moment. He could see none of the creatures he had noted earlier: no birds, no squirrels, not even an insect. The shadows moved, dancing between the trees in ever-changing patterns.

Jim began to growl, crouching low, teeth bared. Troy pulled out his rifle and began to scan the tree line to the left. Brent pulled out his handgun and stared at the trees to the right.

"What am I looking for?" Brent whispered, seeing only the forest and shadows.

"Wogs," Troy whispered back.

"What does a wog look like?" Brent asked.

"It moves," Troy said.

"If I see something that moves...," Brent said.

"Shoot it," Troy said.

Brent stared at the trees, looking for movement. The forest had become even quieter than before, the type of oppressive silence so strong it might as well be a sound. He was not sure how; it had been pretty still already. A dark shadow moved from tree to tree. Brent tried to take aim, but it moved too fast.

"Incoming," Troy whispered before he fired the rifle.

A shadow leapt at Brent and he fired. The shadow disappeared, only to be replaced by another. Brent shot again. He could hear more shots from Troy's rifle as well as Jim's bark, loud enough to penetrate the ringing in his ears. The shadows closed in on them from all sides.

"Run," Troy shouted.

Brent ran, following Jim as they flew through the woods. Shadows continued to jump out at them, reaching for them with dark hands. Troy shot to the left, Brent to the right, and Jim bit the ones

202

coming head on. They dissolved the moment they were hit by bullet or teeth but more kept coming, an endless stream of tormenters.

They sped toward a patch of light up ahead. Brent heard the click, telling him he had run out of bullets. He sped up to stay as close to Jim as he could, hoping the werewolf could keep the shadows away from them both. Troy fell behind, shooting to both sides of the path as they ran.

They stumbled into a glade, sunlight bathing them with light and warmth. Jim collapsed to the ground, panting. Troy quickly pulled a bowl and bottle of water from his bag. He filled the bowl and offered it to Jim.

"What all do you have in that thing?" Brent asked, staring at the metal bowl in bemusement. Troy shrugged.

"Are we safe?" Brent asked, staring at the shadows moving between the trees.

"In sun," Troy said, watching Jim lap up the water.

"We are safe in the sun?" Brent asked.

Troy nodded. He pulled two boxes of ammunition from his duffel, laying them on the grass in front of him.

Brent looked around the glade. It looked exactly like the one where they had their last trial. He glanced around, looking for a giant or a round platform. The glade held nothing but grass, dancing slightly in an unfelt breeze.

"Is this where we have our next trial?" he asked, sliding his gun back into the holster.

"Not ours," Troy said, reloading his handgun cartridge.

"Not ours, what?" Brent asked, looking at Troy.

"Glade," Troy said, looking around the clearing.

"Someone else's glade?"

"Sometimes," Troy said, nodding his head.

"You make no sense," Brent muttered, shaking his head.

Troy shrugged. He began reloading his rifle clip.

"So we'll have to go back into the forest to get to our glade?" Brent asked.

Troy nodded, gathering everything back up and tucking it into one of the duffel bags. He stood, looking around the glade to the forest beyond.

"And those wog things will attack us again?" Brent asked.

Troy nodded, sliding his refilled cartridge into his Colt .45 and holstering it.

"Can they kill us?" Brent asked, pulling his gun back out.

Troy nodded, slinging both duffel bags over his shoulder.

"Great," Brent muttered as he popped the empty clip out of his gun. He dug in his backpack for his box of ammunition and refilled the clip. He also filled his spare clip and slid it into his pocket.

Jim stood back up and stared out into the woods. He sniffed the ground along each of the paths leading from the glade before sitting down in front of one.

"Ready?" Troy asked, picking up his rifle and holding it at the ready.

"As much as I'm going to be," Brent said, walking with Troy to where Jim sat. The three stared into the dark forest for a few moments, taking deep breaths, before breaking into a run.

They darted down the trail and made an abrupt left turn onto another path. Brent could see the shadows darting among the trees and kept his gun ready. The wogs attacked again. Brent fired but kept running. He felt a sharp burning in his shoulder and looked down to see a long gash. He ignored the pain and kept moving, kept firing. Terror filled him as it had in Iraq. He just wanted to curl up, give up.

He forced himself to keep going, keep firing the gun. They turned down another trail and Brent could see brighter spot ahead. He pushed harder, desperate to get to the light. His shoulder had gone numb—in fact, his entire arm had gone numb. He kept running. The numbness spread and he found himself falling, shadowy shapes surrounding him.

Jim dove on top of him, snapping at the shadows. They backed up, giving way. Troy pulled him into a fireman's carry and darted toward the sun lit space. Brent grunted in pain as his shoulder hit Troy's back with every stride. Half of his body lay draped over the duffel bags, and something in one of the bags poked into his thigh painfully. He could see nothing but the ground and Troy's leg.

The first ray of sun hit Brent's face like a burst of hope. He might live through this after all. He stared at the glade from upside down. It looked empty—free of giants, platforms, and wogs.

Troy set him down and tore off Brent's shirt. Brent felt grass poking into his back and the sun warm on his chest. Troy pulled the med kit back out of his bag and began to clean the wound. Jim watched, head cocked as Troy worked. Brent could feel the cool alcohol drip down his arm and his side, but he could not feel the wound itself. Troy leaned back and Jim bent his head to Brent's chest. Jim sniffed the wound and gave it a couple of licks before lying down at his side.

"Spit heals," Troy said, scratching Jim's head.

"Werewolf spit heals?" Brent asked, staring at his shoulder. The jagged cut crossed from collar bone to armpit, but it no longer bled.

"Wog wounds," Troy said, with a faint smile.

Of course werewolf spit healed wog wounds; why hadn't he thought of that? Brent closed his eyes and let the warmth of the sun settle over him.

Chapter Twenty-nine

I woke in my cell, day two of my captivity. It took talent to be terrified of possible execution and bored at the same time. Somehow I managed it. I grabbed the mystery I had borrowed from Domel and tried to read. I tossed the book onto the bed. Who cared who killed the librarian? She sounded like a tedious person before death, and her murder was equally dull. I mean, really, a gunshot to the head? I could write a better mystery than that; in fact, I was living a better mystery than that.

I got up and walked around my cell. It wasn't large enough to really make for good pacing, but I needed to move. I wondered what Troy and Brent were up to; surely they would have made it to the werewolves by now. I wondered what my sniper assassin was up to. Was he still searching for me?

The door entered and Domel came in.

"Did you know you were dead?" he asked.

"What?" I said.

"Come with me. You need to see this," he said.

I followed Domel out of the cell, wondering if the Bigfoots had decided to kill me rather than try me. No, Domel didn't seem worried, though I didn't recognize the scent. We reached the main hallway and turned the opposite direction from the way we had gone before; so clearly not headed to Domel's rooms. He paused long enough to open a door, and we entered a corridor much dingier than the others I had seen. The paint had cracks and some had chipped away, revealing rock beneath it. The Bigfoots here all noticed me. They stared and hissed as we passed.

"Mother killer," someone called out.

Domel moved closer to me, protecting me with his bulk as we walked down the hall. Others hissed insults at me as we walked and I was grateful for Domel's presence. I guessed anger, hostility, and hatred smelled like a decaying skunk who had eaten too many peppers based on the hideous smell that surrounded us. I understood why Seth's stories had said the Bigfoots stunk.

Domel opened another door, and I eagerly skittered through it. Sitting on a chair in front of a small TV set sat a Bigfoot I hadn't met yet. This one had blond fur with sunburst patterns of burnt orange. The pattern would have made for a great shirt.

"This is Neller," Domel said.

"And you must be Kelley," Neller said, gesturing for us to sit down.

"Is it still playing?" Domel asked.

"At least once every half hour or so."

I glanced at the TV and realized he was watching the human news. The news anchor was discussing a hurricane in the Gulf of Mexico that had not made landfall yet. It seemed a little early for hurricanes—it was only the end of July—but what did I know about hurricanes?

"Ah, here it is," Neller said, turning up the volume.

"Humans For Hominid," the announcer said, "has claimed responsibility for the attacks that killed twenty-three members of the organizations known as the Hunter Families. Law enforcement has confirmed that the Heirs of these organizations were all killed by sniper fire."

The screen displayed the pictures of the dead Heirs, mine included. I looked in shock from Neller to Domel, but both of them had their eyes on the screen.

"This domestic terrorist organization has threatened to continue killing members of these Families and those associated with them until Congress passes legislation to disband these groups, labeling them organized crime. To demonstrate their determination, the organization has also bombed two buildings in Rock Springs, Wyoming."

I stared in shock as I saw my apartment building, my own apartment nothing more than a gaping hole. The scene shifted to Dr. Lyman's office, now a pile of rubble. I curled up and lay my head on my knees, staring at the fabric. I couldn't bear to watch anymore. Tears burned my eyes and began to slide down my face. Domel kneeled in front of me and gently stroked my hair with his large hand.

"I'm so sorry," he said.

"That was my home, my workplace. They bombed my life. Did they say who had been killed? Is Lisa alive? Is Dr. Lyman?"

"I don't know," he said.

"We can find out, though," Neller said. "I'm sure we can read about it on the Internet."

Neller pulled up the Rock Springs local news and quickly found an article about the bombings. He confirmed that Lisa's body had been positively identified by the next of kin; however, they had not yet confirmed the number of dead from Dr. Lyman's office. Dental records had only confirmed the identity of five of the victims. I stared into space, numbness replacing pain.

"I think this is what humans call shock," Domel said, watching me intently.

"What should we do?" Neller said, staring at me as if I were an animal in a zoo.

"I don't know; Google it," Domel said, looking over at his friend.

"Keep her warm and hydrated?" Neller said, after typing at the keyboard with a slim claw.

"I think that's for physical shock," Domel said, patting my head.

"Take her to a psychologist."

"I don't think that's practical."

"Dr. Lyman was a psychologist," I whispered, choking on a sob. "He'd have told me to grieve."

Domel sat beside me and put his arm gently around me. It felt like being hugged by a huge teddy bear, bringing back memories of the giant stuffed bear I had slept with as a child.

"Talk to me," he said, voice gentle.

"I don't know where to start," I whispered.

"Wherever you want," he said.

So I started talking. I told him about meeting Lisa in class and how she always made me laugh. I told him how Dr. Lyman would stay late after work to help me with homework or to help me with personal problems. I rambled about any and every memory that flitted through my head. Slowly, the numbness faded and the pain returned. I cried on Domel's shoulder until I ran out of tears. He sat patiently through it all, gently encouraging me.

"I'm sorry," I said, pulling myself back together piece by piece.

"Did you know these people were trying to kill you?" he asked.

"Yes, they'd already tried." I said, my brain slowly thinking over the entire news piece.

"If they announced who they were, can't the police or FBI get them now?" I asked.

"The earlier news reports said they were looking for suspects but there had been no arrests," Neller said.

"They think I'm dead," I said, words slow and soft as I tried to think it through. I couldn't imagine what Ma must be feeling; she had to be a mess. I longed to call her, tell her that I was okay. I wondered if Troy and Brent had heard. Would they believe it? Would they keep looking for me anyway? Troy would. I knew he wouldn't stop until he had seen my body. I had to believe that.

"We'll keep watching the news and let you know if they say anything new," Neller said.

I could only nod.

"Is there anything we can do for you?" Domel asked.

"Let me go home to my Ma and Pa?" I asked.

"After the trial," he said. "I'll take you to their very door, if you want."

"Ma must be going crazy thinking I'm dead," I said.

"I can contact her and let her know you live," Domel said, patting my shoulder.

"The mother-child bond is the most sacred there is. We could not leave your mother to suffer needlessly," Neller said, smelling of the wood ash of sadness.

"Thank you," I told them both.

"I know the timing is bad," Neller said. "But we should work on your defense for the trial."

"The trial," I said, sighing. "Those people in the hall hated me."

"Yes, killing a woman of breeding age is the most horrible crime we can conceive of," Neller said.

"Even if she was the one killing human women and their children?" I asked.

"If we had evidence of that, that would help," Domel said.

"I don't suppose you have a DNA lab," I said.

"No, but one of our scientists has been studying DNA through online classes," Neller said.

"Well, that's usually the standard of evidence accepted in human courts. What evidence could convince your people?" I asked.

"If we could examine the bodies," Domel said.

"Would pictures give you enough?" I asked, staring at Neller's computer.

"If they are detailed enough," Domel said.

"If you're going to contact Ma to let her know I live, can we contact her to get the pictures from the case?" I asked. "It would have to come from an e-mail from me. Ma wouldn't hand the information over to a stranger."

Domel and Neller stared at each other for a long moment. The air changed scents many times, none of them staying around long enough for me to identify them.

"You couldn't say anything about our existence or where you are," Neller said.

"Of course not," I said.

"But you would assure your mother you lived," Domel said.

"Of course," I said.

"We could watch everything you did, everything you typed," Neller said.

I nodded.

"You better get your mother's permission first," Neller said to Domel. "But I cannot imagine she would deny permission to reassure a mother."

"Even if I end up dead after the trial?" I asked.

"We would ensure your family was notified. We would not leave them wondering about your fate," Neller said, sounding indignant and smelling of paprika.

"As her speaker, will you take charge of Kelley while I go ask?" Domel said, looking at Neller.

"Of course," Neller said. "We'll be here until you return."

Domel left and I found myself staring at Neller.

"Domel shared with me the notes he took yesterday," Neller said.

I nodded.

"For me to speak for you, I need to know more about you," Neller said, pulling out a notepad and pencil. "Will you tell me about being Hunter?"

"What would you like to know?" I asked.

"Everything," he said.

I talked until my throat hurt. Neller offered me water and encouraged me to keep going. I'd never really tried to explain to anyone about Hunting; it was just something I did, something I had known my entire life. As I talked, I realized how long it had been since I enjoyed it. I loved other aspects of being part of a Family—the ones where I got to help people. I loved seeing that I had made a difference in someone's life.

I knew Hunting helped people too, protected them from danger, but it never felt like that while I was on the Hunt. I couldn't deny the adrenaline rush or that I enjoyed working as a team with Troy. When we Hunted, it always felt like he and I were one, that we perfectly understood each other. Unfortunately, that understanding did not follow us into our day-to-day lives. I wondered what it would be like to Hunt with another partner, maybe someone like Brent. Could I learn to enjoy it as much as I loved partnering with Troy? Would I still go on Hunts now that I was Heir?

Chapter Thirty

Brent opened his eyes, staring into a blue sky which looked as if a child had colored it with crayon. The sun caressed his face and bare chest, reminding him of the wound. He tilted his head to an angle which would allow him to see his shoulder. The wound had turned a pumpkin-like color but appeared to be healing. He sat up, using his good arm to support himself. He did not feel weak or dizzy; that had to be a good thing.

Troy sat nearby, absently stroking Jim's head and staring into the shadows of the trees. As Brent realized that sitting upright did not hurt, Jim turned his head to look him in the eye. The large wolf got up and made his way over to Brent, thrusting his nose at Brent's chest to sniff the shoulder. Troy turned his head to watch intently.

Jim nodded, then licked Brent's cheek. Troy began to gather up the trash and Jim's bowl, tossing everything back into one of his duffel bags. Brent decided he had better try standing. His legs seemed to hold his weight just fine, and he felt more rested than he had since before they entered this strange place. Troy tossed him a clean shirt, which was clearly meant for someone of Troy's size. Brent shrugged and pulled it over his head, ignoring the loose way it hung on him.

Jim had already moved to stand at one of the paths leading away from the grove. Troy and Brent moved to stand by him, ready for another run. They began their sprint, keeping a steady eye out for shadows. The forest looked just like a forest, albeit a slightly unusual one. A blue bird sat on a tree, head raised in song, though all Brent could hear was the muted sounds of leaves waving in the wind. He looked around, but the leaves remained still. This place could drive him insane.

They moved down the path at a slow jog but saw no sign of the wogs. The adrenaline pumped through Brent's body, pushing him to move a little further, as his senses stretched into the forest, alert for any slight movement. He felt the fear beating at him with every thump-thump of his heart, the rhythm that moved him. The peaceful stillness of the forest wrestled with his fear, lulling him to calm. The rhythm of the run relaxed him; this could be just another morning jog. They turned down another path and began their jog up a hill. Brent felt a stitch in his side and he found himself sucking in air.

They entered another grove, this one containing another giant and round platform. The sunlight hit the platform and it glowed, making Brent's eyes ache after the darkness of the forest paths. This giant appeared female—not that it mattered much. However, the pink polka-dot dress on an eight-foot human seemed distractingly out of place, even for this world. Brent could make no sense of it, tired of this place without reality. He stared at the ground, still feeling his heart speed along, his breathing fast and loud.

Brent bent his knees and lowered his head, gasping for breath after the long run. His shoulder ached from the wog wound and he wondered if the injury had affected his strength. He promised himself he'd work out more whenever he got out of this mess. He would run ten miles a day instead of the five he did now. He would start lifting weights. He would not allow working at a desk to steal his health. Troy barely seemed winded, pausing only a moment to slow his own breathing.

Troy strode up to the platform, as calmly as he had last time.

"My turn to go first," Brent said. Troy turned and looked at him, his face closed off and blank. He nodded and stepped back. Brent stepped forward to meet the giant, confident that he could handle this trial.

"Enter and face your greatest hope," the giant said.

He stepped up onto the platform and a bright light blinded him. When it cleared, he stood outside of a large Tudor-style house, the siding a bright white and the shutters red. He strode up the walkway and opened the door. The sounds of children screaming with happiness gave him a few seconds of warning before three young boys threw themselves at him. He crouched down to better hug all three of them, noting how much they looked like his own pictures from childhood.

"Welcome home, love," a soft voice said, and he smiled as he looked up into the face of his wife. He looked deeply at her face, her features clear. But he could not tell if her eyes were brown or blue. He could not say if her hair was red, brown, or blonde, or if her nose was large or small. Yet, he thought she might look a little like Kelley, if he could just get his mind to register what it was seeing.

He stood up, one of the boys clinging to his shoulder for a piggyback ride. His wife stepped into his arms, giving him a quick hug and a kiss. She released him with a soft smile and led the way. He followed, with the boys telling him all about their day, their chatter flowing around him like a warm blanket, comforting and warming. He heard about mean kids at school, how science was boring, and how T-ball practice had ended in a bloody nose.

They entered the kitchen and Brent smelled pot roast, his favorite meal. The table had been set with china, all waiting for the man of the house. He sat down in his seat as his wife served him, the boys already busy helping themselves to large plates full of food. He took a bite, savoring the taste as the tender meat nearly melted on his tongue.

"How was your day?" his wife asked, pouring him a glass of red wine and handing it to him.

"The Secretary of the Interior called me in today," he said, chest puffed out in pride.

"Your promotion?" she asked, smiling.

"Yes," he said. "The official announcement has to wait for approval by Congress, but it looks like I will be the next Assistant Secretary of the Bureau of Hominid Affairs."

"That's wonderful," she said, raising her glass in a toast.

"What does it mean, Daddy?" the smallest boy asked.

"It means that I will be in charge of the BHA," he said as he reached out to ruffle the child's hair.

"Wait until I tell Tommy," the tallest boy said, pulling out a cell phone and beginning to text.

Wait a minute, Brent thought. The doctors said I wouldn't be able to have kids. The surgery that removed the shrapnel left me infertile. Memories of the forest, the mission, and the trial hit him. He had to get out of here and save Kelley. This was his greatest hope. He wanted a wife, children, and success. Only, he knew for sure that children were out of the picture. None of this was real; none of it could ever be real. He felt his eyes burn. He thought he had accepted the doctor's prognosis, but he looked at the boys sitting at the table. His gut clenched as he realized how much he wanted this, to see his own face reflected in children, to have someone to carry on the family name. He blinked his eyes rapidly, trying to force the tears away.

Maybe he could have the wife and success. Surely he could have that much. Only, he already knew he did not have the connections he needed to rise in the BHA as far as he wanted; he could only hope to be promoted based on merit. That would only get him so far before politics kicked in and determined his fate. He would never be truly successful; just another cog in the wheel. The reality of it felt like a punch in the gut. He bowed his head, staring at his hands. He was no one special. He would never earn his parents' approval. A tear slid from his eye. He could feel its cold path down his cheek. He brushed it away with his shoulder, unwilling to be broken.

He should be able to get married someday; that part of the dream could be true. He looked carefully at the woman across the table from him. The rest of this world looked sharp and clear, yet her features remained elusive. Did that mean that this part might yet be true? He felt his heart burn with hope, felt how much he wanted this one part of his childhood dream.

The hope grew within him; he knew what he had to do. He had to stop focusing so much on work and get serious about dating. He needed to find a woman he could love, someone who would share his life. He could do this, he knew he could. All he had to do was plan it out the way he planned out every step of his life. He had to start as soon as possible and maybe, with all the advances in medicine, he could have children as well.

Hope burned so brightly it hurt. He could hardly breathe from the force of it. He stood, pushing back the chair. He had to get back to the real world and get started. It was time to really begin living his life.

Only, he had to finish the mission first. They had to get Kelley back and then find the hominid killer. Of course, he had to help find who was trying to kill Kelley, too. After that, though, he would go home and start looking. Maybe he could even ask Kelley for a date. He thought of her smiling face, but guilt ate at him. Could he hurt Troy like that? He thought the two of them still loved each other. Why did Troy matter to him, anyway? Of course Troy mattered. If he really did start dating Kelley, he had to accept that Troy would still be her partner and friend. Maybe Troy had become his friend as well. Was that where the guilt was coming from?

He could just go back home and date there. Surely he could find a woman as attractive as Kelley. He was positive his boss would understand if he put in less overtime, spent more time on himself. No, he was lying to himself again. If he did that, he would lose his chance at getting promoted, getting a chance at success. Maybe he should focus on work now and love later. Women loved successful guys, everyone knew that.

I can't stop hoping even when I know the chances are slim, Brent thought. He understood, or at least he thought he understood. The pain grew, blending with the hope. He could break his heart—break himself—continuing to chase his dreams with hope driving him on long after it had become hopeless. How often had hope driven him to keep going even when he lost the good things in his life to do it?

He remembered his last girlfriend, her seductive smile and her lithe body. They had met shortly after he had gotten out of the Air Force and had moved in together while he went to the BHA academy. He remembered her bitter words when he worked late, trying to finish a project. She had left him, packing all of her things from their shared apartment one night when he had stayed late in the library to study for a test.

Hope destroyed that relationship. His burning hope of impressing his instructors with perfect grades and the slim chance that good academic performance would lead to a good position in the BHA had driven him to ignore the woman he loved. That dream, fueled on hope, an emotion more powerful than love, had driven her away. He had to learn to hope less, be more realistic.

He forced himself to stumble to the door. He heard his wife and children calling to him, begging him to come back. He paused, longing to turn around, to live the dream. He moved one foot and then the other, reaching the door. He opened the door, feeling his wife's hand on his shoulder, hearing her whispered words of love in his ears. He jumped through the door and found himself on the circular platform. He stepped down and the giant handed him another token with a one on it. He barely glanced at it before walking over to his travel companions. The memory of the feeling of the little boy's hand in his own followed him, taunted him. He sat down next to Troy and stared into nowhere.

Chapter Thirty-one

Domel returned to Neller's rooms followed by the largest Bigfoot I had yet seen. She stood a couple of feet taller than Domel, and had to duck to come through the door. Her gray and white fur appeared bleached with age and I wondered how old she was. Neller stood immediately and I followed his example.

"Matriarch, this is Kelley Venator Mallard," Domel said, following her into the room.

I had no idea what the proper greeting was, but settled on a small bow. It always worked with vampires.

"Kelley, I understand your family currently believes you to be dead," the Matriarch said, looking me up and down.

"Yes, ma'am," I said, bowing my head politely.

"And your Ma lives," she rumbled.

"Yes, ma'am," I said. Hadn't Domel already told her that?

"And you can get evidence related to your case from her."

"Yes, ma'am."

"I will grant you permission for one communication on several conditions," the Matriarch said. "First, you will write only what Domel gives you permission to, and second, you will give Domel free access to your e-mail so that we can ensure the response has not been tampered with."

"I agree to your conditions," I said. After all, if I lived through this I could change my password. I could even change to a new account.

"Now let me look at you, child."

I stood before her, trying to look polite and calm. She motioned for me to turn around and I spun slowly, feeling like a prized calf up for sale at the fair. She stared at me for a long moment and then turned and left the room. I looked to Domel for an explanation.

"She has never seen a human before," he said.

Neller sat me down at the computer and the two of them watched as I opened the browser to the Western Wyoming Community College and logged on to my e-mail. I stared at my inbox, longing to open the messages, to have contact again with the human world. I forced myself to open a new mail message and then stared at it. How did I write this so that Ma wouldn't panic and would send me the information? I opted for short and sweet.

"Ma," I typed, "I saw the news. I'm still alive. I got separated from Troy. Could you send me the case file? I will explain later. I love you all. Your Heir, Kelley."

Domel nodded permission and I hit send. I reluctantly closed the window before I could be tempted to do more. I wrote out my login and password and handed it to Domel.

"You won't go sending any e-mails from my account or anything crazy?" I asked.

"I will not, but I might do your homework," he said, smelling of oranges and cinnamon.

"What?" I said.

"I believe we might be in the same class," he said. "I'm Joe Smith."

"You are? What?" I asked, aware that I sounded like an idiot.

"I have enjoyed reading your posts on the discussion board."

"So you're the one I've been discussing history with all term?" I asked.

He nodded.

"You're the most interesting one in the class," I said. "Now I know why your view was so different than the others. You truly do see us from the outside."

"Do you really believe humans would have reacted badly if the vampires or werewolves announced themselves?" he said.

"Well, sure; at the time, they were the villains in horror movies. The fact that scientists proved their existence made them seem safer, gave them time to see the truth."

"And how would they react to us revealing ourselves?" he asked.

"New hominids have been coming forward all the time. It seems to work out much better if they announce themselves than if they wait until a Hunter has to go after one of their rogues."

"What about now, when this case is a little of both?" he asked.

"I guess that depends on a lot of factors. If I'm executed, no one will know that the rogue was one of you. If I'm not, well, I guess it depends on whether you came forward before or after I filed my report."

"How would you recommend we come forward?" Neller asked.

"Ask Ma and Pa to represent you. We are the local Family," I said. "Or ask Patriarch Bullend—he heads the local werewolves—to represent you."

"Why werewolves and not vampires?"Neller asked, shutting down the computer.

"From what I've seen of your settlement," I said, "you would want a reservation set up like the deal the werewolves have. They could help you with that. The vampires are too integrated into human society to offer that type of help."

"A reservation would allow us to retain our own laws and independence?" Domel asked.

"Yes," I said. "Since the government had already come up with the idea for the native tribes, it was easy to extend the idea to hominid groups that did not want to be part of human society or could not fit in easily with human society. It limits where you can live, to a certain extent. Anyone leaving the reservation has to follow human laws."

"You give us much to think about," Neller said, nodding his head.

"And you and I can work on next week's assignment together. I always wanted someone to study with," Domel said, smelling lightly of oranges and cinnamon mixed with wood ash. How could someone be happy and sad at the same time? I smiled at him, appreciating the emotional sentiment in his scent.

"When do you think we will hear back from your Ma?" Neller asked.

"Tomorrow, if not later today," I said, knowing Ma would be glued to her computer in her grief, reaching out to all the Venators and the other Families. "I could check the message boards to see if she's online."

"What message board?" Domel asked.

"The Families keep a message board to keep each other informed."

"I would like to see this message board," Domel said, looking at Neller.

"I don't see the harm in it if we're watching her and she doesn't post anything," Neller said, turning the computer back on.

I entered the e-mail address and logged on as fast as my fingers could type. The page loaded quickly and I wondered how they got high-speed internet service. We had to use satellite service to get it at The Range. I scanned for the most recent messages from Ma. I pointed to the screen, showing Neller and Domel her login name. The most recent post had been five minutes ago, asking the community if anyone knew what would happen to a spirit walker seeking a dead person. I could only guess that meant she had heard from Brent and Troy, that they were spirit walking to find me. Domel motioned for me to look at some of her earlier messages. I complied, sad to see her pain but happy to have even this much communication with her.

Most of the messages discussed the attacks. We read that the Families across the United States had evacuated most of their members to vampire safe houses. Some had headed out to either Canada or Mexico, taking foreign Families up on offers of safe havens. I read that Ma and Pa had remained at The Range, trusting in their safety precautions. Anyone who tried to get near would have to approach on foot and would be caught on camera long before they reached the main house. Suddenly, Ma's insistence on not putting a driveway up to the house sounded like good planning.

"Does she always reveal your location?" Domel asked.

I read the message he was reading where Ma said Troy and I had gone hunting in the mountains west of Merna. I scrolled backed and found where Ma had posted my election as Heir, talking about how excited she was to tell me when I got to The Range that night.

"Do you think this is how the shooter knew where to find me?" I asked, looking at Domel.

"If they have access to the message board," Neller said.

"We only let the people we trust know about them," I said, shaking my head.

"Can you think of another way an assassin would be able to find you?" Domel asked.

I thought through who else might have known my location. Several people might have known I was headed to The Range that night, but only a few of us knew I had been heading to Daniel to spend the night. I couldn't imagine that Ma, Pa, or Dave would be involved. The board did seem the most likely.

"Someone's been betraying our trust," I said softly.

"I'm sorry."

I logged off, sorry I had even suggested looking at the board.

"It looks like your Ma has been online recently," Domel said. "She should know you are alive by now."

"That's true," I said, trying to smile up at him. "And she should send those photos sometime tonight."

"That should still allow us time to let our experts look at those photos," Neller said, walking over and turning on the TV.

"And if they determine Sincha killed those people?" I asked.

"Then you have a strong argument in your defense," Domel said, guiding me to the bench and sitting down next to me.

"And if not?" I asked, too emotionally beaten to summon hope.

"We will still make your case," Neller said. "Regardless, we will still need to overcome the prejudice against your species and the horror of losing one of our mothers."

"We will do our best for you," Domel said, resting his hand on my shoulders. "And we will make sure the killer of your people is identified."

"And if a killer is still out there?" I asked. I wondered if I would still need to finish my Hunt after the trial was over. Would Brent and Troy have reached me then, or would I be going out alone?

"Then we will look into that as well," Domel said, rubbing my shoulder with his large hand.

"If there are more killings, other Hunters will be sent out and your existence will become known," I said, looking from Domel to Neller.

"We know," Domelsaid, voice soft and smelling of wood ash.

With that, we changed the subject and ended up in a debate over what to watch on TV. They wanted to watch sports and I wanted to watch the Lifetime movie. Eventually, we settled in to watch an old black and white movie Neller had found.

"Are humans always so violent?" Neller asked as we watched the shoot-out in shades of gray.

"No," I said. "Dr. Lyman said we are fascinated with violence because it's a part of us that we cannot understand. So we make it a part of movies to help us explore it. Plus, it makes for a more exciting movie."

"We can be violent, too," Domel said.

"But it terrifies us that we can and we look on it with repugnance," Neller said.

The scene shifted and the hero kissed the heroine. I smiled. All movies should end with a kiss.

"What about love?" Domel asked.

"What about it?" I asked, looking over at him.

"Do you make so many stories about it to try to understand it, too?" Domel asked.

"Probably," I said. "I never really thought about it." I had once thought Troy and I had a romance straight out of a movie, but it hadn't worked. Since then, well, I guess I wanted the world to prove to me that love still existed.

"Is it as rare as violence?" Neller asked.

"The type depicted in movies is," I said.

"There's more than one type?" Domel asked.

"Well," I said, trying to think through my answer, "what's portrayed on TV is the more extreme stuff. Normal love is about enjoying being together. It's pretty boring compared to this." I waved at the screen.

"We don't experience love like that," Domel said. "When a mating takes place, it's a compulsion to be with that person for the rest of your life. I like you humans and your romance. It seems sweet."

We watched the credits roll and Domel indicated that it was time for me to leave. I got up, not wanting to go back to my cell, but unwilling to get Domel into trouble, either. A short walk later, Domel left me in my cell with a brief hug.

I settled back in to my own bed, grief creeping upon me. I curled up around the pillow and cried. I longed for the familiar feeling of Troy's arms around me. I remembered the feeling of Brent's hand, holding mine after my nightmare, and wondered what it would be like to cry in his arms. I felt the tears slide down my cheek and made no effort to stop them.

I wished Angie were with me to talk to me, or that Ma were here to comfort me. Most of all, I longed to hear Lisa's voice one more time, hear her laugh, listen to another story of one of her dates. The tears fell harder and sobs wracked my body. I curled up around the pillow, letting the grief take me. I fell asleep remembering that last party we had thrown at the apartment and seeing Lisa dance on the tables.

Chapter Thirty-two

Troy placed a hand on Brent's shoulder and Brent shook himself, pulling his mind away from reflecting on his last trial. He could think later; now he needed to focus on Troy. The giant waited by the platform, tapping one foot in growing impatience. Troy strode up to the giant, and they exchanged greetings. Images of his illusionary wife and children danced through Brent's mind, his heart longing for what could never be. He pushed the thoughts aside, focusing on his partner.

Troy nodded and strode up to the platform and was immediately incased in a bright red light. When the light faded, Brent saw Troy standing in a small kitchen with Kelley. Troy's mouth moved, as if speaking, but Brent heard no sound. Troy kept talking while Kelley nodded her head, sometimes opening her mouth with a response. Brent had not yet heard Troy say more than two words at a time; he could not imagine how many pent-up thoughts Troy held in his heart. Brent had always had a way with words and could not imagine the pain of living in such silence.

Brent felt his eyes burn with unshed tears as he continued to watch. Jim whined softly and pressed his body against Brent's. The memories of Brent's own trial flitted in and out of his awareness as he watched the scene on platform.

"It's so sad," Brent whispered to the wolf.

Jim whined a soft agreement and curled up with his head on Brent's lap.

"He just wants to be able to talk to her," Brent whispered. He felt a tear slide from his eyes, which he hastily brushed away. I wanted children I can't have and he wants the words to flow, which never will, Brent thought.

The scene before him continued to play out. Troy's face was relaxed and smiling, an expression Brent had never seen on him. Troy's mouth continued to move and Brent wished he had learned to read lips. It seemed like every word Troy had failed to speak during his life came pouring out his mouth, offering it all up to Kelley. She laughed, smiled, and responded as Troy spoke, occasionally breaking in with a word of her own. She drifted across the kitchen to ruffle Troy's hair. Troy caught her hand gently and pulled her onto his lap.

"He hopes someday he'll be able to do all this," Brent whispered. As I wanted it all: the woman, the kids, the success.

Troy stood, Kelley still in his arms. He gently let her stand, holding her close, before spinning her into a dance. She threw her head back, laughing in joy, as Troy led her in a waltz around the kitchen. He leaned in and whispered in her ear. She turned to look at him, love in her eyes. They kissed gently before Troy swung her back into the dance. They moved as one—graceful, lithe, and young.

"He still loves her," Brent told Jim. The wolf lifted his head for a quick lick on Brent's chin.

A red rose appeared in Troy's hand and he held it out to Kelley, making a small bow. She smiled up into his eyes. With one hand, she reached out, grabbing the rose and stroking his hand at the same time.

His hand caressed her cheek, pushing a strand of hair back behind her ear. She leaned in for a kiss and he leaned down to meet her halfway, a tear sliding down his cheek.

"He knows it can't happen," Brent whispered. "No matter how he hopes, no matter how hard he tries."

Troy backed a step away from Kelley, talking and shaking his head. Kelley began to talk, too, waving her hands, and shaking her head. They hardened their stances, squaring off. Kelley began to shake her finger, face filled with anger. Troy stood still and silent, his face pinched with agony, a second tear slipping down his cheek. Troy turned his back on Kelley, walking away. The scene faded and Troy stepped off the platform. He held his hand out to the giant, who placed a coin in it.

Troy walked over to them without actually looking at them. He slid to the ground and stared off into nothing. Brent turned to say something but found nothing—no words, no thoughts—to express either his understanding or compassion. Jim settled in next to Troy, licking his cheek. Troy reached out to scratch the wolf's head. Jim settled himself across Troy's lap, like a bony blanket, reaching his head up once in a while to lick Troy's chin.

They sat in silence, each lost in their own thoughts. Jim made no effort to hurry them, so Brent lay down in the grass, staring at the abstract-art sky. He emptied his mind of all that had happened, all he had seen. He watched perfectly round clouds drift across the sky as the images from the trial flitted through his mind. He needed to focus on the work at home, focus on the mission, and remember his purpose.

Brent had just found a place of calm again when Troy stood up, his shadow crossing over Brent's face. Troy gazed down on him, his face once again restored to its normal calm. Jim raised his head to watch them. Brent sat up, looking up at Troy. The memories of what they had both gone through returned, driving away the fragile peace he had found.

"I thought hope was supposed to be the emotion that saved us," Brent said. He felt numb from the trial, still not sure he could face the betrayals of hope.

"No, hurts," Troy said, shaking his head, his bangs falling into his eyes.

"But we still need it to keep us going," Brent said as he stood up.

"Yes," Troy said, bending to pick up his rifle.

"Even when it hurts," Brent said.

"And beyond," Troy said, reaching out to touch Brent's shoulder, squeezing for a moment before dropping his hand.

"And beyond," Brent echoed. "Even when we know there is no hope, we have to keep hoping."

"Yes," Troy said, nodding his head.

"That sucks," Brent said.

Troy smiled and grabbed his duffel bags, holding one out to Brent. He took it, slinging the bag over his shoulder. They walked toward the edge of the glade, a few steps behind Jim. A loon sat on the tree above their path, watching them walk forward. As they got close, it took flight, circling into the sky to disappear behind a cloud.

"Is the next trial worse?" Brent asked.

"Sometimes," Troy said.

Brent wondered what secrets they would be asked to face. The only secrets he could think of were his fear and his hope. Since he had just faced those, what could possibly be left? He stepped from sunlight into shadow, the forest reaching out to embrace him.

Chapter Thirty-three

I woke up feeling hungover. It took my groggy brain a moment to remember it was grief, not alcohol. The dull ache in my heart competed with the sharp ache in my head for attention. I sat up slowly. My eyes were all crusty and sore from crying, my throat dry from talking. I took a sip of water from my canteen and then splashed a little on my face.

I stood up and forced myself to stretch and to do some jumping jacks and some sit-ups. I needed to wake up, needed to move. I would have sold off everything I owned for a cup of coffee! Only, my apartment had been destroyed along with all my belongings. What was I going to do? I wished I'd thought to get renters insurance. Dave had told me I needed it. Would it even have covered acts of terrorism?

I sat back down on the bed, staring at the stack of books. If I had counted right, today was day three of my captivity. I needed to find a way to win my freedom and prove my innocence. I scratched my dry ankle, annoyed at the amount of stubble. I needed a shave. For that matter, I needed a long shower and clean clothes. If I stayed here much longer, I'd be as hairy as a Bigfoot. Not that I'd be here much longer;

the trial would be tomorrow. After that, I'd either be dead or on my way home. At least, I assumed the execution would happen right after the trial. I didn't think they kept prisoners on death row for decades while the prisoners appealed.

Domel came in, bearing a plate of what looked and smelled like scrambled eggs. He handed me the plate as he sat down on the bed. He sagged against the wall, looking over at me with a slight smile. He smelled of exhaustion, pride, and concern.

"I have news for you," he said. "Do you want personal news, legal updates, or political updates first?"

"Personal," I said, staring at the eggs. The sight made my stomach heave a little, and I took a sip of water to try to settle it.

"Your Ma wrote back. She said she loved you and would let everyone know you were alive. She also said Brent and Troy have gone to the werewolves," Domel said, smelling curious.

"Did she say anything else?" I asked, forcing myself to take a bite of the eggs.

"She sent the files and we printed them out. Neller took them to our experts earlier this morning," Domel said.

"Is that the legal news?" I asked, taking a second bite as the first settled in without too much trouble.

"Yes," he said. "Neller should have the experts' findings this afternoon and we'll all sit down to plan your defense."

"What else?" I asked, realizing that the eggs had disappeared. I must have been hungry.

"Neller and I spent most of last night talking to the Council. They will meet today to decide whether or not to make our existence known to the humans," Domel said, smelling of the oranges and cinnamon of happiness.

"That's wonderful," I said, looking up at him with a small smile.

"We couldn't find out any more about the assassin, but we did find more about that terrorist group," he said. "I sort of read some of your e-mails. I hoped to find something to cheer you or bring you comfort."

"Did you find anything good?" she asked.

"It was all bad," he said. "Apparently a friend of your partner Brent has been investigating. He sent you an e-mail since he couldn't reach his friend. I guess the NSA has ways of doing that sort of thing. Anyway, the terrorist group has had a long record of violence in their quest to ensure hominids get treated just like humans. Some fights with the BHA as well as other rights groups that led to arrest, that sort of thing. The FBI also suspects them of bombing the site of a new jail built for werewolves."

"Lovely," I muttered.

"He also said the FBI should be moving in for arrests soon, so all you need to do is stay out of sight a little longer," Domel said.

"I'm as out of sight as possible," I muttered. The Bigfoot city would have been a great place to hide if they didn't want to kill me, too.

"I know none of that is useful," he said, smelling of chagrin.

"I didn't think we'd learn anything to help me solve that problem," I said, patting him on the arm.

"After the trial, you could ask for asylum and stay here," Domel said, looking away from me.

"I need to meet back up with Troy," I said. I realized that I wanted to see Brent again even more than I wanted to see Troy. I didn't want to try to explain that to Domel, not when I couldn't explain it to myself.

"That's your ex-husband, right?" Domel asked.

I nodded.

"And the one you Hunt with?" he asked.

I nodded again.

"How do you work together after ending your marriage?" he asked, smelling of curiosity.

"Everyone asks that," I said. "Just because Troy and I couldn't make it work as a couple doesn't mean we can't work as partners."

"From what I've seen on TV, that doesn't seem like normal human behavior."

"Maybe not," I said. "But Troy and I aren't normal."

"Because you're Hunters?"

"Yeah," I said. "But it's more than that. We're outsiders and loners."

"Why were you an outsider?"

"Being a Hunter is pretty weird for a human," I said. "I learned how to talk to all the hominids, but never to the kids at school."

"Why not?" Domel asked.

"Ma would get so mad if I came home and spoke with the local accent or used slang," I said. "Of course, she did it all the time. She's got this whole pioneer woman routine she does to put people at ease."

"But you weren't allowed to do that?" Domel asked.

"She said that the vampires would never understand me if I talked like that," I said. "She made sure all of us kids got tutored by the vampires so we'd graduate top of our classes. Of course, the kids just teased me for being so strange, so old-fashioned, so nerdy."

"That sounds lonely," Domel said.

"It was, until I saw this boy getting teased as badly as I was," I said. "I tore into the bullies picking on him, then took him home with me."

"That was Troy?"

"Yeah," I said. "His mom beat him and he couldn't really talk. Then he'd go to school and get beaten by the older kids. He was a big mess."

"But your family took him in?" Domel asked.

"Ma's got a big heart," I said. "And Dave, my big brother, took a liking to Troy, too. Between us, we kept the kids from hurting him until he learned to defend himself."

"Why did your relationship fail?" Domel asked.

"I couldn't control my temper," I said. I turned away to stare at the desk, not wanting the conversation to continue.

"What happened?" Domel asked.

"I just wanted him to talk to me," I said. "I was so tired of guessing what he meant, never understanding what he was trying to say. I was so frustrated, so angry, so hurt."

"And?" he said.

"We had this big argument and I started to hit him. Only once I started, I couldn't seem to stop. I just kept hitting him and hitting him. He didn't stop me. He didn't defend himself. He just stood there, staring at me," I said, curling up around myself. The tears started again as the memory gripped me. Domel pulled me against him.

"I'd been cleaning out the closet when the fight started. I still had this stupid baseball bat in my hand. I swung it. I wasn't thinking. I broke his arm and he still didn't do anything," I whispered, the horror of the memory shaking me. "He could have stopped me any time, restrained me. He could have walked away, left me to cool down. But he just stood there and took it. He let me beat him, break him."

"What happened after that?" he asked.

"My Ma took him to the hospital and forced him to get a restraining order against me. My own Ma," I said, my voice breaking a little. "She was so furious with me; I never thought she'd forgive me."

"He divorced you after that?"

"No, I ended it," I said, shaking my head. "I couldn't trust myself not to hurt him again, hurt him worse. Ma was right. I was the monster and Troy deserved better, deserved to be protected from me."

"But you work together?"

"Troy's the best Hunter we have, and he won't work with anyone else," I said, shrugging. "Well, I guess no one else will work with him, either."

"So you work with him for the good of the Family?'" he asked.

"I love working with Troy," I said. "We are incredible together on a mission, perfectly balanced."

"Do you still love him?"

"It's complicated."

"Can you explain it?" Domel asked.

"I don't know," I said. "He's family; I can't stop caring about him. He's a part of me."

"Sounds healthy."

"It can be," I said. "There are these moments when it's like we read each other's minds, like we're really one person. I love him then."

"But?"

"But it never lasts. He does something and I'm furious again. I still get so mad I want to hit him, and that scares me."

"But if you learned to control your temper?"

"I'd never trust myself again," I said. "Dr. Lyman says I just have an anger management problem and that once I learn to handle my anger I'll be fine."

"He sounds wise."

"I don't really believe him, though," I said. "There's something about Troy that brings out the worst in me."

"I think you're too hard on yourself," he said, giving my shoulder a squeeze.

"No," I said. "I knew what his mom did to him. I promised myself I would always be there to protect him, never let anyone hurt him like that. But I turned out to be the one that did it, the one that treated him just like his mom had."

"But he forgave you."

"He forgave his mom, too," I whispered.

"And you don't think he should have?" Domel asked.

"No," I said. "I never forgave her for what she did to him."

"You didn't forgive her because she hurt Troy, or you didn't forgive her for leaving the mess of Troy for you to clean up?" he asked.

"I never thought about it like that," I said, staring at my hands. I had always hated anyone who hurt Troy: his mom, the bullies at school, me. But Domel was right; I also couldn't forgive Troy's mom because every day I lived with the damage she had created. In fact, those wounds kept interfering with our relationship time after time. I still felt as if I had to try piecing him back together.

"I think you need to work on forgiveness," he said, stroking my hair. "And I think you need to work on letting go."

"What do you mean?" I asked, looking up at him.

"You've spent so much of your life protecting Troy, taking care of him, that you never learned to take care of yourself," he said.

Was that my problem? I couldn't remember a time when Troy hadn't been with me; my whole life had been with him at my side. Only, how much of that time had I spent acting as his translator, helping him navigate through his life? The only part of my life which had been truly about me had been my friendship with Lisa and my job with Dr. Lyman.

It had been Lisa who had first dragged me out to socialize, helped me build a life without Troy. It had felt good, too—those moments I had been free to be myself and not worry about how Troy was doing. Was that why he had hated her? Because she had taught me to be on my own?

"You know a lot about humans," I said, looking up at him.

"I like Dr. Phil," he said with a smile.

I laughed and shook my head. The door opened and we both turned to look.

"Domel," the guard said. "The Council requests your presence."

What did that mean? Were they moving up my trial?

Chapter Thirty-four

Brent and Troy stepped into the forest. A glowing blackbird flew past them, dipping over their heads. A tie-dye squirrel sat in the path ahead of them. Brent shook his head and closed his eyes. When he reopened them, the tie-dye squirrel still sat and stared.

"Do you see that?" he whispered to Troy.

"Squirrel," Troy said, glancing at the animal.

"That's not normal," Brent said, shaking his head.

"Yes," Troy said, shrugging his shoulders.

"It's normal?" Brent asked, looking at Troy quizzically.

"For here," Troy said.

"Oh," Brent said, watching as the squirrel disappeared up a tree. If this place represented some ideal world, what did a tie-dye squirrel mean? Was it the reality of children's toys or children's dreams?

"No wogs," Troy said, gesturing to the wildlife along the path.

Brent relaxed. Of course; the return of bizarre animals meant no wogs.

They hurried through the forest, Jim setting a tough pace. Brent preferred the fast walk to a full out run like the last time. He looked around him, trying to note all the differences between this world and the one he used to think of as the real world. Some things, like the trees, looked so nearly normal that he had a hard time explaining exactly how they were different. He just knew it. Other things, like multi-colored squirrels, were easy to spot.

They turned onto a left-hand path and Brent spotted a moose, its large rack spread across the entire path, walking along a few feet in front of them. The huge animal looked over its shoulder at them and nodded its head. Jim nodded back. The path narrowed to single file and Troy fell back behind him. Brent continued along, watching the wolf and the moose.

The moose burst into motion, leaping into the darkness of the forest. Brent could not believe an animal that large could move that fast.

Jim became alert, ears back.

Brent pulled out his gun and began scanning the woods. The silence of the forest surrounded him, leaving him with only the sound of his own heartbeat and breathing. He could spot the odd, shadowy movements in the distance. Jim began to run and Brent followed, forcing himself to keep up. He could hear Troy's footfalls behind them, but he did not dare turn his head.

They turned onto another path, running full out. Brent could see light up ahead of them and pushed himself to find a little more speed. A shadow moved and Brent fired at it before remembering to save his bullets for the ones he knew he could hit. He heard Troy fire behind him but kept running.

Jim spun and ran back the way they came. Brent turned and saw Troy lying on the path, struggling to stand. Brent ran back and pulled Troy back to his feet. Jim kept the wogs away, snarling and snapping at any that got close. They ran as best they could, Brent supporting more and more of Troy's weight. He stumbled and pulled Troy's arm more securely over his shoulder, straining to bear the weight.

They burst into the glade, falling to the ground. Brent pulled both of Troy's bags from his shoulder and began to dig through the first one. He pulled out the dish for Jim, water bottles for all of them, and the first aid kit. He put the water out for the wolf and took the first aid kit to Troy.

Troy had a small cut along his right arm, just beneath the stitches holding together the bullet wound. Brent cleaned the new wound as well as he could. He tried to remember what had been used on wog wounds earlier, but all he could remember was the sun. Jim came over and licked Troy's arm after Brent sat back to examine his handy work.

"Did I do it right?" Brent asked.

Jim nodded his head.

"Will he be okay?" Brent asked, looking at Troy's pale face.

Jim bobbed his head again.

"You have had time to tend your wounds," a deep voice interrupted. Brent spun around to see a new giant with the familiar round platform. "It is time for your trial."

Brent looked at Jim. The wolf jerked his head toward the platform, clearly indicating that Brent needed to go. Brent stared at the giant, who beckoned him forward. Brent stepped toward the platform, wishing he could stay with Troy a little longer. It felt wrong to leave him behind. He pulled his shoulders back, pretending a confidence he could not feel.

"You shall now face that which has been secret," the giant said.

Brent nodded and stepped forward onto the stage. The world seemed to spin around him, faster and faster. He closed his eyes. When he opened them again, he found himself staring at, well, Brent. The mirror image raised its hand in greeting. Brent raised his own hand, a brief wave, as he tried to gather his thoughts.

"You lie to yourself," his image said to him.

"What does that mean?" he said.

"I am here to show you your own lies," his twin said, waving a hand. Brent looked and saw new images forming. He saw the house from his last trial emerge before him. He stared at it, remembering the happy family contained within and the moment he had felt on top of the world.

"You know you can't succeed," his image said.

"I know," Brent said, wishing he could enter the house, live that dream for just a little longer.

"Do you?" his other-self asked, waving his hand again.

The image changed and Brent found himself in his high school hallways, staring at a poster with his face on it. BRENT FOR SENIOR CLASS PRESIDENT! Brent shuddered as he remembered. He had worked so hard on that campaign, had been so sure he would win. His sisters had teased him for weeks, telling him he was an idiot for trying. He had ignored them and poured his heart into his campaign. In the end, he had received only one vote: his own.

The image changed again and he saw the giant cement dorm room of basic training. Two rows of bunk beds, home to forty boys, stood in neat rows. Each bunk was identical except for one: his. The pink sheets stood out against the whites and olive green around it. The boys had done him a "favor" by washing his sheets while he had been cleaning the bathrooms. He had been given demerits for having his bed

246

out of regs and earned a new nickname, "Pinkie," which had followed him to his first assignment.

The vision faded and Brent found himself staring at his twin.

"They don't pick on you because they like you," his other-self said. "They pick on you because you don't fit in."

Brent bowed his head, refusing to look himself in the eye. He knew this; on some level he understood this. He could still hear Mike's voice teasing him about being a baby agent. It had always been like that, everywhere he went. He had always told himself it was normal joking; after all, boys would be boys. Believing that had kept him sane.

"I need to believe otherwise," he said aloud as the thought crossed his mind.

"Of course," his twin said. "You aren't strong enough to handle the truth."

"No," Brent said. He fought the knowledge, refusing to believe. Boys were boys. They picked on those they liked as part of the bonding of friends. He had to believe that. If the teasing had been meant to be cruel, then he was a loser, a nobody.

"If you accept the truth," his other-self broke in, "then you can seek friendships with those who really value you."

Brent remembered Sean, the chess champion in high school that had always tried to start conversations with him. Brent had always ignored him; Sean had been such an outcast. The poor kid had had no friends and wore stained secondhand clothes. He'd also had a wicked sense of humor that had always made Brent laugh in class.

He flashed back to Basic Training and the young kid from the depths of West Virginia who had always hung around him, no matter how much Brent had tried to avoid him. The kid had been teased worse than Brent for his crooked teeth and thick accent. But he'd been the only one to help Brent when he couldn't get his shirts folded to meet the impossible nine-inch standards.

"They are the outcasts," Brent said.

"So are you," his image said, shrugging one shoulder.

"I need to be an outcast?" Brent asked.

"You can never be an outcast when you have people who care for you," his image said.

"But," Brent began, but then stopped himself. Values and ideals collided.

All people were equal, all deserving. Only, some people were better than others.

He had all the qualities of a star: good family, brains, brawn, and charm. But he had no charisma; people did not like him easily.

All of these thoughts wrestled with one another. They could not all be true, but somehow he had lived his life as if they were. He felt as if his head would explode from the internal tensions. He put both hands up, cradling his aching brain. He thought of Troy, lying on the grass outside. He might be one of the biggest outsiders Brent had ever met, but he couldn't think of anyone else he would rather have at his back.

Finally, he looked up at his image.

"I am strong enough to accept it all," he said.

The world around him began to spin again and soon he saw the giant. He stepped down from the platform and accepted his coin, another number one emblazoned on it. He looked to Troy and Jim. The wolf yipped happily and Troy sat up. Brent hoped Troy had strength enough to get through the trial ahead of him.

Chapter Thirty-five

I paced the room, waiting for Domel to return. I hated being alone. I needed people to talk to, especially when my thoughts chased themselves around like a cat after its tail. Why had the Council summoned him?

I picked up my notes for the case and looked them over as I paced. I read the words, but they slid through my mind and disappeared before I could get any meaning from them. I kept thinking of Troy, thinking of that horrible night. My thoughts skittered from Troy to Brent, remembering how it had felt when he had held me, kept me from breaking the furniture. I wished Brent had been there that night to stop me from hurting Troy. I wished Brent might always be there to stop me from hurting people.

My mind leaped away from that thought. Where would I live? Ma and Pa would let me stay with them; in fact, they might insist on that now that I was Heir. Only, I still wanted to finish my degree. I might not be essential to run the Family, but it felt like something I needed to do. If I convinced them to let me continue, I'd still need an apartment in Rock Springs so that I could go back to brick and mortar

249

classes in the fall. I guess I could do the rest of my degree online, or at least take online classes until I figured something out.

The pay from this mission should give me enough to get a new apartment and replace most of my things. I might even have enough left over to pay the bills until I could find another job. I wanted just a few more years of living as a normal human before taking on my duties to the Family. I needed to have more of my own species in my life. Could I find another roommate?

Lisa. Lisa was dead.

I forced my mind away from that and stared at the notes for the case again. How was I going to convince the Bigfoots that I was innocent? I didn't feel innocent. I had killed Sincha. I knew I didn't have a choice, but that didn't make me feel better about it. I might be a Hunter, but I had not made a kill. I had always left that to Troy while I would track and collect evidence. I hadn't actually killed since my first hunt as a young child.

We had all been taught to hunt. When Angie had been ten and I had been eight, Pa took us out for our first hunt. We knew where the deer grazed; they often came up to the back door of The Range during the winter. Pa led us out, set us up. Angie and I had both taken aim, both pulled our triggers. I had killed my first and only deer. I had hated it. Angie's shot had gone too high and she refused to try again. We drug my kill back to the house and helped Pa skin it, both of us puking more than once. We had both cried ourselves to sleep that night.

I did love the challenge of the Hunt; I loved proving I was better and smarter than whomever we were after. I liked solving the puzzle, finding the small hints and clues that let us determine a hominid's guilt or innocence. It still felt like something of a game, a test of skill. I knew, in my head, that what we did was necessary. I knew someone had to put themselves out there to protect the lives of the many, the lives of the innocent.

I just didn't want justice to come with blood on my hands. I didn't know if that made me a good person or a selfish person. I didn't blame Troy for killing them; I just felt gratitude that I was not the one to do it. I guess that made me more selfish than good. It wasn't their deaths that bothered me as much as the idea of me being the one to kill. How hypocritical!

The door of the cell opened and I turned to see Domel and Neller walk in my small room. I smiled at them, grateful for the distraction, eager for company.

"They agreed," Domel said. "We are to announce our existence both to your Family and to the werewolves."

"That's wonderful!" I said as I gave them both a quick hug. No matter what happened tomorrow, I had accomplished something. I had brought a new species forward into the growing society of hominids.

"Can you give us e-mail addresses for both?" Neller asked.

I quickly wrote down the contact information and Domel left with it.

"I also heard from our experts," Neller said. "Sincha was the killer you were tracking."

"What does that mean for my case?" I asked. Another problem solved; I had successfully finished my first case as a lead Hunter. It had not ended well, but there would be no more killings.

"We can prove that Sincha had lost her control, had been killing humans," Neller said. "That supports your statement that she attacked you. From there, we have to prove that your life is of equal value to Sincha's."

"How do we do that?" I asked. "I am not one of you, so how will they view my life as valuable as one that they knew?" I knew it had taken humans nearly a decade to recognize hominids as equals; would the Bigfoots be more evolved than we had been?

"I have some ideas on that," he said.

"Will they work?" I asked.

"I don't know," he said. "We've never tried a human."

Domel returned, smiling. The smell of oranges and cinnamon permeated the air. Neller and I turned to look at him, happy to drop our conversation for the moment.

"It's done," he said. "We have taken our first steps to join the rest of the world."

"Will your people accept it?" I asked. Things could become ugly if the Matriarchs forced the Bigfoots to join with the other hominids. It was a huge change.

"I think most will," Domel said.

"Some will resist," Neller said.

"They'll come around when they see the advantages," Domel said.

"You are an optimist," Neller said.

I agreed with Neller. No species had been unanimous in wanting to become part of the greater world. The urge to secrecy died hard. I wondered if I could talk Old Seth into sending one of his older werewolves here for a while. Perhaps having a representative from another hominid group that had struggled to adjust to the new order would help the Bigfoots successfully make the transition.

"About Kelley's case," Domel said, smelling of the scorched popcorn of embarrassment.

"We need to prove Kelley's life holds as much value as Sincha's," Neller said.

"So self-defense outweighs self-sacrifice?" Domel asked.

"What does that mean?" I asked. In my mind, all creatures had to the right to defend themselves. Heroes might be willing to sacrifice themselves, but it seemed to go against deeply ingrained instincts for anyone else to do so.

"One has a legal obligation to sacrifice one's self to avoid harm to one of more value," Neller said. It took me a moment to comprehend that. He must have been speaking legalize.

"How is value determined?" I asked.

"The Matriarchs are valued the most highly, followed by the Chief. After that, children have greatest value, then breeding women, then elders," Domel explained.

"Where does a human fall in?" I asked, my stomach clenching. I had a bad feeling that other species would fall at the bottom of the list. Would the Bigfoots truly accept that another hominid was their equal?

"We have no legal precedence for that," Neller said.

"So we have to determine my value without any precedence and convince those at the top of the hierarchy to agree?" I asked.

"In a nutshell," Neller said.

"If I were one of you?" I asked.

"You and Sincha would be valued equally as breeding women," Domel said.

"Your position as Heir might weigh in if the Ma and Pa of a Family could be considered equal to our Matriarch and Chief," Neller said thoughtfully.

Neller and Domel gathered up the books Domel had brought me and we all walked down to Domel's room. I settled into the comfortable rooms, helping them dig through books in hopes of finding an earlier precedence, maybe a case between competing groups of Bigfoots back when they had been plentiful on the continent. We found nothing that would help.

Domel and Neller began working on their individual speeches, taking their pages of notes and trying to organize it into something simple and coherent. I paced. They practiced their speeches, making changes as comments were made. I answered whatever questions they had, anything to help them defend me.

The more I listened to them, the more I worried that I had no chance. No matter what arguments we tossed around, none sounded powerful enough. We had to convince a group of people who had never associated with other races that I should be held as an equal to one of them. All of the hominids I had worked with held the belief that they were the superior species; most had just learned to hide it.

"It's time for Kelley to go back," Domel said, interrupting Neller's practice speech.

Neller waved a hand. I stood and followed Domel toward the door. We turned into the hall, the door closing behind it.

"I've got it!" we heard Neller exclaim.

I looked up at Domel. He smiled down at me.

"He's the best," Domel said.

"So, this is good?" I asked.

"We'll know more tomorrow," he said.

We walked through the halls that had grown familiar to me over the past few days. The Bigfoots we passed hissed at me or simply avoided me. I inhaled the decaying flesh smell of hatred emanating from them. We got back to my cell and Domel turned to leave.

"Domel," I said.

He turned.

"Thank you for everything."

"You are welcome, my friend," he said with a smile.

Family Heir

Chapter Thirty-six

Troy looked better; his color was back to normal. He stood and walked to the platform, passing Brent. Troy reached out and squeezed Brent's shoulder before stepping forward to meet the giant. Brent watched him exchange greetings with the giant before making his way to Jim.

Troy stepped up onto the platform and faced off with himself. Brent wondered what lies Troy had been telling himself. Brent thought this trial the easiest of the three. He couldn't imagine lying to himself so thoroughly that he never saw a glimmer of the truth. It had been tough, but not as devastating as the other trials.

The image of Troy raised its hand and Brent saw a new image form. A woman who looked like a feminine version of Troy stood before him. The woman smiled at the sight of Troy and reached out to give Troy a hug that seemed to consume him. Troy hugged back, grinning.

The woman pulled back and smacked Troy across the face. Troy stood still, face expressionless. The woman continued to beat him, sometimes with her hand, sometimes with a belt, sometimes with a bat. The woman's face shifted to Kelley's face and then back again.

The woman's face continued to change between the two women, never staying the same for more the minute. She beat Troy and then cradled him, rocking him back and forth. Troy stared blankly at her but relaxed into her embrace. The woman kissed Troy's hair and then smacked him hard on the cheek, leaving a red imprint of her hand. Troy fell to the floor, curling in on himself. With his knees tucked to his chin, Troy rocked back and forth. He buried his face in his knees, refusing to look up at the image of himself. His image continued to talk to him, laying a hand on his shoulder. Troy shrugged the hand off, curling more tightly about himself.

"This has to stop!" Brent told Jim. "I've seen this before, among vets. He isn't strong enough to face this; no one is, not without help. He can't do this alone. Make it stop."

The wolf whined softly and walked slowly toward the giant, his head down. Brent watched as the wolf sat before the giant, the two staring at each other in some form of eerie communication. Brent looked back to the stage and saw that Troy had begun to beat his head slowly and methodically against the deck.

Brent stood and began to move toward the platform. Neither the giant nor Jim moved to stop him, so he picked up his pace. He jumped up onto the platform and the images disappeared. He knelt before Troy as he had knelt by the boys in the barracks.

"Easy, Troy," he said softly. "It's over now. Look up at me, just look at me."

Troy lifted his head slightly, his eyes meeting Brent's.

"That's it," Brent said, keeping his voice soft. "Focus on me. What color are my eyes? What color is my hair? That's it. I'm real. I'm here. Hold onto the details, wrap the details around you."

Troy's muscles relaxed a little and he began to uncurl himself.

"I saw guys go through this before, get swallowed up by the nightmares that haunted them," Brent said, keeping his voice gentle. "If you can find something solid to hold onto, to bring yourself back to the present, it helps. It doesn't fix the pain, but it helps a little."

Troy stood slowly, though his eyes still looked dazed. He took a shaky step forward and Brent paced him, ready to catch him if he fell. They made their way slowly down from the platform. The giant held out a token, bright orange with a six emblazoned on it. Brent settled Troy on the grass and handed him another bottle of water. A quail trilled overhead, circling the glade.

The giant and platform disappeared. Where they had been a doorway now stood, containing the darkest of blackness. The quail swooped down, settling onto the top of the doorway. A blue jay and a loon soon joined it, perching side by side. Three sets of bird eyes gazed down on them. Far above them, an eagle circled, calling a greeting. Jim's wolf form shifted and blurred. Brent looked back at Troy, who stared at the token in his hand.

"The trial is over," Jim said, back in human form.

"What happens next?" Brent asked, keeping his eye on Troy.

"Let me see your tokens," Jim said.

Brent handed him the three tokens.

"When you step through that door, you will arrive back in your world three days from when you stepped into this world," Jim said, tossing the tokens into the air. The eagle swooped down, swallowing the tokens.

"I'll find Kelley?" Brent asked.

"As you step through the door, think only of Kelley and you will arrive wherever she is," Jim said.

"And Troy?" Brent asked.

Troy held out his tokens. Two were emblazoned with a one, and the last held a six.

"Troy will arrive eight days from when he stepped in here, five days after you return," Jim said softly, tossing the tokens up. The eagle swallowed them and settled on the door frame.

"I'm sorry," Brent told Troy.

Troy looked up at him, not truly registering the world around him.

"I can't leave him like this," Brent said.

"We can rest a short while, but both of you must step through the door before it closes," Jim said.

"How long is that?" Brent asked.

"An hour, maybe two."

"What would happen if it closes?" Brent asked.

"You stay here forever," Jim said. "Eventually you fade until all that will be left is the shadows we call the wogs."

"And if he steps through like this?" Brent asked.

"He will arrive back in your world in eight days, wherever he was thinking of," Jim said.

"And if he doesn't focus?" Brent asked.

"It can be unpredictable," Jim said.

"Troy," Brent said softly. "We need you to come back to us. I need you. I couldn't have made it this far without you, and I don't know what to do next."

"Save Kelley," Troy's voice came out harsh and broken.

"What about you?" Brent asked.

"I follow," he said.

"Can you make it to her?" Brent asked.

"Always," Troy said, looking up and meeting Brent's eyes.

Brent nodded. He looked up at the door and took a deep breath. Troy pulled the bags to him and dug around, pulling out an old army-style helmet. It looked like the same one he had tried to get Kelley to wear. Troy handed it to Brent.

"What am I supposed to do with this?" Brent asked, holding the helmet before him.

"Protect Kelley," Troy said.

"I'll do my best," Brent said, glancing from the helmet to Troy.

"I know," Troy said, nodding.

"Since we don't know where Kelley is, you need to be prepared for anything," Jim said.

Brent nodded. He checked his gun, reloading the cartridge.

"Brent," Troy said as he stood up, slinging the bags over his shoulder.

Brent turned to face him.

"Date Kelley," Troy said, looking over Brent's shoulder at the doorway.

Brent stared at him, searching his face for any clue of what he might be feeling. Troy's face remained blank and unreadable.

"You love her," Brent said, eyes widening.

"Not mine," he said, shrugging one shoulder.

"She's not mine, either," Brent said, echoing Troy's shrug.

"Ask her," Troy said, looking Brent in the eyes.

"Are you sure?" Brent asked, staring back.

Troy nodded, holding out his hand. Brent reached out and they shook.

They walked forward toward the door. Brent stared through it, looking for light, but could see nothing but a dark void. Tendrils of darkness crept out of the door and wrapped around his wrist. Troy stood next to him, staring as well, with tentacles of black wrapping themselves around his legs. Brent felt panic building within him as he tried to move closer to the door.

"Picture Kelley; hold the image in your mind as you step through," Jim said.

"Are you coming with us?" Brent asked.

"No, I have my own way home," Jim said.

Brent stared at the door, trying to picture Kelley. He remembered her dusty red hair pulled back into a ponytail, her smile as she teased him. He tried to hold the image, but it dissolved in a wave of fear. The doorway reached its limbs of shadow toward them. His pulse raced and his body tensed for flight. He could not step into that darkness, into nothing.

"No fear," Troy said, bumping Brent with his elbow.

Brent looked over at him. Troy nodded toward the door.

"Together?" Troy said and held out his hand. Brent took it, feeling uncomfortable to be holding hands with another man. Troy squeezed his hand gently and Brent looked up. Troy smiled slightly and winked at him. Brent relaxed and smiled back. He would never admit this moment to anyone back home. Ever.

"On three?" Brent asked, staring into the void.

"A blue jay for fearlessness," Jim said, and the blue jay spread its wings, drifting through the doorway.

"Picture Kelley," Troy said, body tensing.

Brent nodded.

"One," Troy said.

"A loon for hope," Jim said. The loon launched itself into the air before diving through the doorway.

"Two," Troy said.

"A quail for secrets kept hidden," Jim said as the quail hopped down and skittered through the doorway.

"Three," Troy said.

They stepped forward. The black tentacles drew them near in a hug, pulling them through the doorway. Brent clung to the memory of Kelley's laugh, letting it fill his mind as he stepped into darkness. The darkness swallowed him and he could see nothing, not even his own hand. He could no longer feel Troy's hand in his. Panic began to claw at his mind, trying to drive away the image of her red hair. He thought of Kelley's amazing blue eyes, the strawberry scent of her hair. The blackness held him in a firm embrace, and for a moment he felt weightless. Then he was falling.

"Kelley!" he screamed as he fell faster and faster.

Chapter Thirty-seven

The morning of the trial dawned like all the others. I woke up in my tiny little cell and stared at the ceiling. One way or another, I would not be sleeping here tonight. I would either be dead or on my way home. It felt like years, not days, since I had last seen another human being. I thought about just rolling over and going back to sleep. Domel would come to get me soon enough.

My stubborn eyes refused to stay closed and I reluctantly admitted that I was awake for the day. I stumbled through my morning routine, only to end up sitting back on the bed much too soon. I stood back up and grabbed the note pages with all of my notes on the Bigfoot legal system. I looked them over, hoping for one last insight that would help my case.

Domel came in bearing breakfast and a small bag. He handed both to me, and I could not resist peeking in the bag. I saw my own clothes, clean and waiting for me. I looked up at Domel, smiling.

"I thought you would feel better facing the Council in your own clothes," he said.

"Thank you," I said, biting into breakfast. I savored the taste of the meat (deer, I thought). After all, this could be my last meal.

"After you eat, you can bathe in my room," Domel said.

"How long do I have before the trial?" I asked.

"About one of your hours," he said.

I ate as fast I could, unwilling to give up the chance to clean up as well as possible. Soon we were on our way to his suite of rooms. The hallways stood mostly empty as we walked, and I wondered where all the Bigfoots were this morning.

I had intended to take a long bath, but anxiety sped me along. Soon I was clean (if hairy), and stepping into my own clothes. I longed for a razor and some deodorant. Oh, yes, and toothpaste. I couldn't even remember what clean teeth felt like. I pulled the old army cast-offs on, reveling in the feel of human clothes. I would have preferred my dependable jeans, but real pants felt like heaven. I slipped the sports bra on, amazed at how good it felt to have a bra on again. Wow, I was a spoiled prima donna! Four days without my own clothes and here I was, embracing even a bra. The T-shirt slid on, nearly completing the outfit. I pulled on the socks and the boots, amazed at the difference clothes made on my outlook.

I stood up straight, feeling the familiar clothes settle around me. I was back. I, Kelley Mallard, could handle anything! I strode back to the living room and saw Domel and Neller waiting for me.

"Ready?" Domel asked.

I nodded.

"You look like a warrior," Neller said.

"I feel like one," I said as we walked out the door.

I followed the two Bigfoots down the hall and through a new door. This led us to a hallway filled with light, covered with paintings. I looked around, noting the scenes as we walked. They all appeared to be naturalistic, forest and mountain scenes. Not a single depiction of a Bigfoot.

Domel opened another door and we entered a new room, filled with Bigfoots. The large woman I had met before, Domel'smother, sat in the center of a half-ring of Bigfoots. Others sat in rows behind them. Domel led me to a set of chairs in front of the half-circle and indicated that I should sit. I crawled up onto one of the oversize chairs and tried to look confident.

"Remember, do not speak," he whispered to me. I nodded.

"We have gathered to hear the case of Kelley Venator Mallard, accused of murdering Sincha, a woman of the Sasquatch Clan of breeding age," Domel's mother intoned. The crowd hissed. "Neller, do you speak for the accused?"

"Yes, ma'am," Neller said.

"Begin," she said.

"This human, Kelley, is the Heir of the Venator Family. She represents, protects, and assists the hominids of this region," Neller began.

"We do not need her history," a voice interrupted. I looked over to see a chocolate and vanilla-striped Bigfoot standing to our right.

"Tolnar, her place in the human world bears directly on this case," Neller answered, looking at the other Bigfoot.

"Go ahead," the Matriarch said.

"She was assigned to investigate the killing of human children and human females of breeding age. Her investigations pointed her on the trail of Sincha," Neller said.

"We obtained copies of these crimes from the humans," Domel said, handing over a stack of papers to the matriarchs.

"When she came upon Sincha on the mountain trail, Kelley simply observed her. She made no hostile movements. In fact, her original intention had been to follow Sincha and look for evidence that this was the killer she had been seeking." Neller continued to detail the events that had occurred that afternoon, speaking of my hesitation and doubt.

"Kelley does not deny that she killed Sincha and it is clear she acted in self-defense. So at the heart of this case is whether Kelley's life is of equal value to Sincha's."

Neller sat down as he finished speaking.

"Sincha was a well-respected member of our community," Tolnar said as he strode to the center of the semi-circle of Matriarchs. "She had borne our community three children, two of which live Motherless because of the actions of this creature."

He pointed at me, staring at me as if I were no more than an insect.

"Sincha's third child was brutally killed, slaughtered like a helpless fawn, by one of these beasts who call themselves human," Tolnar said. "This vile animal not only shot an infant, but walked away, laughing with his friends."

I straightened, mouth open to argue. What that hunter did was a crime—by human laws as well as Bigfoot laws—but that did not excuse Sincha's killing spree. Domel's hand came down hard on my knee, squeezing. I looked up at him and he shook his head. I clamped my mouth shut, silently fuming.

"In her grief," Tolnar said, "Sincha lost her mind, trying to take revenge on the creatures that murdered her child. We had restrained her once, offering her the help she needed, and she had begun to recover. Only when she heard gunshots in the distance, while out helping to bring in our crops, did she once again seek revenge. Sincha was sick and we could have treated her but this creature, sitting here in our courtroom, took that choice away from us."

I opened my mouth but closed it again at Domel's glance. I hadn't wanted to kill Sincha. In fact, I wished to spend the rest of my life helping those like Sincha. I longed to heal the wounds of the heart and the mind.

"We do not recognize any value in a species so prone to violence," Tolnar said. "We have watched our TVs, witnessing the horrendous cruelty these humans inflict on one another. No species so in love with bloodshed can be held as equals, can be considered civilized."

Tolnar finished and sat down.

"Kelley is a female of breeding age. Her place in the human world is one of great esteem. She will inherit the Venator family upon her Ma's death or retirement," Neller said, standing. "So the case now hinges, as Tolnar pointed out, on whether we accept humans as our equals. This is a decision that only the Matriarchs can provide to guide our people in the future, as we enter into a new age of interaction with not just humans, but with the other hominids."

"Humans are plentiful, while we are few," one of the matriarchs said.

"This is true," Neller said. "However, human Families with their long traditions of dealing justly with other hominids are rare. In fact, in the United States, Kelley is the only living Heir, the sole human left to inherit both the traditions of her own clan and of the clans that served the hominids for millennium."

Neller's words hit me in the gut. The weight of millennia of tradition, of the Families' responsibilities, settled on me. As a psychologist, I would be able to heal hominids, but only the few that came into my office. As the leader of the Venators, even as their Heir, I could help so many more. If I stepped aside, left Ma and Pa to choose another Heir, I walked away from that obligation and the opportunities that came with it.

"This human has sought peaceful ways to resolve situations," Neller continued. "She has built her life on the principles of aiding others and protecting others."

"I want the human to speak," another unknown Matriarch said. Domel's mother nodded.

"Stand and answer their questions, but say no more than needed," Neller whispered.

I stood and faced the Bigfoots, trying to appear confident.

"Did you know that you were the only Heir left when you went after this killer?" the Matriarch asked.

"Yes, ma'am," I said.

"Why did you endanger yourself?" the Bigfoot asked.

"It was my job," I said. "I had two young men with me to offer additional protection, but they alone could not handle the case without me there. I had to balance my duties as Heir with the risk to my life."

"And you valued your life as less important," the Bigfoot asked.

"No, ma'am," I said. "I trusted my partners to protect me and I trusted my own abilities."

"And your Ma let you go?" Domel's mother asked.

"I do not know how your children mature," I said, "but among humans a time comes when a child must use their own judgment, take their own risks. I am of that age. My Ma did not like the risk before me but knew that if I were to lead my Family, I had to make my own decisions."

"Why did you put yourself in danger?" she asked.

"The danger was everywhere," I said. "I saw no path forward, no place to go that would not have been equally dangerous. It was not a choice between safety and danger. It was a choice between facing the dangers that came with the responsibilities I had, or facing a danger while knowing I had failed to do my job."

"And you view these responsibilities as worth more than your safety?" Domel's mother asked.

"I grew up knowing that my Family had an obligation to help those hominids that looked to us," I said. "Humans are indeed the most plentiful of the hominids. The Families chose to act as a bridge between the smaller hominid groups and our own, to help them live comfortably and peacefully with each other and with us. I wanted to serve the hominids in the role of a healer of the mind and put aside the Hunting, the violence, and the danger. But my family chose to make me their Heir. I did not want it; I still don't know if I want it. But being here, among you, I realized that I cannot live the life I wanted. There is no one else that can ensure that people such as yourself can step forward and join the rest of the world. Sometimes, that means that I will have to search down those who have violated the one rule all hominids agree upon. No one has the right to kill an innocent, a sentient hominid. I must protect those who cannot protect themselves. I am a servant. I serve those hominids who have chosen to accept the assistance of the Families and those who have not yet chosen to come forward. I work for the betterment of all hominids, including my own species. I believe we are all equal."

I stopped talking. My mouth had gotten ahead of my mind and had somehow discovered a truth that I had not realized. Regardless of my personal desires, I had to be the Heir; I had responsibilities now that I could not put aside.

"And you view yourself as an intelligent being?" Domel's mother asked.

"Human beings have grappled with what it means to be sentient since we discovered the existence of werewolves and vampires," I said. "How do you define intelligence? One of our great philosophers, Plato, believed that in another plane there existed the ideal and our reality held only inexact images. Perhaps, in that other plane, all sentient beings look exactly alike: the same face, the same hands, the same eyes. In our world, we all look different. But we cannot deny that those who look different from us can be the same underneath. You and I, we speak the same language, can communicate our thoughts to one another. We both value life, though we both recognize some life has more value than others. We do not hesitate to eat the meat of the deer, but we look with horror at the killing of a small child. We have much more in common than is apparent in our different appearances. We are varying images of the same ideal."

"Where am I?" Brent's voice echoed in the silent room. Voices rose in protest as two Bigfoots grabbed Brent and dragged him forward.

Chapter Thirty-eight

"That's one of my partners," I whispered to Domel. "Do something!"

Domel stood and the Bigfoots parted for him, letting him reach Brent's side.

"What is going on here?" Domel's mother demanded, standing and striding toward Brent.

"I came for Kelley," Brent said, eyes wide with shock.

"How did you find us?" a Matriarch demanded from her seat.

"The werewolves," Brent said.

"Can you explain this?" Domel's mother looked at me.

"Not very well," I said, shaking my head. "The werewolves have ways of doing things that I don't understand. Even though I've done it myself."

"Do they know where we are?" she asked.

"No," I said. "It doesn't work like that; he thought of me and came to wherever I was."

"You sought this woman?" she asked, turning back to Brent. "Why?"

"I—I—I—" Brent stuttered, looking at me. I met his eyes and the room faded. The Bigfoots and possible death disappeared and all I could see was him.

"I came to protect her," Brent said, voice soft, "because it's my job. I would give my life for hers, not because it's my job, but because she is the most incredible woman I've ever met."

Domel's mother gestured for Brent to join me, and the others in the semi-circle stood. Brent followed Domel through the crowds, making their way to where Neller and I had remained.

"We shall confer," Domel's mother said, and the five Matriarchs and one Chief left the room.

"I could have said that better," Brent whispered as he reached me. "That wasn't as romantic as I wanted."

"It sounded good to me," I said, smiling up at him.

"What's going on?" Brent said.

"It's a long story," I said, "and this isn't the best place to tell it."

"She's on trial for murder," Domel said.

"What?" Brent looked at me, eyes wide.

I pulled myself back up onto my seat and motioned for Brent to join me; the seat had plenty of room for two. He crawled up beside me and held my hand. I stared at the remaining Bigfoots. The room held so many smells that I could not decipher the predominate mood of the audience. I looked over to Domel and Neller, but neither looked toward me.

The Council returned and I held my breath.

"We have decided," Domel's mother said. "The Council made the choice to join with the other hominids in this new world. As a consequence of that decision, we must view all hominids as equal before our laws. Therefore, Kelley Venator Mallard has equal value to Sincha. We do not require her death for Sincha's death. We do find Kelly Venator Mallard guilty of inadvertently causing the death of a breeding mother and require her to serve penance."

"What penance do you require?" Neller asked.

"Kelley Venator Mallard, do you agree to serve my people as our spokesperson as we negotiate for a place in your world?"

"I do," I said.

"Do you agree to take our chosen representative with you, ensure his protection, and assist him in all things necessary to function in your world?" she asked.

"I do," I said.

"Domel, we have chosen you to be our representative," she said, looking fondly at her son. "Go with Kelley Venator, form alliances with her family, the other hominids, and her government."

"Yes, ma'am," Domel said.

Domel gestured for me to follow him from the room. I left, unsure of exactly what had happened or what I agreed to, but I would live. I would go home. Brent walked beside me, still holding my hand. We reached Domel's room and I crawled onto his bench.

"What did all that mean?" I asked.

"I'm going to go home with you," Domel said.

"And then what?" I asked.

"You tell me," he said. "We do what we need to do to get my people acknowledged, to join your world."

"It could be a long process," I said.

"Then I shall pack for a long trip," he said, smiling. I watched as he packed books and blankets into a large bag. When he had finished, or at least had stopped adding anything, I stood back up.

"How do we get home?" I asked.

"I will take you back to where we met," he said. "From there, I trust you can find our way."

I nodded.

We went back to the jail long enough for me to get the rest of my gear. I shrugged the flak vest back on and checked that the weapons were still loaded. We made our way back through the Bigfoot settlement and down to the level we had come in on. Domel led us to a platform and onto a subway car. The car started moving before we had gotten settled and I nearly fell from the sudden movement.

Brent stared around him but remained silent. I could not take the suspense any longer and broke the quiet.

"Where's Troy?" I asked.

"I had three days, he had eight," Brent said, still staring around in a daze.

I explained spirit walking as quickly as I could to Domel. Then I had to explain the basics of what had happened to me to Brent. Once both of them seemed more relaxed, I turned to Brent.

"Is Troy okay?" I asked.

"He had problems with the last trial," Brent said.

"But is he okay?" I asked.

"I don't know," Brent said. "But he said he could always find you."

I nodded, trying to tuck my concern for Troy far away and refocus on the task in front of me.

"I received bad news before we left," Brent began.

"About the bombings?" I asked.

Brent nodded.

"We saw that on TV and they took credit for my death, too," I said.

"Will that mean no one will try to kill you?" Domel asked.

"I'm pretty sure the assassin saw you leave the hotel," Brent said.

I nodded. Brent handed me a helmet and I just sat it on my lap, staring at it.

"Once we get back, you'll need to wear it."

I nodded.

"I'll protect you," Domel said.

"You represent your people now," I said. "You aren't expendable."

"I have status," Domel said, his voice quiet and slow as the thought sunk in.

"We aren't going to let you die," Brent said.

"Do you have a plan?" I asked.

"Once I have a cell phone signal, we can find out what's going on," he said.

"I really want a vacation," I muttered.

"As soon as we know this is over," Brent said.

I stared at the map on the wall, watching the little light move along its track. I wanted my life back; I wanted to go an entire day without wondering if I was going to be killed. I really wanted to sleep in my own bed, the one blown to bits by a bomb.

The car slowed to a stop. I put the helmet on, feeling like a fool wearing the thing, and gathered my guns. Brent stood as well, and the three of us exited back to the bottom of the mine shaft.

"I guess I'll carry you up one at a time," Domel said eyeing us and the long ladder back up to the surface.

Chapter Thirty-nine

I stepped out of the mine, turned my face upward, and let the sunlight bathe me. I tried to tip my head back.

"I hate these helmets," I muttered as the back of the helmet dug into my neck.

"The newer models aren't as bad," Brent said. "I think that one's from World War I."

"We have some of the newer ones, but not small enough to fit me," I muttered as I started walking. "Maybe the men back then had smaller heads."

"The military doesn't measure head size when you sign up," Brent said, matching his stride to mine.

"Are you saying head size doesn't matter?" I asked, glancing at him through my eyelashes.

"I believe that's for the woman to decide," Brent said, blushing.

"Do human women have a preference for head size?" Domel asked.

Brent's cheeks shifted from pink to bright red.

"Humans also call the male sex organ a head," I told Domel, keeping my eye on Brent's blush.

"So human women prefer large sex organs," Domel said, straightening a bit.

"Don't even go there," I told Domel. "As a rule, hominids do not have interspecies relationships."

"Rules are made to be broken," Brent said, winking at me.

"Men," I muttered, walking a little faster to get ahead of them. They took the hint and fell silent. The wind rustled through the leaves, brushing against my face. I inhaled deeply, savoring the scent of pine, dirt, and fresh air. It felt good to be back in the open. I led the way over the game trails, heading to the nearest road. If we could get a cell phone signal, we could call Ma and Pa to send someone to pick us up.

"Look at the trees," Brent said. "Each one has so many unique features."

"Thinking of the spirit world?" I asked, glancing over my shoulder at him.

"Yes," he said, "Troy tried explaining something about Plato, but I didn't understand."

"They call it the theory of forms. It's scattered throughout Plato's writing," I said.

"And is Plato part of Hunter training?" he asked, eyebrow raised.

"No. Troy loves reading philosophy," I said. "I got frustrated with his two-word explanations and read some of it myself."

"And this theory of forms?" Brent asked.

"It's about as good an explanation for the spirit world as I can think of," I said. "Plato posited that the objects we see are not the true form, but that in another realm the pure form or the ideal form of a tree exists. These ideal forms include all that makes up the concept of tree and the world we see holds the imperfect reflections."

"That doesn't make sense," Brent said.

"Philosophy rarely does," I said. "I certainly don't claim to really understand it. But my imperfect understanding tells me the spirit world contains all the ideal forms while the uniqueness of this world stems from those imperfections, those deviations from the ideal form which arise in the reflection."

"Still way over my head," Brent said.

"It makes sense in my head, but I can't really say it well in words," I said.

"You're doing better than Troy," Brent said.

I laughed and shook my head.

"How did you and Troy manage on your own?" I asked.

"I think we were beginning to make a good team," he said.

I stopped walking to stare at him. Troy couldn't even work with my brother, someone he'd known most of his life. He got too impatient when others didn't understand him. Of course, the same held true for those who tried to work with him.

"I kept losing my temper at first," Brent said, "but then I just tried to mimic what you did."

"Would you partner with him again?" I asked.

"Sure," Brent said. "After what I saw in the spirit world, I think I understand a little. I admire him."

"There's a lot to admire," I said, "if you can keep from killing him."

I flew backward, landing on my back. Domel and Brent hit the ground. Domel pulled me behind a tree, crouching over me. Dang it, not again!

"What?" I mumbled.

"Sniper," Brent said, crouching behind a tree a few feet from us.

"Where?" I asked, trying to look around, but all I could see was Domel's furry body.

"Not sure," Brent said.

Domel sniffed the air. He stared at the trees around us for a moment before pointing.

"There," he said, pointing to one of the pine trees in the distance. It would have been a long shot, but possible with a good scope.

"You're sure," Brent asked, staring at the tree.

"There's a human in that tree," Domel said.

I rolled over onto my stomach and pulled my rifle out. I aimed in the direction Domel pointed, sighting through the scope. I could see him, a man dressed in camouflage stretched out on a tree limb, his face obscured by the branches. I had a clear shot and aimed for his chest. I flicked the safety off and steadied my arms against the ground. I breathed out, ready to pull the trigger. One shot, he'd be dead, and this would be over. I just had to kill. Again.

He moved, beginning to climb down the tree, and I lost my shot.

"Lost him," I said, flicking the safety back on.

"I can track him," Domel said, muscles tense.

I nodded. Domel kept his nose to the wind and his eyes on the trees.

"Have you ever killed?" I whispered to Brent.

"No," Brent shook his head.

"Even in Iraq?" I asked, turning my head so I could see him better.

"Never had to," Brent shrugged.

Great. Of the three of us, I was the only one who had taken an intelligent life, ending all of the possibilities of that existence, their future. I couldn't ask them to kill for me, not when they had never crossed that line before, never dealt with that guilt. Troy wasn't here to bear the burden for me; it fell to me to act.

"He moved to that tree," Domel said, pointing to one with a much clearer shot of our current position.

We shifted to better cover as the sniper climbed into position. I pulled the rifle out again, aiming carefully at the climbing figure. I breathed out and pulled the trigger. The shot echoed, leaving my ears ringing. Brent, with his gun out, moved quickly. Domel kept me down, still shielding me with his bulk.

"He's dead," Brent called.

I closed my eyes and lay my head on the forest floor. I had done it again, killed to save myself. Only this time had been in cold blood, not in the heat of a struggle. Domel got up and moved toward the body, leaving me to collect myself. I forced myself to breath in and out, letting all the pain and guilt pour into the dirt beneath me. I stood slowly and went to look at the man I had killed.

Brent rolled the body over as I approached and I stopped, mouth falling open. I fell to my knees as my stomach emptied its contents, tears streaming down my face. I stayed on my hands and knees, gasping for air, guts clenched. Shaking my head to deny the reality, deny what I had seen.

"Kelley," Domel said in a low voice as he approached.

"Do you know him?" Brent asked as he knelt at my side. I nodded, not trusting myself to speak yet. I forced myself to crawl away from the vomit and curled up, hugging my knees. I let the numbness creep over me, let my mind empty as shock took hold.

"That was Dr. Lyman," I whispered.

"Your boss?" Domel asked.

I nodded.

"He killed Lisa, blew up his own business," Brent said, stroking my back.

"He was my friend," I whispered, refusing to look at either of them.

"He betrayed you," Domel said, resting his hand on my hair.

"That just makes it worse," I said, sitting up to better glare at him. "He betrayed me and everyone. But I knew him, I cared for him, I shot him."

"Your life was more valuable," Domel said.

"I don't know how to deem a life more valuable than another life," I said.

"You did what had to be done," Brent said.

"I know," I snapped, "but I don't have to like it."

"No, you don't," Brent said.

I forced myself to stand up, shaking off their offers of support.

"Come on," I said. "We have a long walk."

I yanked the helmet off as we walked, tossing it to Brent. Then I pulled the flak vest off and handed it to Domel. Neither of them said a word as I scrambled ahead of them, trying to find peace in the nature around me.

We stumbled onto the road midafternoon and Brent confirmed he had a cell phone signal. He pulled my cell phone from his pocket and handed it to me without a word. I unlocked it and stared at the notifications. Texts and a voice mail from Lisa greeted me. I closed my eyes, holding back tears. I would look at them later, listen to her message when I could bear to hear her voice again. I scrolled down, noting a call from Dr. Lyman's office and several messages from Ma.

I dialed home.

"Ma," I said, tearing up again at the sound of her voice.

"Kelley!" she said.

"I'm going to need a ride and it better be a pickup," I said. "I have Domel of the Sasquatch Clan with me."

"Troy?" she asked.

"Still in the spirit world, but Brent's with me," I said.

I told her where we were and she promised to send someone out to pick us up. She passed the phone to Angie while she went to make arrangements.

"Angie," I whispered into the phone, "it was Dr. Lyman. He was the sniper."

"Oh my…oh," she said. "How are you?"

I poured out everything. I talked, I cried. Angie talked, she cried. The boys settled further up the road, far enough to give me privacy.

"Are you going to stay at The Range for a while?" Angie asked as I ran out of heartache to share.

"Probably," I said. "I don't have anywhere else to go right now."

"Then I'm going to run into town and get everything we need for a girls' night," she said.

"And that's going to fix everything?" I asked with a choked laugh.

"No," she said. "Only time will fix things, but I never met a problem that couldn't be helped with a chocolate overdose."

I giggled, remembering too many adolescent nights spent gorging and talking.

"Hey, sis," Angie said, her voice soft and serious.

"Yeah," I said.

"I really love you," she said.

"I love you, too."

"Now go take care of those boys before they get into trouble," she said.

I laughed as we hung up and went to find the boys.

Chapter Forty

I saw Brent talking on his cell phone while Domel stared up and down the road. He watched me as I approached and I waved a hand at him. He waved back. Brent put his cell phone away and turned to see me. His face lit with a quick smile before settling into a frown.

"Feeling better?" Domel asked.

I nodded.

"I have news," Brent said as I sat down.

"The FBI arrested all the other shooters," he said. "Dr. Lyman was the only one they were still hunting."

"They knew it was him?" I asked.

"Yes," he said. "They arrested the head of Humans for Hominids and he was willing to tell everything in exchange for a plea deal."

"But why did he do it?" I asked.

"We may never for sure," Brent said. "But the FBI found Dr. Lyman had connections with the group from its inception. He may have hired you in hopes of getting close to one of the Families. He had also been a competitive shooter in his younger days."

"I feel like there should be something more," I said.

"Just be happy it's over," he said, wrapping an arm around my shoulder. I leaned in, enjoying the feel of his solid warmth.

"Do you watch football?" Domel asked Brent.

"Of course," Brent said.

"Can you explain it to me?" Domel asked. I rolled my eyes at them, but they ignored me.

Brent launched into an explanation of football that somehow drifted into basketball, baseball, and hockey. Domel peppered him with questions. I sat, nestled in Brent's arms, listening to their voices and watching the sun set. After the week I'd had, this moment felt perfect.

Just as dusk settled into darkness, we saw headlights coming our way. The boys stood up in front of me, shielding me from view. The vehicle slowed and came to a stop before us. It was Troy's Chevy pickup. I stood up, pushed the boys aside, and walked toward it. The driver rolled down the window.

"Miss Kelley," Don said with a soft smile.

I bowed.

"I heard you were back," he said.

"And in need of both a police officer and a ride," I said.

I explained about the body in the woods and gave him the location. Don called it in on his cell phone, assuring me that someone would be out to recover the body. Domel settled in the truck bed as Brent and I slid into the cab.

"I need to take you to the station to get your statement," Don said as we pulled out.

I nodded.

"And where's my truck?" he asked.

Brent took over the explanations, detailing their trip to the werewolves and all that had happened since then. The two men began debating all the logistical options of getting trucks swapped back. I never understood men's fascination with such details so I closed my eyes and let their voices flow around me.

The police took our statements in record time, spurred to speed by the imposing form of Domel, sitting on the floor and attracting most of the attention. It helped that Dr. Lyman had made the Most Wanted list, so the police did not question my need to kill in self-defense. Domel listened intently and I hoped he was comparing our system to his. At least this time I wouldn't be charged with anything.

At my request, we made a quick stop for a razor, toothbrush, fresh clothes, and other basic supplies before heading back to Don's. I made directly for the bathroom and threw myself into the shower. Somehow, the act of cleaning and shaving washed away much of the pain along with the dirt. Even better, I got to brush my teeth. In fact, I brushed until my teeth felt smooth and my mouth tasted of nothing but mint. I followed that up with gargling enough mouthwash to kill a small horse. Overkill? Oh yeah. But days without brushing and vomiting all over the forest called for some serious measures. I did have a gorgeous man waiting for me in the other room to consider.

I emerged, feeling like a new person—or at least feeling more like a human female than I had in some time. I could smell the delightful combination of tomato, garlic, and other spices which heralded a good meal as I stepped back into the hall. I followed my nose to the kitchen.

Don's partner had joined our small group, and they all sat around the kitchen table eating pizza. Domel grinned from his seat on the floor as I came in, holding up his slice of pepperoni. I smiled back. I dug into my own slice, savoring all of the flavors. I had missed cheese. I had really missed spices. Maybe I'd send a care package to Domel's mom with every spice in the supermarket.

"Your Pa will be here in the morning," Don said. "He would have come tonight, but they spent the day making sure all of your Family members returned from their sanctuaries."

"Did you end up taking anyone in?" I asked.

"Your Aunt Bertha and Uncle Harold stayed with me until last night," Don said. "I found them to be pleasant company. Not many humans remember the days before your scientists found us."

"They sure do have some stories to tell," I said, picturing the three of them swapping tales of life before computers and complaining about us young kids.

"You and Domel head back to The Range tomorrow with your Pa," Brent said. "James and I will go get Don's truck. I'll drive back to The Range with Troy's when we're done."

"Are you sure?" I asked.

"I haven't been much use so far; let me at least handle this," he said.

"I think you've been tremendously handy," I said, grinning at him. "You helped the FBI solve the case and made sure I had family to come home to."

Brent ducked his head, blushing.

James stood, gathering the paper plates and other debris. Don pulled out the trash can and soon the table was clear. Brent and James got their things and walked out of the kitchen to begin their journey to the reservation. I sat, nibbling on a piece of pizza as they headed out, wishing I had a little more time to talk to Brent before he left. The door opened back up and Brent motioned to me. I joined him on Don's small porch.

"This may not be the best time," Brent began.

I looked up into his emerald eyes, losing myself for a moment.

"When I get back, would you..." he started to say. "Could we? Maybe go out on a date?"

I smiled and nodded. He leaned in slowly, giving me plenty of time to duck. His lips met mine and I wrapped my arms around him. His solid warmth felt right, leaning against me. The kiss deepened as he pulled me closer. I felt my body respond as I pressed myself against him. He stepped back slowly and sighed with regret.

"I'd better get going," he said.

I nodded.

I watched him get into the truck and drive off into the night. I sat, listening to the crickets, and stared at the stars. I had a date with Brent. I wished I could tell Lisa about it; she would have been so excited. I heard the door open and glanced up to see Domel come out. He sat on the step, staring out at the street.

"I don't fit any of the furniture," he said, waving his hand to indicate his large bulk.

"No. We'll have to get creative about that," I said, smiling at him. I tried to picture him at The Range, sitting on one of the sofas. They might just fit him. Having a ten-foot hominid around was going to create more than a few challenges. He wouldn't fit in my VW, that's for sure. I wondered if the police would ticket us if we kept carting him around in the bed of pickup trucks.

"I liked the pizza, but it didn't taste like I imagined," he said, smelling like oranges and cinnamon.

"I suspect most of our world will be different than you imagined," I said. "TV lies."

"Do you think it's over? Will people stop trying to kill you?" Domel asked, smelling of the dried leaves of concern.

"I hope so," I said, sighing. "But the rest of the group is out there someplace."

He nodded, patting the back of my leg.

"Is Brent going to be your new mate?" Domel asked, smelling of scorched popcorn. I really hated that smell. He needed to stop getting embarrassed so easily.

"I don't know," I said. "We'll need to see how the date goes."

"You don't sound excited," he said.

I looked at him and smiled. I guess I didn't sound excited. I liked Brent more than I wanted to like him. I loved the idea of the two of us out on a date, somewhere nice and normal, preferably with no one shooting at me. I even thought we had excellent chances at making a relationship work. The problem wasn't Brent; it was everything that had happened.

"I've had so much happen the past few days. I'm not sure what I'm feeling," I said.

"I like him," Domel said.

"I do, too," I said, smiling. I hoped that liking would grow into love when I got a chance to get to know him without all the drama and adventure. I wondered if he would come to Angie's wedding with me and if he would find a way to stay in town for a little longer. I leaned into Domel, my living teddy bear, and stared into the night. I could deal with all of my problems tomorrow. Tonight, I just wanted to enjoy the possibilities.

Chapter Forty-one

Angie and I sat in the attic at The Range, packing boxes. Well, unpacking, sorting and repacking boxes. Thanks to the generosity of the hominid communities, I had received enough donations to set up a new apartment. We unpacked the donated boxes, dividing the goods into keep boxes and donate boxes. So far, I had more donate boxes then keep boxes. As much as I appreciated the generosity, I had the feeling I had received other people's trash. It's the thought that counted, though, right?

"How is Domel going to fit in on campus?" Angie asked as she wrapped a bright blue bowl, placing it gently in a keep box.

"It'll be an adjustment for everyone," I said, wrapping a pumpkin orange bowl for the keep box, "but he's excited to go to class. We're taking most of the same classes, so I should be able to help."

"And you two are really going to share an apartment?" she asked, wrapping up a cherry-red plate with tiny white flowers and putting it in a keep box.

"Sure," I said. "His people are making some decent money from the mines and his mother is giving him a stipend for acting as their representative to the world. He'll be able to pay half and that will be a huge help."

"That's not what I meant," she said, holding up a brown chipped plate for my examination. I shook my head and she placed it in a donate box.

"I know," I said, pulling out a crusty brown frying pan. I handed it to Angie for the donate box.

"Well?" Angie asked as she broke down the box we had emptied.

"We get along fine," I said. "And I don't want to live alone."

"And Bigfoot will be enough company?" she asked, tossing the flattened box onto a pile of finished boxes.

"Don't you like him?" I asked, putting down the plate I was wrapping to look at her.

"Of course I do," she said. "I just worry that you are shutting yourself off from humans."

"You don't need to worry," I said, picking the plate up and putting it in a donate box.

"It's part of being your big sister," she said, standing up and looking at the stacks of unopened boxes.

"I promise to hang out with human kids, Mom," I said, tossing a ball of packing wrap at her.

She laughed and dodged the ball, moving to a small box on top of the nearest stack of donations.

"Will you be safe?" she asked as she brought the box back over and sat down.

"Brent said the FBI arrested the leaders of the People for Hominids group. They don't think they'll be able to reorganize anytime soon," I said.

"So you're going to accept being the Heir?" she asked, using a knife to open the box.

"I'm still going to finish my degree," I said. "But I'll start acting as Heir, too."

"Are you okay with that?" Angie asked, ignoring the box to look at me.

"Yeah," I said, shrugging. "It's not what I wanted to do, but it's what I need to do."

"Hey, look at this," Angie said as she peered into the contents of the box she had just opened. I peered over Angie's shoulder to see a picture album on top of some clothes. I pulled the picture album out, flipping it open to see pictures of Lisa and myself. I touched Lisa's face, feeling tears sting my eyes. I missed that smile.

"It's from Lisa's mom," Angie said, handing me a card.

"I thought they hated me," I said, beginning to read. "Kelley, Lisa would have wanted you to have something to remember her."

"That's all it says?" Angie asked.

I nodded. It didn't say much, but it was enough.

"Where was this taken?" Angie asked, looking over my shoulder at a picture of Lisa and me.

"That was at the fair last year," I said, torn between laughter at the memory and the pain of the loss. We flipped through the rest of the album and I told Angie stories. Most of them were simple things, moments of friendship caught on camera, but each memory brought ten more behind it. The laughter beat out the tears and Angie joined in, teasing me about some of Lisa's and my sillier adventures. I put aside the memories and the book, carefully packing it in one of the keep boxes.

We moved on to a new box; more clothes, most of which wouldn't fit me. We worked in silence, tossing clothes into one of the donate boxes. We found enough clothes to keep that I might have a wardrobe again. Not a sexy one, but it was a beginning.

"How're things with Brent?" Angie asked as she held up a jean miniskirt. I smiled, picturing Brent's face if he were to see me in it.

"We're going out again on Friday," I said, smiling at the memories of our first date. He had taken me for a steak dinner and had even brought me flowers. Romance was not dead. Best of all, we had talked until morning.

"But what about when he goes back home?" Angie asked, tossing the skirt into a keep box.

"He's requesting a job at the Salt Lake office," I said. If he got the transfer, he'd only be a few hours away.

"That's still quite a distance," she said.

"I know," I said. But it was a huge chance he was taking in hopes that our relationship would work out.

"How will Troy handle it?" she asked.

"Handle what?" Troy's voice said from behind me.

"Troy," I squealed, jumping up to give him a hug. He lifted me off my feet and spun me around.

"Welcome back from la-la land," Angie said, smiling at him.

"Missed you," Troy said into my hair.

"Kelley's dating Brent; Kelley's dating Brent," Angie said in a singsong voice.

"Good," Troy said, setting me back on my feet.

"What?" Angie exclaimed, eyes wide.

"And I found Bigfoot," I told him, grinning.

"What?" he looked at me, one eyebrow creeping into his bangs.

"She did. Even brought one home to live with her," Angie said, smirking.

"Angie," I said, glaring at her.

She laughed as she stood up. With an elbow to my side, she moved me out of the way to give Troy a quick hug and kiss on the cheek.

"I'll leave you two to get caught up," she said, heading for the stairs.

"Are you okay?" I asked him, studying his face. I could see the tracks of pain along his eyes and his forehead, evidence of the toll the spirit world had taken on him. I noted the additional cuts and bruises he had collected and wondered if we needed to get Uncle Mack back for a visit. He shook his head and sat down among the boxes and piles.

"Brent told me some of what happened out there," I said, still looking him over for damage. I could see the lines of exhaustion and suffering crisscrossing his face.

He nodded.

"You have to let me go," I said, trying to meet his eyes.

"I know," he said, head bowed, refusing to make eye contact.

"That doesn't mean we're not still family, still friends," I said, offering the only thing I had.

"I know," he said, shoulders hunching in on themselves.

I wanted to reach out to him, comfort him, but I held myself still. I didn't get that right anymore; I had to let him go as much as he had to let me go.

"I want you to be happy," I said, needing him to look over at me.

"I know," he said, still staring at the floor.

"Can't you say anything else?" I snapped.

He shook his head.

I took several deep breaths, calming myself. I would not let myself be mad at him, not anymore.

"Are you going to be all right?" I asked.

He shrugged.

"I never meant to hurt you," I said, reaching out a hand to touch his shoulder.

"I know," he said, looking up to meet my eyes. The raw pain and love in his eyes broke my heart.

"But I'm a danger to you," I said, dropping my eyes to stare at his chin.

He shook his head.

"Yes, I am," I said, nodding my head. "I hurt you more than you'd let anyone else."

He shook his head again. I'd rather his normal caveman words then this silence.

"Why didn't you stop me?" I asked.

He shrugged.

"Love is not about pain," I said, willing him to hear me.

He looked away, staring at the wall.

"Troy, I know the secret you can't face," I said. "Your mom did love you. I love you. But that doesn't give us the right to hurt you. Love does not excuse it."

Troy curled his legs up, burying his head into his knees.

"But that's not what you can't face," I said, moving to wrap my arms around him. "You can't bring yourself to believe that you deserve better."

I felt his shoulders shake as he leaned into me. I held him tighter, resting my head against his.

"You deserve someone who will cherish you, someone who will treat you gently," I whispered into his hair. "You need to love yourself—cherish yourself—first."

I held him, rocking him back and forth as he cried. I wished I knew if he understood what I was trying to say. I hoped he'd believe it. I knew it all sounded like cheesy pop psychology, but it was all the wisdom I had to give, all I could hope for him.

He gently unwrapped himself from me, pulling back to look me in the eyes. He leaned forward and gently kissed my forehead before standing. He walked toward the door, silence surrounding him. He turned as he reached the stairs, looking at me for a long moment.

"Be happy, Kelley," he said.

Acknowledgements

I need to thank Jen, first and foremost. I could write a whole page listing all of the things you've done to help make this book happen. I'll try to keep it simple. Your editing made this work better than I could have imagined, you have a gift. That's the obvious one. I also owe you a debt of gratitude for loving the story, encouraging me every step of the way, helping me figure out what I'm doing, and believing in me and my Bigfoots.

Thanks to Paramita for the beautiful cover. You are a true artist! I have no idea how you took my vague ideas and turned them into an image that reflected what my hindbrain pictured.

Thanks to my Dad for listening to babble about my thoughts as I wrote. I appreciate it more than I can express. Also, thanks to the rest of my family for being there. Oh! Kelley, thank you dear step-sister for letting me use your name and promising not to take this character as a personal reflection!

Lastly, thanks to my friends for support, encouragement, and lying to me (telling me how wonderful I am) when I needed it. Jen, Ed, Aleks – I thank you. Ed, you have my gratitude for making me laugh when I needed it and having patience with my absent-mindedness as I wrote. Aleks, I owe you for keeping me sane and focused when I needed it. I should also thank all of my coworkers who've been understanding as I ventured into writing and who have acted as my cheerleaders from the beginning.

Of course, any errors or problems with this book are my fault!

About The Author

Sara developed a severe book addiction as a young child. Eventually, her concerned parents attempted an intervention and cut off her supply. These desperate times called for desperate measures forcing her to write her own stories, which grew to book length over time. Since a human being cannot live on books alone, she has worked as a stage hand, care giver, active duty Air Force member, college instructor, mental health counselor, and civil servant. On the theory that more pay equals more books, she's often juggled two jobs (or more) to the detriment of her social life. Outside of that, she spends time developing a reputation as a crazy cat lady, perpetual student, and irritating introvert.

If you want to learn more go to: http://saramdrake0.blogspot.com

Feel free to contact the author at: saramdrake0@gmail.com